THE SUPERNATURAL ENHANCEMENTS

THE

SUPERNATURAL
ENHANCEMENTS

A NOVEL

EDGAR CANTERO

DOUBLEDAY

NEW YORK LONDON TORONTO
SYDNEY AUCKLAND

All rights reserved. Published in the United States by Doubleday, a division of Random House LLC, New York, and in Canada by Random House of Canada Limited, Toronto, Penguin Random House companies.

www.doubleday.com

DOUBLEDAY and the portrayal of an anchor with a dolphin are registered trademarks of Random House LLC.

Grateful acknowledgment is made to Music Sales Limited for permission to reprint an excerpt from "John, I Love You," words and music by Sinéad O'Connor, copyright © 1994 by Nettwerk One Music Limited. All Rights Reserved. International Copyright Secured. Reprinted by permission of Music Sales Limited.

Selected art created by Ocabrita and Jordi March
Book design by Pei Loi Koay
Jacket art and design by Michael J. Windsor

LIBRARY OF CONGRESS CATALOGING-IN-PUBLICATION DATA
Cantero, Edgar, 1981–
The supernatural enhancements :
a novel / Edgar Cantero. —First edition.
pages   cm
ISBN 978-0-385-53815-2 (alk. paper)
ISBN 978-0-385-53816-9 (eBook)
1. Heirs—Fiction.   I. Title.
PQ6653.A5775S97 2014
863'.7—dc23
2013027730

MANUFACTURED IN THE UNITED STATES OF AMERICA
3 5 7 9 10 8 6 4

First Edition

```
L X G P V B I P O D M I C M Q C P X P H D G M I
P T F N A N I P G D M E V I I P C Q M C T F Z G
P S S D E C O C H K D B K U F C C B K Z A N M I
L P Q O W H S P R Z A F T Q G P K L R Z C O C E
A O W O D B L T O H N C M P F C K B T H M I F K
L V L S U B W S S D P F L D P G O C S W W N M S
G P T K K Z N F N B K Z C Z V T W C Q C P K B S
H Z K N K D H P T K O H D E B S H Z V N E S C Q
K M A O F N Z H K D M W B S P W M W P Z H P G Z
M C M V L D P G M I L S S K D K G C X L P F R C
Q A E D S E C O W B V A U H G Z L K W H G S Z G
S U H W P O X S E V T V O D F C K B F A M I H W
K Q Z G Q I L K P L M K V S A O R A X M D L K M
F A G D E D W N M S G P R Z D G G P V L O P N U
O C E T C W A O L P C B P W W N P O P T F C E D
R Z A F H W D N C F P W P F H C R K G C L R X G
R T H L K M O A S L K X T V L V S L O A Z W P U
```

THE SUPERNATURAL ENHANCEMENTS

The following collection of documents details the events that occurred at Axton House, 1 Axton Road, Point Bless, Virginia, during the months of November and December of 1995.

The footnotes are the editor's only contribution. The first page is missing.

[. . .] Axton House and all of its contents." I could hardly conceive a harsher interruption to my lifestyle than that of the Thomas Jefferson stamps, the news of my deceased relative, and his posthumous gift, which I finally accepted as an amendment for his failure to produce any Christmas presents for twenty-three years. Several long-distance calls and a few faxes contributed to knock down my incredulity, which gave way in the end only because the name of Wells was not completely unfamiliar to Aunt Liza, who in an exercise of reconstructive genealogy established that Wells was the surname of the family into which my great-great-grandmother's sister had married before emigrating to the States in the 1890s. Therefore, my having a distant cousin in Virginia (until last September, that is) was fairly plausible. His being rich, though, I found unlikely. And his awareness of my existence was positively unreal. So much, indeed, that what little I collected about Ambrose Wells' odd habits, his furtive behavior, and the rumors surrounding whatever he used to hide in his solitary manor in Virginia seemed hardly extraordinary in the context of this sudden turn toward the interesting that things had taken. I did not hesitate to quit my courses and leave my apartment, feeling as detached from everything as only at twenty-three one feels, when all is temporary and settling down means to stagnate, and flew to America with no big picture and no other company than a friend whose fondness of me seemed the only thing worth preserving. On November the second, we landed in Richmond. On the third, we met the lawyer, Glew. On the fourth, he's driving us in his Mercedes to our new home.

Niamh, sitting in front, snatches the notebook out of my hands, reads the paragraph above, represses a laugh, then contributes from her own pencil:

Worst beginning ever written.

And then she nives. This is a verb I made up to signify a facial expression she often summons—a tiny tight-lipped smile held through a long, amused stare. It will be a frequent word in these pages.

She's probably right. But I've noticed that all manuscripts are bad; any book randomly opened in a friend's house is good; the same book in a bookstore is bad. When this story is completed, that beginning will turn better.

PART I

Above us lies suspended a gold-trimmed cloud the size of one of the big states (say, Arizona), threatening to plummet over Virginia. The low sun beneath casts its rays along the dirt road we travel, exalting the yellows and oranges, turning aluminum into gold and the skin on Niamh's arm into apricot. Crop fields dash across her irises as she feasts on the continent. She's going to be difficult not to fall in love with.

The road goes on from Point Bless in a westward direction for miles.

"How are we supposed to come and go when we're on our own?" I ask.

"Just stay on the good road," Glew replies. "Don't worry; in your car it's a ten-minute ride."

"We have a car?"

"Two, actually. Your cousin's—an Audi—and a Daewoo he bought for the butler."

"We have a butler!"

"Strückner. He is closer to a housekeeper, actually. There used to be other servants, but reading your cousin's will to the letter, 'the house and all of its contents,' it was interpreted that only Strückner came in the package, for he is the only one to live there. Anyway, I am not sure you should rely on his assistance."

"Why's that?"

"He is missing. Left in mid-October without a word. I've been trying to contact him since."

Niamh scribbles on her notepad and shows me: *The butler did it.* I smirk. Glew hasn't read it, but he guesses something.

"I suppose he needed some vacation," he says apologetically. "He seemed fairly upset. After all, he found the bodies."

"Bodies? I thought Ambrose Wells committed suicide all alone."

"He did. In the same fashion as his father, thirty years ago."

About three miles from the center of Point Bless, the car takes a right turn down the stem of a T; then we travel along a gravel driveway that shoves the house deep into the estate, hiding it from the main road. The roadside crop fields have been replaced by untamed woods that might once have been gardens. But then the trees halt well before the building, respecting the vast empty court at whose center sits Axton House.

The house must have looked Georgian on the blueprint, three stories high, with a mansard roof. From the front yard, however, it shows none of the comforting Greek sense of proportion. It had a rather somber effect upon us, with its boasting grandeur and excessive verticality. Doors and windows and windowpanes consistently push the golden ratio a little further, stretching higher and narrower. The stone skin of the building seems able to adopt the hue that best fits the landscape. It looked dirty gold when we first saw it. Only the hedge maze beyond the conservatory dares to green the place. The estate teemed with the voices of birds and trees.

Two sets of French windows open on each side of the front door onto the November-carpeted platform. Three windows on the second floor stand on each side of the protruding spine that rises from the portico. On the third floor the front wall recedes, yielding room for two balconies. The attic has only two dormers, and the spine in the middle peaks in a mansard, then rises a little farther, then ends for good in a sort of belfry. Inside this stands what must be a weathercock, though it more closely resembles a sailor's sextant. According to Glew, it is both a weathercock and a calendar: When its shadow licks the foot of a certain oak in the front line of the woods, it is signaling the winter solstice. The design was first patented by Benjamin Franklin.

LETTER

Axton House
1 Axton Rd.
Point Bless, VA 26969

Dear Aunt Liza,

I'm aware that the occasion calls for filling several pages of this luxurious letter paper found in Mr. Ambrose Wells' desk with a thorough description of Axton House.

Unfortunately, I can't give you that. I am indeed writing from Axton House, about to turn in for the very first night; Niamh and I share a bed big enough for each of us to throw an orgy without her guests disturbing mine. Glew gave us a tour around the house this evening, but we haven't really seen it. Not in the way you meant that day, when you said that a passenger on a ship doesn't see the ropes the way a sailor sees them. Having seen the house would mean to be able to go around it and predict which room awaits behind each double door. Having seen the house would mean to understand the use of each room and each piece of furniture. We haven't seen the house. We have merely perceived a circular sequence of empty halls, large windows, fireplaces, chandeliers, spiderwebs, canopies, and a cluttered desk on every floor.

I believe I have caught some patterns, though—such as that the whole house seems to revolve around the library on the second floor, its central and largest area. I mention this, perhaps, because it suits your notion of the Wells as people who lived and died for their studies.

Other features (such as the great number of long galleries whose only purpose seems to be the exhibition of curtains) bewilder me.

I don't think I'd be able to find any of those rooms right now if my life depended on it. In fact, I wouldn't dare go to sleep had Niamh not laid a trail of chickpeas to the nearest bathroom.

No trace of ghosts so far, but we'll stay alert.

Tomorrow morning I plan to start socializing around. We also have to find the missing butler, Strückner. Niamh and I agree it's not a good name for a butler.

We wish you were here, but purely out of courtesy; truth is we're managing quite well. Niamh says she'd like a dog. Can we?

Kisses,
A.

—What's the most formal clothing you brought?

—*Green summer dress.*

—Good. We're going to church tomorrow. I guess you have no problem with that.

—*I think they Baptists here, but I'll live with it.**

—Puritan.

—*I have a bad feeling about the butler.*

—Me too.

—*But he wasn't in the will, so he free of suspicion?*

—I guess so, but something doesn't fit. I don't know what kind of bonds people have with their servants, but if you lived with somebody for fifty years and left him nothing, you probably didn't like him that much, and sympathy tends to be reciprocal. So why is the butler so deeply affected?

---

* Niamh often excludes the verb *to be* in writing. Also, she ends sentences with a question mark whenever she expects feedback. Consider it an abbreviated tag question.

Despite my reluctance to borrow any clothes from Ambrose Wells' wardrobe, which fell out of fashion together with pocket watches and airships, we succeeded in getting noticed in church. I was the guy disguised as a history professor from midcentury Oxford (with sneakers), and Niamh was the kid with her hair hoisted in a loose ponytail like an explosion of blue-violet ribbons, and a green dress too short for both the season and the occasion. I noticed some curious looks during the service, and on our way out, the human flow lingered in too small groups, gossiping in unnecessarily low voices. Niamh greeted them all with dazzling smiles and had even the most uptight judges eating out of her hand.

Nobody tried an approach in church, but later in the day we received three visits.

The first of them were the Brodies, at about five o'clock. Their farm is visible to the south from the higher windows. They're our closest neighbors; in fact, their land used to belong to the Wells. Actually, from what I understood, Mrs. Brodie's family worked that land before the Thirteenth Amendment abolished slavery, but I didn't dare to confirm that for fear of having misheard and sounding rude. Truth is I felt pretty lost during our introduction: She had a very tough accent. Anyway, whatever the relation between Brodies and Wells was in the past, I gather it was a pretty warm one in Ambrose's times, and Mrs. Brodie meant to keep that friendship alive.

Mr. Brodie was clearly not so keen on the welcome visit, but he did open up when, after my asking Niamh for drinks and her returning from the kitchen with half a bottle of 7UP, he pointed out that Ambrose used to keep some bourbon in his office.

He meant the first-floor office, the one used for "public" business— one of the rooms I don't like. The perfectly hexahedral anteroom, with its gondola chairs in every corner and double doors on every wall, is just too symmetrical, and the office's dark paneling and grumpy-looking books remind me of a school principal's den. Brodie didn't seem intimidated, though; he just walked straight toward the American history volumes displayed on the back shelves to impress visitors and pulled out Champfrey's *Rise and Fall of the South.* The panel on his left opened with a click, and from the secret compartment he produced a bottle of fourteen-year-old Wild Turkey. He said Ambrose revealed it to him the day they sealed the lease for the orange grove. I said I ought to invite him more often, just in case the house held any more secrets. He solemnly replied, "It does."

(Of course, he doesn't know them, but his faith is a good enough hint. I know how deeply this man can believe in what he hasn't seen. I saw him in church.)

As he closed the panel, I noticed an envelope on Ambrose's desk. I wonder how I failed to see it before, because then and there it so loudly announced itself that I would have banged my head on a wall for missing it, had someone else not found it and opened it already. I have the envelope in front of me now, empty. The outside reads "Aeschylus."

I just slipped it under a pile of papers then and postponed the thinking—it would have been discourteous to leave the women alone too long, even though Mrs. Brodie seemed the kind able to chat for hours before realizing that her interlocutor is mute.

She had just found out when we joined them in the music room (long hall across the foyer with a piano, hi-fi, and TV). We arrived in time for her delivery of the well-known line, "But you do hear me, don't you?" in a very loud voice, carefully shaping each phoneme (a considerate effort on her behalf—see accent issue), and I had a new chance to see Niamh's nod and silent laugh before I covered the customary explanations—that she's mute, not deaf-mute; that it's an acquired condition; that her English is actually better than mine, for she's from Dublin, whereas I only took it up in high school, reading classics; that she communicates through mime, mouthing, or writing, plus a whistle code and a knock code; that she carries a notepad and pencil with her at all times, and she spends the evenings filling the gaps between her own lines with the answers she got, thus recording long dialogues by doing just fifty percent extra work, and keeping a complete log of every significant conversation she's had across every notepad she's ever used, each page notated for where the conversation took place, when, and with whom; and that they would never have a quieter neighbor.

That last thing I said on purpose, and it caused an awkward silence. Mrs. Brodie tiptoed around the subject. I chose to feed her some of the existing rumors: half lies in exchange for half truths. I listed Ambrose's odd habits, the noises, the lights, the rites held in the house, and even mentioned the ghosts *en passant*. Mr. Brodie quickly said, "The noises bit is not true."

His wife made a heartfelt apology for Ambrose Wells, claiming that "people in town" might have considered him a bit of a hermit, but she would often stand up for him, pointing out that his door was always open and he had been very generous to them. In her words, "He had learned from his father's mistakes." She regretted this phrasing a second later, on remembering Ambrose's end.

I availed myself of the opportunity to ask about John, Ambrose's father. Her words:

"John was an even more obsessive scholar. He lived for his studies."

"And for his son," Mr. Brodie added. "But that was a close second."

I asked about the nature of those studies. They hesitated. Then they mentioned some scattered disciplines: history, geography ... anthropology? Mrs. Brodie remarked that Ambrose used to go on long trips. "He's been to Asia and Africa. He quit traveling when his rheumatism got worse."

"The father was interested in math too," said her husband, as if having spotted an incongruity. "He was a cryptographer in World War Two."

I brought up the odd habits and rites again. Again they looked embarrassed. Again Mrs. Brodie vindicated one's right to do whatever they please at home, as long as it doesn't disturb the peace of the community. Once she'd run out of fuel, I cued her: "But . . . ?"

She gave way at last, much to her husband's contrariety:

"The Wells used to hold some reunions. In December. I guess there would be nothing weird about it, but it's because they had so few visits during the year that suddenly so many cars parked out front called people's attention. Some would lose their way and reach our farm, and we'd give them directions. They were always men, traveling alone. They used to stay for two or three days."

"Until Christmas?"

"No, they'd leave just before Christmas."

Niamh lipped for me the words *winter solstice.*

"Maybe they were celebrating Ambrose's birthday," I said.

They gave the idea some thought, but then Mr. Brodie recalled that this tradition stretched back to pre-Ambrose times. They didn't seem aware that Ambrose's birthday was in February.

"And those were the only visitors in the whole year?"

"In such big groups, yes. At other times, they'd drive by one or two at a time, but that didn't happen often. Some did come more often—like that young gentleman Caleb . . . something. They went on trips together, Ambrose and him."

Mrs. Brodie seemed to foresee a quarrel with her husband when they got home, but she said this nonetheless:

"Some people think they're Masons."

Her husband dived into his palm.

I feigned surprise and appeared to meditate for half a minute (which I really spent imagining how fourteen-year-old Wild Turkey would taste mixed with 7UP) and then said, "Well, if that's the case, we'll find out soon, won't we? By Masonic law, a Mason is allowed to identify another Mason only after that other Mason is dead. So when a friend of Ambrose's turns up, I'll ask him and will report to you."

I think my tone served to thaw the ice; Mr. Brodie laughed at the prospect. They were about to stand up when Niamh showed them her notepad: *What about the ghosts?*

Mr. Brodie said cheerfully, "That's probably false too."

LETTER

Axton House

Axton Rd.

Point Bless, VA 26969

Dear Aunt Liza,

[. . .]* The second visitor arrived at dinnertime. We were sitting at
the table when we heard a car braking on the gravel. Niamh meant to
take his picture for you, but I told her not to. Mr. Knox (so he introduced himself) epitomizes the anachronistic Virginian high class I
told you about when describing Glew: Nothing about him belongs to
this era—not his car, not his hair, not his handshake, nor his accent
(says Niamh). However, framed in the doorway of Axton House, he fit
perfectly. Had he rung the doorbell of my old apartment, I would have
mistaken him for a time traveler.

He apologized for the late hour; he was just driving past on his way
to Lawrenceville (about thirty miles northeast) when Glew informed
him of our arrival; naturally, as an intimate friend of Wells', he wished
to welcome us. He wouldn't join us for dinner, but he didn't mind
watching us eat. He's younger than Ambrose was, somewhere in his
forties. Reminds me of Jeremy Irons.

Niamh took some Polaroids of the dining room (second door on
the right from the entrance) so you can picture the scene. I doubt we'll
be using the room a lot: The pink arras and high, dark beams seem
to stare down on our food with disapproval. The Gothic atmosphere
demands a bleeding carpaccio; instead, we were having spaghetti and
meatballs. Picture us sitting at the north end, Knox at the south, nearest to the fireplace. He seemed surprised that Niamh was laying the
table.

"Shouldn't a servant be doing that?"

---

* Some paragraphs in these letters are omitted to spare the reader redundant information. All omissions will be signaled like this.

"If you mean the butler, he deserted even before seeing how we leave the bathroom in the morning."

"Strückner has resigned?" I think he regretted the incredulity in his pitch as soon as the sentence parted his lips.

"Do you know him? If you see him, tell him he won't get his job back easily—Niamh cooks like God."

Niamh was anacondaing a meatball as big as her head. Knox watched us eat like we were on the Discovery Channel.

"It's funny. I knew Ambrose for so long, and yet he never talked about you."

"It's okay; he never mentioned you either. Of course, we never talked much, what with having never met and everything."

"And what exactly was your kinship?"

"Ooh, wait, I know that one—I'm his *second cousin twice removed.* Meaning his grandmother Tess and my great-great-grandmother were sisters."

"Mm-hm. I suppose I could have a second cousin twice removed myself and not know about him."

"It came as a surprise to me too."

"And he left you this house."

"And all of its contents."

"Was that the extent of his will?"

"Oh, no, there was more. There was us, then something about the lands . . . Glew is working on it. I'm told I have the last word on that, but I guess we'll just give it away to its current tenants."

"Give it away," he parroted. "Do you know how much that land is worth?"

"Very little, compared to what we've got now. You must understand: I just realized I don't need to work again in my life. Not that I've worked a lot, really."

"What did you used to do?"

"I was a student of geography."

"Ambrose liked geography too," he observed, while his mind attended some less trivial matter. "Didn't the will say anything else?"

"You're certainly curious. Did you have your eyes set on the silverware or something? Because we can talk about it."

"No, no, not at all." He almost blushed here. "I am just looking for an explanation for what Ambrose did."

That invoked a mournful silence. We tried to suck pasta quietly.

"So, nothing else? Not a note? No instructions for Strückner or anybody?"

"I'm afraid not. Although . . . Wait, what was your name again?"

"Knox."

"Caleb Knox?"

"No, Curtis Knox."

"Oh, nothing then."

"But I do know Caleb. If you mean Caleb Ford."

"Ford! That was it. My mistake—Ford, Knox . . ." I realize I was behaving like an ass, but that's fine. It proves I have many registers.

"What was in it for Caleb?"

"I don't know. Glew is looking for him; he's missing too."

"He's on a field trip."

"Really? Please tell Glew; he'll be glad to know. Where is he?"

"Africa."

"Where in Africa?"

"Central Africa."

"You can be more specific; I've seen a couple maps in my life."

"Kigali."

"Wow." He almost got me there. "Rwanda."

"That's just where he started; his work must have drawn him deep into the country. He can be untraceable for months during these excursions."

"How long has he been gone?"

"Since April."

"He might not even know of Ambrose's death."

Knox just nodded irrelevantly. After a minute or two he resumed: "It's funny he left you this house."

"Didn't we go through that just now?"

"No, I mean . . . not in that sense. Somehow, Axton House is a poisoned gift."

This silence here was somewhat heavier, lonelier than the preceding one. The former was an elevator silence; this one was a walking-through-the-woods-by-night silence.

"I mean," he clarified, "that this house is not a real treat."

"Excuse me; could you speak a bit louder? I didn't hear you from this end of the room."

"Yes, I know: the three-story mansion, the ten-thousand-volume library, the conservatory . . . But besides that, the house comes with a dark background."

"I see. The rumors, the nocturnal noises . . . The secret rites . . ."

He didn't even blink. On the contrary, he added, "The ghosts . . ."

"Bullshit." I would have never dared to say that in front of the Brodies, but I could afford it now.

"Sure, nothing but fables. But they make one of Axton House's features; fables come in the package. 'A house with supernatural enhancements,' as I think Edith Wharton put it."

"They don't affect me."

"They did affect your predecessor," he replied, visibly grateful for my walking into that. "And his father too."

Niamh asked on her notepad, *Did they really kill themselves the same way?*

"Yes, they did," he said, leaning back after squinting at the message. "Same age, same time, jumped from the same window."

"Which window?"

"Third floor, third on the north side, main bedroom."

That's where we sleep. It's where I'm writing this now.

Mostly to deflect his attention from the deep impression on Niamh's face, I challenged him:

"How come it affects members of the Wells family and nobody else?"

"Who else is there to be affected?"

"Strückner?"

"I would have admitted he was not affected until you told me he resigned."

"Touché. What about the women?"

"Ambrose's mother died when he was a child. Breast cancer. His father raised him. Well, mostly the Strückners did: Strückner senior as a nanny and male figure, then Strückner junior as his butler and friend."

"And higher in the family tree? Ambrose's grandfather Horace?"

"Sadly my knowledge doesn't reach that far back."

"Isn't it more reasonable to take Ambrose's death as a consequence of his father's death, i.e., to assume that he was traumatized and bore the scar throughout his life, until he reached the same age, and the old wound reopened, and he followed his father's steps just to end the pain, rather than speculating that two different people were independently induced to commit suicide the same way at the same age by some unknown agent?"

"Good application of Occam's razor," praised he.

"How old was Ambrose when his father died?"

"Eighteen."

"And they died at the same age, you say. Fifty, isn't it?"

"Correct."

The only argument I could come up with to comfort Niamh and myself was that I still have a twenty-seven-year grace period.

NIAMH'S NOTEPAD

(In bed.)

—You forgot to ask if they Masons.

—You're right. Anyway, if Knox is a Mason, he didn't seem the kind who would be open about it.

—I don't like him.

—Nor do I.

—He doesn't like us either—like we're in his way.

—You mean, like he wanted the house for himself? Why?

—*I think Knox part of the Xmas party group, & Wells their leader. K. expected W. to pass him the baton.*

—Right. That's why he kept asking what was in the will. Or if there were any messages for him, or Strückner.

—*Maybe Strückner & Knox in cahoots?*

—Or Knox hoped to be handed the baton through Strückner.

—*You made him jealous. Now thinks Caleb the one to succeed Wells.*

—Yeah, I just said that to probe him. But it's true there was a Caleb in the will. I'd forgotten until the Brodies brought up the name. It's exotic.

—*I think I'll like Caleb better.*

—There's a better prospect yet. If Wells runs these yearly meetings that Knox and Caleb attend, and now Wells is dead and Caleb doesn't know . . . how many more don't know?

—*You mean they coming back for Xmas?*

—Why not? Ambrose wasn't a notable man, just rich. His death didn't make the papers. It was unexpected; he wasn't ill or anything. Most of his associates drop by only once a year. Caleb was one of the assiduous, and he knows nothing. Conceivably, neither do the others.

—*So, we don't interfere? We stay silent & have the dining room ready for winter solstice?*

—Could be fun. Tomorrow I'll go through the office. I might find a guest list or something. You search Strückner's room: Check if he did receive any instructions. Any questions?

—Can we move to another room?

—Why?

—I'd rather have you sleep on the 1st floor.

—There aren't any beds on the first floor.

—Isn't it like tempting fate?

—That's why you're here—to protect me.

A.'S DIARY

I woke up after midnight. I'm not sure about the time. The bed is so vast that lying in the middle of it my elf eyes can't read the LCD clock. Niamh must be sleeping somewhere else on the mattress, in hollow silence—not a swish, not a breath. Outside the canopy lay the immeasurable dark void.

I rolled over to my left and sat at the edge of the bed, ready to leap into space. I almost didn't expect to touch a floor under my feet. I stood up and went for a glass of water.

Luckily, the bathroom is just across the hallway. Like a bat, I guided myself by sound: first the creaking floorboards of the hallway, then the silent tiles of the bathroom. I did have some trouble finding the light switch (they're all too high). With the lights on, I noticed for the first time that the ceiling is vaulted like a tunnel. I drank some water from the sink and glanced at the mirror. I could see my skin with outstanding detail. I checked the bulbs and saw the light grow brighter. I squinted at the white glow reverberating on the sink, the wall tiles, and the shower curtain, haloing them all with an aura that seemed to corrode the outline of all objects and that of a shadow on the curtain. *Not my shadow.* A shadow *behind* the curtain.

As soon as I understood that, the bulbs went out.

I stood there, waiting, until my scorched eyes got used to the dark. Quietly the moonlight redrew the room: hardly a whisper, compared to the recent electric cry.

Then I strode to the tub and pulled the curtain open.

It would be stupid to pretend I found anything. I couldn't even tell whether the whole episode had been a dream when I woke up in the morning twilight, next to Niamh wrapped up in the quilt like an insect in a cocoon. But I did remember the shadow. I remembered the position of the light above the mirror and I knew it couldn't have been my shadow. There had been somebody standing inside the tub.

Niamh stirred, stretched herself out of her patchwork chrysalis. She turned over, and a good-morning nive froze on her lips.

I asked what was wrong. She ran to the dresser and brought me a mirror. I have a burst vessel in each eye—both my sclerae dyed crimson.

The bathroom lights are burned out. And of course there's no trace of anything or anybody in the tub.

That was the third visit.

The second-worst thing that can happen at a medical exam is having the doctor call in a colleague because *he* needs a second opinion.

And the worst thing that can happen is that they ask you permission to take a picture.

Despite their attentions, though, our visit to the little Point Bless clinic has been overall useless. Though I enjoyed the ride and the horror in the pedestrians' faces as Niamh drove me there doing a hundred and twenty in our mile-snouted Audi.

We had breakfast at Gordon's, the local café on Monroe Street that youngsters around here must consider the definition of tedium. I loved the place. It was quintessential U.S., with its window tables and the many sauce bottles and thingies against the glass, just like in the movies. It made everything we said very interesting. Not that it actually wasn't; Niamh did find my account of the bathroom poltergeist pretty transcendent. And the sunglasses I was wearing at the time certainly added some mystery.

*

—*Shouldn't we call someone?*

—"Who you gonna call?"

—*Electrician!*

SECURITY VIDEOTAPE: RAY'S HARDWARE AND ELECTRONICS

1995-11-06 MON 11:02

An unshaven YOUNG MAN in sunglasses looks straight at the camera.

> *[A WOMAN, in a down vest and wool hat, comes behind the counter.]*

WOMAN: Hi.

YOUNG MAN: Oh, hi. Uh, the woman at the café said if I want an electrician I must come here and talk to … Sam?

WOMAN: Wait, I'll call him.

> *[She leaves. Behind the man, a skinny KID in punk rags, fifteenish, is browsing through the shelves. Her dark hair falls in ringlets down her temples, ends à la garçonne at the back, and freezes in a volcanic eruption of dreadlocks and wool ribbons on top.]*

> *[The man turns to see her unwrapping a box.]*

YOUNG MAN: Who's going to pay for that?

KID: *[Distractedly points at him.]*

YOUNG MAN: Am I? God, I don't know what to spend my money on. What a piece of nouveau riche scum I am.

[Kid presses some buttons on the voice recorder she has pulled out of the box.]

RECORDING: —ce of nouveau riche scum I am.

YOUNG MAN: Cool. *[Inspecting the device.]* Where do you put the tape in that?

KID: *[Indicates a word on the box.]*

YOUNG MAN: "Digital." Wow. Seems like yesterday we went to see *Arrival of a Train* and ran out of the theater in panic.

[The woman comes back.]

WOMAN: Is it a problem with your car?

YOUNG MAN: Uh, no, no, it's my house, I just wanted an electrician to come by.

WOMAN: Is your power out?

YOUNG MAN: No.

WOMAN: Any twitches, tension drops…?

YOUNG MAN: No, quite the contrary. It works too fine. I'd just like somebody to check it out.

WOMAN: Well, you know, we mainly sell appliances and tools. Sam only goes to homes for emergencies.

YOUNG MAN: Oh. I see.

[The woman eyes the kid tampering with the voice recorder in the back.]

WOMAN: Are you from nearby?

YOUNG MAN: Yes, we just moved to… *[He stops, reads the kid's lips. Then to the clerk.]* We live in Axton House.

WOMAN: Axton House.

YOUNG MAN: Yes.

WOMAN: Oh. Well, uh… Maybe Sam can drop by sometime this week. Actually, I'll kick his ass off the couch if I have to.

YOUNG MAN: Oh, great. Thanks.

WOMAN: *[To the kid.]* Can I help you, dear?

[The kid replaces the device in the box and leaves it on the counter.]

WOMAN: Are you buying this?

KID: *[Nods.]*

WOMAN: *[Checks the price tag.]* Okay, that's … eighty-five ninety-nine.

KID: *[Whistles and snaps her fingers to the man.]*

YOUNG MAN: *[Pulling his wallet out.]* Do you take Visa?

WOMAN: Sure.

YOUNG MAN: *[Producing his credit card, to the kid.]* Aunt Liza warned me
            you'd do this.

[She grins. The woman runs the credit card, hands out the ticket, he signs.]

WOMAN: Thank you. And welcome to Point Bless.

YOUNG MAN: Thank you. *[To kid.]* Let's go.

[Woman leaves through the back; they start for the door, kid carrying the box.]

YOUNG MAN: So what did I buy that for?

[She pulls up the string around her neck, retrieving a small note-pad from inside her shirt, tied to a ring together with the stub of a pencil. She scribbles a message and shows it to him.]

YOUNG MAN: Either I'm dense or you abbreviate too much. What does "e vee
            pee" mean?

LETTER

Axton House
Axton Rd.
Point Bless, VA 26969

Dear Aunt Liza,

It's half past six in the evening and I'm lying on the sofa in the music room (first door on the left from entrance). The yellow paper light from the side lamp fights the remains of dusk outside. At the other end of the room, about half a mile away, I hear Niamh on the piano. Where did a brat raised in the streets of Ireland learn to play the piano?

Nuns taught me! *

Anyway. The day's been gloomy and memorably sad, so we spent most of it indoors. We plan to start lighting up some of the hearths; otherwise, as winter besieges these long, windy halls, the whole house will become unlivable except for the inside of the quilt in which Niamh wraps herself at night like a Chinese spring roll.

We explored the maze today. It's beautiful, as Niamh's pictures show. Perhaps even more so with the box hedge overgrown and the floor so dirty with cracking leaves and twigs. I think decadence becomes a labyrinth. Same goes for the house: downfall and smut romanticize it.

The maze isn't all that challenging, though. Niamh told me about the tip you gave her once, "Always turn in the same direction, and turn around only if in a loop." We reached the center pretty soon. The intricate path makes the finding of four stone benches and a statue of Ariadne winding a ball of thread a little treasure. We sat down, despite the drizzle and the fear that the creeping fingers of ivy under the seats would clutch our feet and drag us into the hedge, and we stayed there,

---

* This appears written by Niamh herself on the margin.

breathing that cold little square, realizing that a maze is one of the craziest, coolest *real* things one can aspire to own.

There's not much else new. I went through Ambrose's office here on the first floor and found nothing but the reassurance that this was the workplace he meant for people to see, the one dedicated to his futile public business. The rest of the paper-towered desks about the house surely hide worthier prizes.

Meanwhile, Niamh explored Strückner's room and the servants' quarters. They fit under the main stairs, and except for a useful little bathroom have long been deserted. According to Glew, Strückner was invited to occupy one of the nicer guest rooms in the refurbished second-floor south wing. Though he accepted, I think he took the smallest one out of modesty. I wonder if he ever dared to untidy it.

By the way, we drove to town this morning and Niamh bought a voice recorder. She plans to leave it on in the bathroom through the night and capture "electronic voice phenomena." I'm concerned that I'll have to flush the toilet at launching time to cover up the splash. And talking about splashes, she also picked up a brochure from a swimming pool installer. I'll try to keep her from turning this place into a holiday resort before you see it, but you'll have to hurry up. I don't know how long I can hold her.

Yeah, that might be my way to say I'm beginning to miss you a little. So does Niamh, I'm sure. I don't let her read these letters anymore; she keeps laughing at my prose and pointing out how pompous I sound. She says I read too much Lovecraft.

Well, at least it taught me *some* form of English. And we live in a haunted house now, so that background might come in useful.

Oh, and Niamh *really* wants a dog.

Kisses,
A.

*

P.S.: I considered this was worth a new page. While looking for an envelope for this letter, Niamh stumbled across the one found in Ambrose's office, the empty one with "Aeschylus" written on it, and she noticed this:

A E **S** C H Y L U **S**
S T **R** Ü C K N E **R**

EXCERPT FROM SAMUEL MANDALAY'S *ARS CRYPTOGRAPHICA.* LONDON, 1977

Among substitution ciphers, the simplest form (and therefore the most transparent) is monoalphabetical substitution, which consists of individually replacing each letter for another symbol. A memorable instance of this cipher is found in Edgar Allan Poe's "The Gold-Bug." Sherlock Holmes cracks a similar code in "The Adventure of the Dancing Men," by Sir Arthur Conan Doyle. The high incidence of this kind of cipher in crime fiction actually denotes its inefficiency to safely conceal information in real life.

There are several common ways to assign new values to each letter. The simplest of these involve transposition of the alphabet. For example, shift the alphabet one letter forward, thus replacing each letter by the next: $a = b$, $b = c$, $c = d$. We call this a Caesar cipher. An even more puerile method: Write out the twenty-six letters of the English alphabet in two rows of thirteen; then replace each letter by the one below or above. So: $a = n$, $b = o$, $c = p$.

The following method allows one to encode and decode a message quickly by knowing a single key word: Write out the alphabet in one row; then below write one key word, the longer the better, omitting repeated letters, and fill the rest of the row with the remains of the alphabet. In the following example, we used the word *Mozambique.*

```
ABCDEFGHIJKLMNOPQRSTUVWXYZ
MOZABIQUECDFGHJKLNPRSTVWXY
```

And again we replace the letters in the upper row with the ones in the lower: $a = m$, $b = o$, $c = z$. [...]

If the language of the message is known, breaking a monoalphabetic substitution code is extremely easy. This is due to the recurrent character sequences discussed in §Appendix II. An example: By far the most frequent word in the English language is *the*. If a ciphered message contains several occurrences of a word such as *123*, it is not unwise to start by verifying whether $1 = t$, $2 = h$, $3 = e$.

In order to counteract the breaker's efforts, the messenger may wish to reduce these sequences to a minimum by *a*) omitting or cutting down on common words such as articles, demonstratives, and personal pronouns; and *b*) omitting spaces and punctuation marks. Still, some recurrent character sequences will remain detectable (as exposed in §Appendix II.3). For instance, if 4 is always followed by 5, but 5 can be preceded by other symbols, then most likely $4 = q$ and $5 = u$. This applies to all languages in Western Europe.

Furthermore, the message will still be susceptible to a frequency analysis as detailed in §Appendix II—as Legrand does in Poe's tale: Take all the symbols in the coded message and sort them by number of incidences. If the message is in English, the symbol on top of the list is most likely the letter *e*.

The definitive way to strengthen your substitution cipher is brevity. It is estimated (see Zangler, 1949) that any message longer than eighty characters falls within the reach of a more or less laborious aficionado. On the other hand, a message written in a single row, without spaces or punctuation, even using a childish Caesar cipher, may very well be indecipherable.

But, of course, an indecipherable message is not a message.

*

(Bedroom.)

—What does this mean?

—*That Ambrose DID leave a message for Strückner.*

—How was Strückner supposed to know he was Aeschylus?

—*They'd used the code before? Wells Sr. a cryptographer.*

—Of course. And he had a Strückner serving him too. It isn't much of a code, though. I guess it had to be within Strückner's skills.

—*Not as easy if the message inside short. Like "CALLCALEB."*

—That's going to the other extreme: from pastime to indecipherable.

—*But the key is the envelope. Strückner knows 8 letters already:*

$$A = S$$
$$E = T$$
$$S = R$$
$$C = U$$
$$H = C$$
$$Y = K$$
$$L = N$$
$$U = E$$

—And from here he can work out the rest. Whereas someone who came across the envelope by accident, not knowing whom it was for, would need to start from zero. Ingenious.

—*Pity we only got the envelope.*

—What might he have done with the message?

—*Destroyed.*

—I guess so.

A.'S DIARY

Just a while ago I was standing in a dazzling white desert. The heat was intolerable, but the sun was not to blame. A fire was burning behind me. I heard distant screams. Light engulfed me. I was carrying a gun.

I blinked into blackness. I thought I'd carried along a gasp from the dream; I heard it dissolving into silence. I waited for Niamh to move, but she didn't.

I stayed in bed for a while until I felt clearheaded, and then I got up and felt my way along the edge of the bed and around the canopy to the bathroom. If something out of the normal was going to happen, I wanted to be awake enough to record it properly.

I closed my eyes at the bathroom lights. The new bulbs worked fine, but my eyes had grown sensitive. Squinting, I washed my face, trying not to sprinkle water on Niamh's voice recorder lying on the sink. I looked in the mirror, and my reflection stepped back. My sclerae seemed cleaner, but the contour of my eyes was scarlet, like I'd been crying for weeks.

I must have heard something. I can't remember what. I know I instinctively turned to the bathtub. I didn't see a shadow.

As I stepped closer, I imagined the sound track to this scene. Either two single piano notes in rapid succession, or a tremolo of violins growing as my imprudent hand rose to the curtain.

I pulled the curtain, and a guitar blast shook the foundations of Axton House.

It actually came from the music room, right through two floors and strong enough to blow the ceiling away. It was the same Dead Kennedys album that Niamh had been listening to earlier in the afternoon, but I didn't recognize it at first. What I did recognize was a whistle from Niamh on top of Jello Biafra's voice that almost cracked the mirror from side to side.

I ran—no, I flew downstairs, regretting the whole way that our house is too big: a long corridor, the third-floor landing, a long flight of stairs, second-floor landing, two flights of stairs, another corridor lit by the music room from where the punk music blasted, and the anteroom across, which I stomped into just in time to see Niamh bursting open the double doors to Ambrose's office.

She ran to the window and scanned the garden. Later she claimed to have seen somebody; I saw no one.

The doors had been blocked from the inside. The carpet was littered with papers. On the center panel behind the desk, where a painting of black plantation workers praying had hung, an open safe yawned.

Niamh had not been asleep when it happened. I guess her mutism has somehow sharpened her hearing; otherwise I can't explain how she could pick up the breaking of a glass two floors and several closed doors away. She heard nothing else, but it was enough to set her in motion. She walked downstairs, barefooted, and began checking all of the rooms in the dark. Once she located where the intruder was, and judging it too dangerous to face him, she opted for scaring him away. So she went to the music room, where she'd been playing the piano first and her CDs later, turned up the volume to the max, and pressed play to scare the intruder; then she whistled to call me over; and finally, she charged at the office doors without opening them to force him out—she only pushed strongly enough when I got there. Of course, the burglar had left by then.

*

(Living room, later.)

—*I think it was Knox.*

—You think or you saw?

—*Think.*

—Not good enough. I doubt it was Knox. If I were him and wanted something from that safe, I wouldn't come in person.

(Meditating.)

—Anyway, forget about the who. Think about what. Knox expected Ambrose to leave him something; we know that. But what Ambrose left was a coded message for Strückner.

—*& Knox very interested in Strückner.*

—True. We know it was a brief message; it was bound to be. Most likely, it was meant to lead Strückner to a longer message kept somewhere else. So it probably said . . .

—*"Check the safe."*

—Exactly. We're assuming Strückner knew where the safe was. Maybe he didn't. But let's assume he did.

—*So he opened it, took what he looked for & left. & when Knox came after him, found nothing.*

—*If* it was Knox. Are you sure he left empty-handed?

—*90% sure.*

—But it doesn't make sense. If the safe contained Ambrose's final dispositions, and if they concerned Knox, as Knox believed, if all that were true, Strückner would have transmitted them to Knox, period.

—*What if Str. DIDN'T open the safe?*

—Why shouldn't he?

—*Maybe he wouldn't follow the instructions?*

—Why wouldn't he?

—*Maybe he didn't decipher them?*

—And yet he destroyed them?

—*Maybe he didn't?*

—No, if he hadn't understood them, or hadn't understood they were for him to read, he would have put them back in the envelope. Anybody would do that.

(Meditating again.)

Okay, let's say he did read it, but chose not to follow it. It's strange, but . . . let's go from here. He says the hell with it, he leaves, deeply affected . . . Then we come along . . . Then Knox comes along . . .

—*Knox does what Strückner wouldn't do?*

—Very risky. Plus, here's something puzzling—how long was it between you hearing the window breaking and giving the alarm?

—*5–10 minutes.*

—So he knew in which room to look, knew where the safe was, and spent ten minutes searching it?

—OPENING it.

—See? There's our hypothesis castle tumbling down. He doesn't even search the house; he goes straight for the safe; he even breaks in by the nearest window. Why is he so confident about the safe? Why is he so sure it's worth the trouble?

—Strückner told him!

—And didn't give him the combination?

—Good point.

(Depression.)

—Why didn't you come upstairs when you realized someone had broken in? He could've been a professional! He could've killed you!

—I'm here to protect you.

(Meditating . . .)

—Oh, okay, get yourself a dog!

*

I guess we felt profaned enough for one night, so we refused to go back to bed. After coffee and chocolate milk, we began to inventory the contents of the safe (mainly a coin collection, a jewel case, and a folder of title deeds whose original order I failed to reproduce), and return them to their nominal place.

The revelation came at dawn.

The safe had been opened, not forced. Once all its contents were returned to it, I realized that if we closed it we wouldn't be able to open it again. I decided that a thief wouldn't come back for what he didn't take the first time, and left the safe ajar; then I started to look for another place to hang the painting. As I carried it around, I noticed in the back of the canvas the same blue-headed thumbtacks I had seen among Ambrose's desk supplies.

I stood there holding the painting for about two minutes before I figured it out.

The instructions left for Aeschylus were not "Check the safe." They were "Look behind the painting."

Both Strückner and Knox thought it meant to look in the safe, but neither had the combination; that was why one failed to follow the instructions and the other sent someone to open it.

Actually, it was as simple as removing the cork sheet behind the canvas. Morning was breaking when we found Ambrose Wells' letter taped to the back of the painting.

2/14/1995

Dear Strückner,

This will be the twenty-first letter I hide behind the old Van Krugge. Yet I have the dark presentment that this one will be read. Surely you understand why.

I have adhered to this yearly ritual since my twenty-ninth birthday, after returning from India, when I first noticed I was too closely following my father's steps. I will ask you about him often this year. I will be eager to hear what your father used to say about mine. It is indeed remarkable: No physical threat looms ahead; no clock is ticking my time away. And yet I feel that if I live to replace this letter in a year's time, I will be reborn.

You understand now why I chose to be childless. I cannot permit this fate to continue devouring souls of Wells. Nor can I tolerate any more Strückners wasting their lives serving honey tea to eccentric occultists. Both our families deserve a rest.

If you are reading this, the Wells have already taken it.

For you I have a last request. There are further letters I keep prepared for this eventuality, and I rely on your diligence to post them as soon as possible: to Curtis Knox in Lawrenceville and Caleb Ford in

Clayboro, regarding our sad Society; and to Dr. Belknap in Midburg. You shall find these letters hidden between the pages of that wonderful book of our childhood, the one you used to read by a tree.

That will be all, Aeschylus. Good night.

Affectionately yours,
Ambrose Gabriel Wells

P.S.: The Van Krugge is all yours. Happy retirement.

NIAMH'S NOTEPAD

(At Gordon's Café, 9 am, waiting for Glew.)

—You seem affected.

—It's sad someone takes so much trouble to send a message to the right person at the right time, & still they fail.

—That's true. But hey, at least it got to us.

—Come to think of it, I can't remember any dead whose last wishes were carried out exactly as they wanted. Like we don't respect them anymore.

—I guess the trend now is disappointing our fellow men. And the dead are no different.

SECURITY VIDEOTAPE: PONOPAH COUNTY ANIMAL SHELTER

```
1995-11-07 TUE 11:51 CAM6
```

STAN walks onto the path between the kennels, announced by a boisterous ovation of dogs.

STAN: These are the stray adults. They're all found in the wild and unclaimed.

[A young GUY in sunglasses and a teen GIRL with dread falls come in tow.]

GUY: *[To the girl.]* Okay, you choose.

[The girl catwalks down the path, studying the dogs on both sides. Her companion stays at a distance, arms crossed. The ruckus is saturating the audio.]

[The girl turns around, retraces her steps, stops halfway to the start point. She stands there, arms akimbo, avoiding eye contact, letting the animals bark themselves hoarse.]

[Stan checks with the guy twice in the next two minutes; he just signals to wait.]

[The barking commotion has now fallen to a senseless dialogue between two or three animals.]

[Eventually, one utters the last word.]

[The girl walks to his cage, a few steps behind, kneels, and leans her hand forward. The barking stops automatically.]

STAN: Noisiest of the lot.
GUY: Most extroverted too.

STAN: *[Reaching the cage, unlocking the door.]* The black pariah. He's been here awhile. *[Cage is opened.]* Here. I'll let you guys fraternize while I get his release papers.

[Stan leaves. The kid is now petting an excited (yet silent) medium-size dark mongrel, the man kneeling to greet it.]

GUY: I like him. What are you going to call him?

[The girl retrieves from under her pullover a small notepad and short pencil on a string around her neck; she writes.]

*

—*Your choice—I'm not calling him.*

**PONOPAH COUNTY
ANIMAL SHELTER**

30 Culbreth Rd. Clayboro, VA 26960
Phone: (755) 963-3979
Fax: (755) 963-3991

TEMPORARY ADOPTION AGREEMENT

ADOPTER

Name: ....Niamh S. Connell...

Birth date:...............10-29-79...

Address: ....1 Axton Rd., Point Bless, VA.... ZIP: ...26969.........

☒ I agree to foster this dog for a test period of 2 weeks, feed it, provide it a space of its own, look after it, and train it if necessary.

☒ I agree to be visited by an inspector from the Ponopah County Animal Shelter at the end of the test period to check that the dog is properly attended.

☒ I hereby make a non-refundable down payment of ....$50 for the adoption fee, which shall cover up-to-date vaccination and/or neutering costs.

ADOPTEE

Name: ......Help..

Breed: ....Mixed (possible McNab collie cross)..........................

Gender: ....Male................... Age: ....3 (estimated)..........

History: ..Unclaimed stray, captured in Clayboro, March '95.
Signs of malnourishment. Nameless collar. Tested
positive for vaccines...

Height: ......19 in....... Weight: .....28 lbs.......Fur: .....Black.....

Distinctive marks: ....Dented left ear. Talkative...................

Adopter's signature

Connell.

LETTER

Axton House
1 Axton Rd.
Point Bless, VA 26969

Dear Aunt Liza,

And so, there are three of us. Let me introduce you to the newest member of the family. We called him Help, so as to ensure he'll assist us in case of peril. Niamh is committed to turning him into our personal security guard in a matter of weeks. Until then, I'm not even sure whether he'll raise the alarm in the event of (another) break-in (more on that later). He hasn't yapped since he met Niamh, though he was the loudest barker in the shelter.

So. The break-in. [. . .]

AUDIO RECORDING

[BACKGROUND: Gordon's Café, morning rush.]

A.:	Sir. Thanks for coming.
GLEW:	As soon as I could. Miss. First things first—are you both all right?
A.:	We're all right. It was just a shock.
GLEW:	In all these years, I never heard of Axton House being burgled. Did you leave the shutters open?
A.:	I'm afraid we did, yes.
GLEW:	I see. Strückner used to take care of that every night; now it is your responsibility. But I guess you already learned that the hard way.
A.:	So we did.

GLEW: Hello. Coffee, please. Have you reported the crime? Can I assist you?

A.:   Well, we don't know what they took. If they took anything. Did you know there was a safe in the office?

GLEW: Yes, I knew. I just forgot to mention it.

A.:   Do you know the combination?

GLEW: No. But if it's open now, you probably will be able to change it.

A.:   Didn't you think that the safe could contain relevant documents? Like deeds and stuff?

GLEW: I already have copies of everything.

A.:   Did you go through his papers after he died?

GLEW: Strückner did, but he found nothing. *[Over coffee being poured.]* Thank you.

A.:   Didn't he leave any note behind, a message for Strückner or something?

GLEW: No—why are you asking me all this?

A.:   Well, there's … There was a note from Ambrose to Strückner in the safe. It said that the watercolor that hangs over the safe is a present for him.

GLEW: A watercolor … Do you mean the Van Krugge?

A.:   That's it. Is it valuable?

GLEW: Well, to Strückner, it is the difference between a modest retirement and a life pension.

A.:   Then we should give it to him.

GLEW: The will doesn't mention it. Legally, it is still part of "Axton House and all of its contents," so it's yours to dispose of.

A.:   Well, if Ambrose meant to give it to him, I want to do it.

GLEW: That's very noble of you, but where is Strückner? That's what I would like to know.

A.:   Is it possible that he returned to Europe?

GLEW: It is.

A.:   Was he German?

GLEW: Swiss. I should know, because Wells used to ascribe all of his virtues to the Swiss heritage—the Swiss thoroughness, the Swiss discretion, the Swiss cheesecake, and so on. His father, Strückner senior, worked in Axton House before him, serving

Ambrose's father. Then mother and child were reunited with the father, and he joined the staff.

[Sound of writing. Blank.]

A what? *Spider-Man?*

A.:   Yeah, in the safe. It seemed a regular comic book to me, but since it was in there, I thought it'd have collector value. Or sentimental value, to Ambrose.

GLEW: A comic book? *[Chortle.]* I'm sure not. Truly, I am surprised; I've known him since we were boys and he never showed any interest in such things. *[More writing in the background.]* Let's see, what is that now? *[Pause.]* A Mason, you say? Well ... Of course, one might never know, but I'm pretty sure he wasn't.

*

[. . .] As for the windowpane, the glazier in town will come by tomorrow. There's really no hurry, now that we've been reminded the shutters are there for a purpose.

Still, despite the statistical improbability of two burglars on consecutive nights, I will not sleep soundly tonight. This fortress of ours is too big to defend. Even Help, who's been stocking up energy for months in a kennel, burned it all up in one morning running about the property.

I wish you could see the house as I see it now. The Polaroids don't do it any justice. In the distance, when its grandiose form slides into view at the last turn of the road, it stands proud like an attempt at futuristic architecture in the plantation era. In the close-up, though, when you're near enough to touch it with your fingertip, it just feels old. Not respectable old, but godforsaken old. Like a sepia-colored photograph, or Roman ruins that miraculously avoided tourist guides.

This house ages differently. It's like those bungalows that endure decades, but are awake only three months a year in summer, so that they live one year, but age four. This happens to Axton House and the things within, "all of its contents." They stand on the brink of the twenty-first century, but their age pulls them back. Maybe that's why everything in it is or seems anachronistic; a newspaper in it is outdated; any accessory falls out of fashion; Ambrose Wells lived in 1995 looking like a gentleman from 1910s London.

I am starting to feel it myself—like time is running faster than me, and I have to catch up. Like I'm stuck on the bank of a river while the space-time continuum keeps flowing. Like I'm being forgotten from the universe.

Okay, let me describe for you what I'm seeing now: I'm sitting on the porch and Niamh and Help are about fifty meters away in the garden, and I can't see exactly what she's saying to him, or how she's saying it, but the dog is sitting, standing, and coming to her, *following her orders.* And every now and then she rewards him with corn flakes.

How the fuck does she do that?

Kisses,
A.

AUDIO RECORDING

[Blank.]

[Slight stir of blankets.]

A.:   *[Gasping sounds.]*

[Silence vibrates. The air is about to crack.]

          NO!!

[Blankets flutter away like a startled murder of crows, leaving A.'s accelerated breathing in the foreground.]

[After some seconds, the breathing slows down, not progressively, but in clear, self-aware drops of speed.]

[Then it ceases, tentatively.]

     Niamh?

[Seconds later, breathing is resumed.]

     [Almost in a whimper.] Help?

[The breathing yields to a subtle shudder. Blankets crawl back to the head of the bed; a body rolls on the mattress.]

[Then all goes blank again.]

?

I was walking barefoot on muffin snow along the spine of a steep roof with stair-shaped battlements. The sky was unnaturally yellow above. And below, an ashen fog covered the ground, nothing but bare trees sticking their heads out.

I was half-naked. My shoulders burned with cold. I couldn't feel my hands.

Somewhere down on the street it's still snowing and it's daytime and cars honk at a red light and passersby smell of alcohol. There is one female driver trapped in the traffic jam, and she's half-naked too, her skin warm in the winterproof universe inside the car. And she's gorgeous. More than gorgeous: blazing hot, mindblastingly sexy, the kind any nonstupid person should kneel before. And she wears nothing but a pretty set of flowery lingerie, and the seat belt and the seat are unworthy of caressing her silken body.

I am on the passenger seat, twisting a Rubik's cube in my hands. Now and then I peek at her ridiculously long legs.

A human skeleton stares back at the Renaissance men, his empty sockets filled with equal curiosity.

I slam a door open into the glaring white desert. I'm carrying a gun. My eyes hurt.

My eye hurts. The black soldier's holding it open, and the surgeon sticks the pincers around my eyeball. I'm strapped down on the operating slab. I'm conscious, and screaming to prove it, until my throat's torn and bleeding, but they don't mind. He's pulling my eyeball out, measuring the nerve's resistance, until he yanks and it snaps like a whip and I don't wake up—I stay there to feel the pain. I'm in the dark for a million years hearing them giggling at my eyeball.

Then I wake up and kill them and wake up.

SECURITY VIDEOTAPE: POINT BLESS POST OFFICE

1995-11-08 WED 09:42

NO AUDIO.

> [Skinny TEENAGER walks in straight to the admissions window, a
> long scarf kiting behind her. She hands a letter to the CLERK and
> she fishes some coins from her pockets. As she waves her hand
> and starts to leave with a long, uncommonly kind smile, the clerk
> calls her over again. She is handed another letter. Off her guard,
> she flips the unexpected envelope in her hands, lips moving to
> both addresses.]

LETTER

165 Wheat Row
Milburn, NY 12984

Axton House
Point Bless, VA 26969
Nov 1st

Dear Leonidas,

I am forced to give up, for once, two months before the end. My task
has provided me little fruit and much visible wearing. Dr. Herbert in
Watertown is urging me to take some rest. I've been relying on sleeping pills for six months now, and my only relief is that I don't look
worse than Asterion: I visited him in April and he was taking Xanax as
Mentos. I am able to sleep with a double dose of Starnox, but I keep
dreaming. I tried the tablets he recommended to you to inhibit REM
sleep. They are effective, but sleeping without dreaming is hardly sleeping at all.

I'm concerned about Asterion's health. Honestly, I am concerned about your health as well. I am concerned about your dreams and I am concerned about what slipped into your note dated August 4th.

I have tried to answer your questions about John Wells. Unfortunately, my father is not a good conversationalist anymore. Age is slowly gnawing away his memories.

I confess, there have been times when I envied him.

I am not sure I am interested in attending our next reunion. But I do look forward to seeing you as soon as possible, in whichever circumstances.

Yours sincerely,
Prometheus*

NIAMH'S NOTEPAD

(At Gordon's, over the letter.)

—What do you think?

—*If this Wells' Society, I don't like the game they playing.*

—I'm not sure you actually have to play the game.

—*What do we do?*

—We go on. What do you want to do?

—*Must search for those letters, "Inside that wonderful book of our childhood."*

---

* The sender's initials on the envelope of this letter were "S.W.L."

—True.

—What does it mean?

—Just another code. A safer one, because it's based in personal experience: "The book you used to read by a tree." That Spider-Man card you played was a good try, by the way.

(BLUSH!)

—I could start shaking books until something falls out.

—There're about ten thousand books in the library. Not to mention the rest of the house.

—I have time.

—Maybe you shouldn't. It's just what you said about the wishes of the dead. Ambrose took so much trouble to ensure that those papers were found by whom he intended. We should be worthy of it.

—To be worthy, you must be Strückner.

—Not really *be*. We could ask.

So Niamh began raiding the library while I returned to the office on the first floor, where the official papers are kept (in a pretense of order that all other workspaces around the house fail to observe) and found the latest phone bills. The volume of both outgoing and incoming international calls is staggering for someone labeled a hermit. I guess this intense communication made up for Ambrose's unfitness to travel. However, he did not live alone, so I expected some of these calls to be Strückner's. I highlighted some numbers in Switzerland, but failed to find any in the September–October bill, which lay unopened in the unread mail pile.

Still, I dialed the last number, just to give it a shot. Only while waiting for the tone I remembered I don't speak German. A woman answered, and all I could babble was, "*Strückner, bitte.*" She replied impatiently and hung up.

I'm afraid that was most of my work plan for the morning. So I sat back and put my feet on the table and I studied the records again. And mused. And began writing this.

So okay, maybe he hasn't left the country. Still, people make calls whenever their lives take a sharp turn. But to whom?

*

Blue Ridge Bell
Telephone Cooperative, Inc.

BRB Data Communication Services
(Internet access, dial-up and DSL)
available NOW!
More info: (546) 802-4873

ACCOUNT	DATE	CHARGE
755 963 4000	10/08/1995	68,91

*NO.	DAY	DATE	TYPE	NUMBER	RATE	MINS	AMOUNT	
01	FRI	09/08	INTERNATIONAL	+44 20 36272687	I	05:35	6.41	→ UK
02	FRI	09/08	INTERNATIONAL	+44 20 38723841	I	15:57	17.07	
03	FRI	09/08	INTERNATIONAL	+49 030 23967555	I	02:01	3.13	→ GERMANY
04	FRI	09/08	INTERNATIONAL	+49 030 39394044	I	05:09	6.40	
05	FRI	09/08	INTERNATIONAL	+44 22 2402711	I	:57	1.63	
06	FRI	09/08	INTERNATIONAL	+44 20 36272687	I	03:19	4.07	
07	SAT	09/09	INTERNATIONAL	+49 030 20399135	HI	01:12	2.03	
08	SAT	09/09	INTERNATIONAL	+41 22 2402711	HI	04:39	6.23	→ SWITZERLAND
09	SUN	09/10	LOCAL	755 9632740	H	:30	0.05	
10	MON	09/11	INTERNATIONAL	+49 030 26589617	I	:57	1.63	
11	TUE	09/12	AREA CODE 540	540 7053866	D	03:27	0.26	
12	TUE	09/12	LOCAL	755 9632740	D	05:34	0.37	
13	THU	09/14	INTERNATIONAL	+49 030 2388382	I	10:18	11.35	
14	THU	09/14	INTERNATIONAL	+250 252596400	SI	01:55	3.94	→ RWANDA
15	THU	09/14	INTERNATIONAL	+250 933827771	SI	:40	1.36	
16	THU	09/14	AREA CODE 757	757 1673897	S	03:16	0.26	
17	FRI	09/15	EMERGENCY	911	E	:43	0.00	→ HERE'S WHEN
18	FRI	09/15	LOCAL	757 9653318	D	01:30	0.10	IT HAPPENED
19	FRI	09/15	LOCAL	751 9630952	D	02:01	0.13	
20	FRI	09/15	INTERNATIONAL	+250 252596400	I	:28	1.36	
21	MON	09/25	AREA CODE 434	434 2910971	D	02:49	0.22	
22	TUE	09/26	AREA CODE 434	434 2910971	D	07:04	0.53	?
23	THU	09/28	AREA CODE 434	434 2910971	D	:59	0.07	
24	MON	10/02	AREA CODE 434	434 2910971	D	01:39	0.13	
25	THU	10/05	AREA CODE 434	434 2910971	D	02:22	0.18	

AN ANSWERING MACHINE TAPE

LINDSAY: Hello. Thank you for calling Whateley's Domestic Staff Agency. Our business hours are nine a.m. to three p.m. Monday through Friday, and nine a.m. to noon on Saturdays. If you wish to be contacted, please leave your name and number after the signal.

[BEEP.]

MAN: Uh. Hi. This is—

[Sudden burst of techno music in the background.]

YOUNG MAN: *[Off the mike.]* Niamh?! NIAMH!! Ssshit.

*[Sound of the handset being dropped. Two minutes of uninter-
rupted music follow, until the time allotted runs out.]*

A CUTOUT ARTICLE FROM *SPEED* MAGAZINE, APRIL/MAY 1994

Ann K. Sassari

We first heard about Ann K. while looking for a DJ for our acid-
issue presentation party in '91, and we haven't missed a gig in London since. If you live on the forefront of dance music, you must
attend one of her sessions. It's not enough to stick with the many
imitators who saw her once and live off the experience. She's not a
trend, but a line; she doesn't read a score; she writes the score. And
has written more pages in the history of techno trance than any
other guru from Ibiza.

Sassari was born in Sardinia to a Malay father and a French
mother. At 15 she became the adopted groupie of Parisian pop
band Piqûres. While on tour she took up drums and guitar, along
with other more frownable habits. She spent the following four
years as a piece of Eurotrash living for nothing but acid and sex
on the road. She finally found her epiphany on a nudist beach in
Minorca, where she settled down—once again the Spanish islands
cure a lifelong traveler. She is now a resident at Vis à Vis club in
neighboring Ibiza and flies to Paris and London every now and
then.

Persuaded by friend and coproducer Iris Lerroux, Ann K. agreed
to release a CD with a random sample of her frenetic innovation.
The EP's title is *Meuf,* and the edition is superlimited (2,000 copies
all over the world), but its four tracks are worth it. Even the most
glorious seconds in "Bluenips" barely capture for an instant the
musical ecstasy that Ann K. drives relentlessly from one orgasm

to another, higher and unexplored, light-years from anything any other musician can conceive.

REVIEW FROM *ROCK SPOILED*, JUNE 1994

Meuf / Ann K. Sassari

EP / PRODUCED BY ANN K. SASSARI & IRIS LERROUX / BISOU RECORDS / PARIS 1994

If you're a sick enough raver to have risked treading in a Spanish airport, and crazy enough to spend £8 on four sodding tracks, it better be the new EP by the resident bitch at Vis à Vis Ibiza, who, beside her local fame as an easy fuck, is generally regarded above other turntable zombies for having renewed trance music. For the first time in years, her permanent XTC hangover allowed her to sneak into a recording studio on the continent (something destiny is not planning to let happen again), so you might as well seize the chance. "Bluenips" is even tolerable; "Flow" sounds like Kate Bush on the didgeridoo. Hell, if anyone wants our copy, we're giving it away half price.

REVIEW FROM *CUTTING EDGE*, JULY 1994

Ann K. Sassari: *Meuf*

EP / BISOU RECORDS / £7.99

Let's face it: At 25 you've outdrunk both your parents; you take antidepressants Monday thru Thursday and acid on Fridays; your days as a marathon raver running on mineral water are over. If you must think about the future, put your money on *Meuf*, the very rare four-track CD by resident DJ at Vis à Vis Ann K. Sassari. We guarantee that "Bluenips" will make you drop both the feeding bottle and the feedee baby and move your body like married sex hasn't in years. Once this investment is settled, you may return to your usual house club and dance Jiminy Cricket to death.

A.'S DIARY

It wasn't an alarm this time. It was music for the sake of music. That I realized when I stampeded into the living-room-turned-into-dance-floor to find Niamh bouncing on the sofa, blue and violet extensions whipping the air. But something wasn't right. I know Niamh's music; she listens to trashy punk and garage rock, the kind she head-bangs to along with a crowd of skinheads in a basement, all drinking beer from Dixie cups. This was different. It had synths droning and sending saltwater waves under my feet. It had drumbeats bursting like fireworks, rumbling the furniture out of place, and then a crazy, irregular, disharmonious, spiral crescendo of pure electric noise, like a typhoon dragging our bodies into it. It featured brass orchestras and choirs of mermaids and a piano in Iceland, all of them right there, visible, touchable, in Axton House. It shook us, fucked us, suspended us far above the reach of Help bouncing on his hind legs. It spoke of magenta sunsets and plastic patio chairs growing moss under summer storms rolling on caterpillar tracks. It sprinkled a bokeh of car lights rushing through night highways and slapped our faces like the wind at a hundred and twenty miles an hour. It pictured Niamh playing guitar, washed up naked on a beach in Fiji.

I can't explain it. All I know is I felt like lying three feet over the floor while the last chords of the dream sailed away, and from beyond the dream came the doorbell.

We ran to the door, soaked in sweat. I saw Niamh's eyes glistening. I felt my wounded eyes glistening. Even Help's. Music had just touched every living thing in this very old house.

Even the thick man at the door noticed.

"Hi. I'm Sam. I heard you have a problem with the power."

"Yeah," I panted. "Too much of it."

Later I learned where the CD had come from. Niamh found it in a folder labeled "4" in Ambrose's hand, stacked in a Babel tower of paper on the library desk. Enclosed together with the album are some cutout articles from magazines and a telegram.

THE TELEGRAM

From: Edward Cutler
Ibiza, Spain

FOUND! STOP THANK YOU STOP I FEDEX YOU A COPY OF
THE BEST ALBUM OF 1994 STOP LOOKING FORWARD TO
SEE YOU IN DECEMBER

AUDIO RECORDING

[Sound of steps, and a dim crackling noise like that of a Geiger counter.]

A.:   Nothing really happened here, just the bathroom incident.

SAM: I'm just measuring the voltage drop—see if there's any sig-
        nificant loss of power.

A.: Uh-huh.

SAM: Yeah, you see that a lot in old farms. Too much power gets lost on the way from the intake to the plugs because of bad wiring. But not here, apparently. Wells had all this changed in the eighties. Not the plumbing, though. You might want to look into that. Say, what's that machine, li'l lady?

A.: Don't mind her; she just records stuff.

SAM: That's a recorder?

A.: Digital. She bought it at your store.

SAM: Did you? Well, that's some nice toy you got there. Here, check this one. This baby here is a voltmeter. It measures the current running inside the wires. *[...]* Cat ate your tongue, miss? *[...]* Oh, you can't speak? Sorry! But you can hear me, right?

A.: Should we go on to the third floor?

SAM: Yeah, sure, sure.

[Steps climbing upstairs, creaking wood.]

  Very nice house, yes, sir.

A.: This way. This one's the bathroom of doom.

SAM: It's okay; I can read it from here.

[Thick crackle, sounding like static.]

  Interesting. It reads one twenty-six.

A.: I thought the voltage in this country was one twenty.

SAM: It is. *[...]* Very interesting. Wanna see, miss? Here, check yourself.

A.: So, instead of a voltage drop, I get extra power?

[Question lingers, unanswered. Then Sam sighs.]

SAM: Not too strange for this house.

A.: What do you mean?

SAM: Oh, I'm—I'm sorry, I didn't mean that as ... Uh, the high voltage could cause the lightbulb to explode, I guess. That's known to happen.

[One character's footsteps start walking away on the moaning wooden floor.]

A.:   Are you frightened of my toilet, Sam?

SAM: What? No, no. It's just … You know. There's not really much I can do.

A.:   I see. A house with supernatural enhancements, right?

SAM: Hey, I'm not the kind of folk who listens to *Tales from the Crypt*, but …

[The party resumes its way, now at promenade speed.]

            The house has its background, you know.

A.:   What kind of background?

SAM: Well, you know.

A.:   No, I don't.

SAM: But you heard the stories.

A.:   What? The lights, the noises, the bleeding walls …?

SAM: The what?

A.:   That's from a movie. Seriously, what is there for a fact about the house that's so creepy? I mean, apart from two members of my family jumping out a window.

SAM: Look, I don't mean to be rude. Your family were the best thing about the house, okay? Nice, charming people.

A.:   Actually, I heard they were hermits.

SAM: Charming hermits, then. Lovely, when compared to the previous owners.

A.:   Previous owners?

SAM: Yeah, well, you'd call it "Wells House" if they'd been here first, right?

A.:   I know Ambrose's grandfather was the first to arrive. He found the house deserted.

SAM: Before that, the last to live here was Charles Axton, surviving his wife and son, in the eighteen seventies. He's the one who gave the house ...

A.: Its bad reputation?

SAM: I was going to say "the supernatural enhancement." The Ngara girl.

A.: The who?

[The creaking floorboards shut up.]

SAM: You know. The ghost of Axton House.

[A big door unlocks. Gentle rain and sparrows can be heard in the background.]

That's the *Tales from the Crypt* part.

A.: Okay. How much do I owe you, Sam?

SAM: Nothing, sir. Nothing's done; nothing's owed. It's been great to visit the house, though. If something else turns up ...

A.: I'll tell you, sure. Good-bye.

SAM: Good-bye. Miss.

[Hurried footsteps on the gravel marching away from the microphone. Seconds later, a car door slams. Engine starts. A van skids on the gravel and rolls away. Rain remains.]

[Crackling noise.]

A.: He'll come back for his toy; you know that.

*

—*No, he won't—he just shat his pants.*

[After an hours-long meaningless blank.]

[Light switch. Bare feet on tiles. Faucet squeaks on, tap water running. Somebody rinsing their face. Then they stop.]

[Water keeps running.]

A.: Niamh?

[Faucet is turned off.]

Niamh?

[A.'s breathing reverberates inside the tiled, vaulted bathroom. Nothing else, except for flat audio noise stretching through a whole minute.]

[Then, a single tap on the sink, as if trying to mark a beat.]

[Nothing.]

[A. produces a slow sequence of four taps, always at the same beat.]

La-lah … Da-dah …

[In the background, off beat, approaches the clickety sound of paws on wood, stopping near the microphone.]

Help. Do you hear it? *[…]*
Come on, dogs are supposed to be sensitive; tell me you hear it.

[Blank.]

[Bare feet and paws exit; light switch.]

Wandering through lifeless woods. There's a little girl in a turquoise dress, spinning, blindfolded, red hair orbiting around her, playing hide-and-seek in the stone-barked grove. Winter fog clings to the trees like amber around prehistoric insects. One shivering sparrow sings.

An identical little girl in an identical turquoise dress is watching, blindfoldless, at a scream distance. Same red hair, blue eyes, a coarse hand across her mouth, her throat exposed. A hideous man is holding her captive. They both gaze at the seeking twin, in her clumsy post-rotation stagger, inquiring arms in satin reaching out. Her seven-winter-old fingers grasp the fog; footfalls on the crunchy soil make her only guidance. Her head turns slowly, ears scanning her whereabouts. A milk-teeth grin has just flashed past. The sparrow's fallen silent.

At the Renaissance men's table, the skeleton's empty sockets look down. Its machinal phalanxes clutch some playing cards.

Saltpeter-crying gargoyles watch the near-naked tomboy skedaddling along the roof spine under the low yellow night, reaching the farthest dormer and slipping through the window left ajar.

Inside the cryptish bedroom lie two rows of iron beds, and one's blanket's held open for me, a red-haired girl inviting me in. I scuttle inside and she pulls the blanket over our heads. In the giggling dark the cold vanishes; I feel my toes again, at the first caress of prison wool. I can't see her face, but I smell her freckles and feel her gossamer lips.

Lesbians melt in a mushroom-cloud kiss in the liquid crowd of

MDMA-eyed dancers swirling to the music (the same tune we danced to yesterday), and the priestess raises her arms to the shafts of light from the surface of the ocean above, where a giant, catastrophic wave is rolling on, curling like a snake a second before biting the sun.

And the gas tank explodes, fireball engulfing the guerrillas attacking me. Through my only eye left I see their internal organs wrinkle and crumble to dust. I have a gun.

I'm defenseless. I'm still stumbling through the corridors of that nightmare house that smells of mildew and putrefaction, retching at the view of the sitting-up corpse against the wall, trying to outrun the monster behind me. But the windows are boarded up, and I'm yelling, not for help, just to wake me up, just to invoke the light of day. And then I see it, an empty room and dust particles playing in the sunlight, but I trip on something soft and fall, air slammed out of my lungs, and he just sinks the pitchfork through my torso, and my rib cage collapses in an explosion of blood.

The guy in the mirror looks like hell. No wonder half the café is staring at him.

People in Point Bless must be guessing our routine by now. We drive to town every morning, park on Market Street; then we split up. One drops the daily report to Aunt Liza at the post office; the other goes to the shops; then we meet at Gordon's for breakfast. The regulars know us as the Wells heirs. You can feel the calm before the gossip storm when we leave a crowded store. I'm afraid some of them believe us to be siblings, but all in all, it's not the worst wrong assumption they could make. Nor does it bother me that waitresses and storekeepers address me as Mr. Wells. I would tell them it's not my name, but there is such respect in the way they say it, even a hint of care or pity, as if the family were some sort of run-down attraction of Point Bless, I don't have the heart to tell them otherwise; I go along with the charade.

Besides, I could use the extra deference. Because right now, scribbling these words in a corner of the café, shielded by sunglasses, I must look to every good Christian in Point Bless like I'm squandering the family fortune in coke and prostitutes of assorted genders.

(In the car, after breakfast.)

—What are you doing today?

—Library searching. You?

—Phone calls, I guess.

(Takes glasses off. Eyes are scarlet rimmed.)

—Do you dream, Niamh? What do you dream?

—I sing.

—You dream that you sing? That's so sweet.

(He strokes my cheek.)

—Do you feel like driving?

(I shrug.)

—Like . . . 200 kilometers?

—FUCK YEAH.

—Let's get Help and get out of here.

A.'S DIARY

I won't pretend it felt better just by driving away from the house. That would be like crediting the house with some sort of unnatural power, as if it were a dark spot on the surface of Earth. It is not. I checked as we sped between the crop fields, a crest of yellow dust on our tail: There is no dark aura around Axton House, no permanent storm brewing in its general direction. There was a storm lingering about, but that was probably yesterday's rain on its way off. Axton House *is* just a house. A beautiful cliché at best. It cannot pretend to be the source of all evil.

Neither can it focus all of our attention. There's stuff to be done, clues to be followed, people to talk to. I guess I could just phone them, but I'm bored anyway.

So here we are, all windows down, arms leaning out, punk music blaring, crossing the state of Virginia, due in Alexandria for lunchtime and with a new mission to excel in. Niamh manning the billion-horsepower-engined Audi, me in care of the stock of Fanta and Twinkies, Help lean-

ing out of a window, a foot-long tongue slapping in the wind: the very
image of happiness.

[Muzak in the background.]

A.: Do you have to carry that around? It's supposed to stay in the
house recording while we aren't home. How do you expect to
catch any e-el-vee or whatever? Besides, you never listen to
the recordings anyway.

[Sound of scribbling.]

Oh, yeah? So do you. Help. Help, that carpet's not your territory; don't you dare claim it.
NIAMH: *[A two-syllable, imperative whistle.]*

[Dog steps approach; playful panting.]

A.: We got ourselves the Hernán Cortés of dogs.

[Door opens.]

WOMAN: Good afternoon. Please come in, Mr....
A.: Wells.
WOMAN: Esther Hutchinson. Pleased to meet you.
A.: How do you do. This is my ... associate, Niamh Connell.
WOMAN: Pleased to meet you.

*[The whole company migrates; Muzak is shut behind a door.
Heels, rubber soles, and paws settling in; chairs scraping the
floor.]*

	So, Mr. Wells, I understand you're in the market.
A.:	I'm … what?
WOMAN:	You're hiring staff for a house you just inherited—is that right?
A.:	Oh, yeah, but not staff, just a butler.
WOMAN:	*[Keying in computer.]* All right, looking for a new butler …
A.:	Not a new one, actually. Our old butler. See, I know he left after my predecessor died, but I'd like him to resume his position.
WOMAN:	*[Skeptical.]* I see. But, truth be said, Mr. Wells, we can only offer you the personnel who choose us to find a workplace for them—most experienced people, by the way …
A.:	Yeah, well, I know he came to you.
WOMAN:	A butler.
A.:	Mark Strückner.
WOMAN:	Mm-hm.
A.:	He must have come by three, four weeks ago.
WOMAN:	Uh-huh. Well, I am not the one interviewing the staff; I talk to employers …
A.:	Yeah, I could have guessed that. I mean, that lamp over there is not meant to impress a maid.
WOMAN:	Well, anyway, you know, you can't just hire a domestic servant because of his ties with your family in the past. If this man resigned his position in the first place, he is unlikely to be interested in taking it back. And we can't force him to.
A.:	I understand, but the thing is, I think he resigned because he didn't know I was coming. I think he'd love to come back.
WOMAN:	*[After a short pause and a diplomatic puff.]* Mr. Wells, I seem to recall this … Strückner you're looking for, and I don't think he would.
A.:	He told you so?
WOMAN:	Again, I'm not the one who interviewed him, but he seemed to be … *[Looks for a word; desists.]* Servants often witness uncomfortable situations in their houses. He was quite in a hurry to find a new position, and with his résumé, it wasn't very difficult. I remember having recommended his name to some good customers in D.C. not three weeks ago.
A.:	"D.C."? Oh, Washington! Hey, that's not far, is it? Could we—

WOMAN: Sir, our customers' data are strictly confidential, as you will surely understand.

A.:   But you must have a way to contact Strückner—

WOMAN: Same goes for the staff, sir. I'm sorry; I must ask you not to inquire any further. Now, if you wish a perfectly trustworthy—

A.:   You do follow-up, don't you?

WOMAN: Beg your pardon?

A.:   Well, an agency of your reputation surely does some follow-up calls. To make sure servants and employers get along.

WOMAN: Well, yes, we—

A.:   So, next time you call him, can you give him a message? Just a message.

[Scribbling in the background.]

WOMAN: This is most irregular, sir.

[A paper is torn off the notepad.]

A.:   Just that. Please. When you call him, tell him exactly that. I won't call again. And please tell me how much I owe you for your excellent service.

LETTER

Axton House
1 Axton Rd.
Point Bless, VA 26969

Dear Aunt Liza,

Life at our family's ancestral manor is still tolerable despite the place's multiple flaws, such as the house being severely understaffed—a circumstance largely contributing to my failure to completely spoil our young protégée. The lack of personnel is noticeable by the growing marks of our presence in all rooms—not only the ones where we dwell (i.e., this bedroom and the kitchen), but also in those where we just camp during the hike from ground floor to attic. No matter how long a virgin room remains impregnable, hidden at the end of a windowed gallery or in a particularly dark corner under the main stairs, after we discover it and claim it for our rightful patrimony, it will never look untrodden again. There will always be at least a piece of Niamh's colorful clothing or some hair accessory of hers to signify our passing, if not a much less subtle hint from Help. Niamh is addressing the latter problem, though, so we expect not to need a servant to look after that. But anyway, a butler would be so cool.

[. . .] I'm sad to admit the return trip was significantly less fun than the runaway, mainly owing to the uncertain results of our investigations. Objectively, none of us walking up the porch stairs looked as happy as in the morning when we left. Okay, maybe Help was; he *does* feel the house as home. The whole of it. That's some mind-stretch, considering his previous home was a kennel.

But then again, it's not the house. I think it's the homework: the burying ourselves again in books and desks. Also on that issue, Strückner would be of great help. But I fear we just shot our last flare.

Tomorrow Niamh and I are working the library together; we'll concentrate on finding that book of Ambrose's childhood—the one Strückner "used to read by a tree." I hope that being side by side will keep our spirits up.

I wish I could have her by my side in my dreams too. I recently started a dream journal, if only to prove to myself that the dreams are recurring, that it's not just déjà vu, but I haven't shared it with her. At least she's there, delicately sleeping when I wake. That's nice.

Okay, so maybe I do miss you. Happy now?

Kisses,
A.

I am sleeping on a bench, in the park, in the snow. I hear boots on the walkway. Cops prod me with their truncheons and speak in some language I've forgotten. I'm too tired to answer.

The über-sexy woman in lingerie, in the car, in the traffic jam, in the snow, in daylight, in Scandinavia, is wearing magenta blush. I'm not moving the Rubik's cube; I've made up my mind that I won't move it until I know exactly how to solve it.

The Renaissance men dressed like Jacobean doctors and the skeleton are playing poker.

A book slips from the reader's brown hand, and watery music.

I hear them laughing at my stolen eyeball in the surgeon's pincers, optic nerve dangling, interrupted messages of useless pain sparking out the severed end. They laugh at it. So I sit up and grab the surgeon's skull who just pulled my eyeball out and shove his face into a rack of syringes, needles up; I kick the general, snatch his gun, execute his fucking skull; I run for the door, a hand covering my vacant eye, feel the breeze through my fingers inside the cavity, shoot my way along the corridor, black soldiers with Kalashnikovs splattering their useless brains on the walls; I kick the metal door, feel my remaining eye burning with the light of a white desert, white sun, white air, black guerrillas aiming at me, white gas tank behind them; I shoot at it and it blossoms into a fireball, roasting them alive; I hear their blood sizzling, smell their flesh burning, see their charred skeletons falling to their knees and crumbling, skulls frozen in a cry of pain, and I hope it fucking hurts.

LETTER

Axton House
Axton Rd.
Point Bless, VA 26969

Dear Aunt Liza,

Some words to accompany Niamh's Polaroids of the library.

It feels like an amphisbaenic church. It certainly echoes like a church and has the size of one, but when you come in through the massive double doors from the hall stairs, you don't see an apse at the other end, but another set of double doors that open out to the front gallery. We leave both doors open to create a corridor across the floor, which otherwise shows a peripheral path.

The two long rows of bookcases separate the central nave from the narrower aisles. Four spiral stairs, one in each corner, climb up to the balcony. There are no windows, no walls—just shelves spanning all around the court.

The cases, the shelves, and the books are all unlabeled.

On one side of the central nave sits a card catalog, each entry painstakingly handwritten. On the other side there's a small desk—the workplace of someone who was abruptly interrupted from their labor, and whose butler came cleaning after them, doing his best to arrange the mess into an illusion of order by aligning and piling solidly the misplaced books and papers that no one knows where to put anymore. This is where Niamh found the folder containing the CD and the magazine clippings. It is also where today we found a curious document. The original was handwritten by Ambrose on a torn sheet from an accounting ledger; I copied it for you.

A LEDGER PAGE FOUND IN THE LIBRARY DESK

1994 Quest Status Report—August

1	Leonidas			
2	Hector		*On field*	
3	Archimedes			
4	Sophocles		*FOUND*	*Ibiza, Spain*
5	Zosimos		*On field*	
6	Socrates	*(Gone)*		
7	Cybele		*FOUND*	*Sonora, Mexico*
8	Dioskuri			
9	Anchises			
10	Elpenor		*Quit*	
11	Coroebus		*On field*	
12	Phoenix	*(Gone?)*	*On field*	
13	Amphiaraus			
14	Tyche		*On field*	
15	Alexandros		*FOUND*	*Monrovia, Liberia*
16	Asterion		*On field*	
17	Chronos			
18	Prometheus	*(???)*		
19	Heracles	*(Betty)*	*Quit*	
20	Zeus		*Quit*	

LETTER

[Cont'd.]

Regarding the library contents: I reckon that works of fiction make up less than half of it. The majority of the collection is a gold mine of knowledge from every time and place, in multiple languages, with ancient philosophers fraternizing with twentieth-century geopolitics. These books are roughly sorted by area. There's also an astounding map collection. It even includes a chart of Mars.

The fiction section takes up the shelves in the balconies, and it's sorted alphabetically by author. There is no children's literature area. It's a perfect place to hide a book forever.

[Five minutes of pages slowly flipping.]

A.:   Niamh? Niamh, why's the recorder on?

[…]

Turn it off. If a ghost were to haunt this library, she'd be bored to death. Again.

[Cont'd.]

By three p.m. Niamh collapsed. The research part of the job doesn't fit her. After a whole day in the book woods tracking and hunting down possible candidates for "that wonderful book of our childhood" as I checked them in the catalog, something just snapped in her little fantasy-dressed head. She probably screamed (thank God I didn't hear that), gave up solving the riddle, and attempted to crack it. She started to pull out books and shake them, hoping for Ambrose's letters to flutter out like autumn leaves.

She went through a whole shelf while I timed her from the desk. Then I did the math while she panted her frustration away. It took her three minutes and twenty-six seconds to check the forty-something books on one shelf. That bookcase is eight shelves high. The balcony runs for a straight row of ten cases, plus two in each corner. Multiply by two for the opposite side. Multiply by two for the lower level. Add fourteen cases along the central nave. I reckon thirty hours would be necessary to shake out any document, marker, or train ticket from all the books.

Unless, of course, Ambrose actually fixed those letters inside the book with tape. Which, now that I come to think of it, I would have done.

So, in short: We do need a butler.

Kisses,
A.

P.S. From the vast continent of uninhabited wilderness that is Axton House, I feel we could begin to consider the annexation of this music room into our conquered territory. I admit it's a big step forward (I dare compare it to the acquisition of Tennessee), but it is, after all, the place we go home to after a day's work in the library. Here Niamh plays the piano or listens to her EVP (I scolded her today for just recording stuff and never listening to it) and I write and watch TV (did you know *The X-Files* is on its third season here?)

A.'S DIARY

It's midnight.

The uncharted regions of Axton House sleep in utter shadow. Between this music room and our bedroom lies a swamp of silence. We don't dare to cross it. We'd rather stay here, where there are many lights, and a TV, and things that won't desert us. We sit on the sofa and comfort each other. Suddenly, we shiver with cold and frailty.

I watched *The X-Files* tonight (it's even creepier here in Axton House). There's a poster in Fox Mulder's office in the basement that reads, "I want to believe." I think that's the way I've felt all my life.

I'm not a religious man. I'm not sure why. I guess I never needed a religion. Niamh is a Catholic, and I went to a Baptist church with her last Sunday and stood through the service like Livingstone might attend a ceremonial rite in Africa: amused by the exotica, and somehow honored to be accepted, but spiritually untouched. I'm actually *so* atheist that I'm reluctant to use the word *spiritual.*

Same goes for anything fitting in the X-files cabinet. I don't believe in, nor let myself be affected by, anything that requires empirical reason to stand aside. So there go gods. There go souls. There go ghosts. There goes the paranormal. I don't need it.

And yet, like Mulder, I'd like to believe.

It's not that I envy people who believe. I don't see them getting any advantages. Niamh would have endured her shitty childhood without God just as well. Those who believe in the soul fear theirs might burn in hell. Those who believe in ghosts fear they will be haunted. Those who believe we're not alone end up glancing over their shoulders at all times and despising their unreliable senses.

No, I think I *want* to believe because I need that limbo between the real and the unreal to exist. I don't want this wall imposed by my precursors, a border to which my reason must abide: "This side is real; that one is not; bacteria and hallucinations exist; ghosts and UFOs are bullshit." I don't want my reality set, my world defined.

I guess believing wouldn't be enough, though. I'd like to know. Not even empirically: just as I know Australia is somewhere out there, though I've never actually seen it. Because if there were a minimal chance for those things to exist, it would improve my universe in the same way that coming to America improved it: Everything would be more like in the movies.

But I can't believe. The older I get, the more solid the wall becomes, like everything that was to be explored has already been. True things grow truer, and unproved things fade away. Because we don't need them. Like I don't need a god.

And I'd like X-files to exist. I'd like to have plausible testimonies of unexplained phenomena as I have news of countries I've never been to. I long for the slightest evidence of it that doesn't require me to relinquish reason, because a natural mystery and reason to face it make the happiest combination of all.

But there is no hint. No plausible clue for anything we now call superstition, religion, or bullshit to be real. And the ones who should provide it, the ones who believe, are also nearing extinction.

And I blame them. Yes, I blame believers for my skepticism. Because they're not up to it; they're no challenge; they're so easily proved fools, I hate them. All those psychic wannabes, those women holding séances and faking so unconvincingly, expecting me to lower my standards to their puerile level; those self-proclaimed parapsychologists pretending to be scientists, who can't even tell when they started to con themselves; all those pathetic lonely people fooling one another into their clumsy games of afterlife and cosmic relevance just to avoid noticing the nauseating sadness of their real lives. How could such a fascinating realm end up in the hands of idiots who stripped it of any glamour? How could it sink that low?

That's how I used to feel, bound by reason to boredom.

And then along came Axton House.

We've spent most of the night here in the music room, not daring to go upstairs, because Niamh was listening to her EVP and I asked her to play the recordings from the bathroom two nights ago, on the eighth. At first, it seemed the recorder had captured nothing but a thick layer of noise and my voice swimming in it. But Niamh heard something else.

She browsed the wire drawer for a connector and jacked the recorder into the hi-fi speakers. We heard the same static through the stereo. She dialed up the volume until the floorboards trembled with the drone and Help escaped the room. Then she played with the equalizer to raise a certain frequency over the rest. I thanked God (that is, Niamh's God) for having our closest neighbors more than a mile away.

But finally she succeeded: a single string of sound emerging from the static, one dyed fiber in the pattern, droning at a different beat. With a rhythm. Making notes. Singing exactly the same melody. And then my own voice on top of it all, repeating the melody in a whisper that had the chandelier rocking in the sound blast. That was me in the bathroom two nights ago, repeating what I thought I had heard: the same indelible four notes from the orgiastic tune we danced to that afternoon. Hours after we danced that day, the tune was still echoing in the bathroom—or being echoed. Niamh has heard it too.

Music had touched every living thing in this house. Living or whatever.

But that isn't proof enough. This is.

Niamh replayed bits of every recording at the same frequency. Most gave nothing. One did. The one from the bathroom on the sixth.

It features, after hours of pure white noise: the light switched on. Me pouring water over my face. The faucet squeaking off.

And then a voice—the same exact bar on the equalizer screen, the same dyed fiber, saying something.

Then plain noise, for a few seconds.

And then the Dead Kennedys, in a brutal shock wave of punk music coming from this very stereo, played by Niamh to warn me that Curtis Knox or somebody else had broken in.

Niamh spun the volume down and we locked eyes. That voice before the music exploded was a girl's. And what she'd said—actually, she'd said *to me*—"*We're not alone.*"

It's a fountain—the watery music is. There was a Moorish window before I quietly closed my eyes. The book falls out of my hand. And I savor the last words I read, but I can't understand them.

I am the skeleton. And I'm holding a pair of fives. And the ace of hearts. And a three, and a four. (Should I go for a flush?)

I'm playing Scrabble, but the words look all fuzzy.

I reach for the window and trip and fall. And the monster thrusts the pitchfork through me and nails me to the floor.

*

(Late night.)

—You babbling in your sleep.

—Sorry.

(He clutching his chest.)

*

[Later.]

I'm flying over a shirtless man under tropical rain clouds. He peeks over his shoulder, startled, but he can't see me. He sees through me. His skin *feels* me.

It's a corpse he trips on. And as soon as he touches the floor I thrust the pitchfork through his back.

(Cellar—facing the wine racks.)

—I think the older the better.

—Yeah, but I also think there's an age when it just turns into vinegar.

—You should've insisted on having them come over here.

—Next time I'll pass you the phone and see you handle it. Look, just take anything that looks pompous and old.

(I hug him.)

—I just walked into that, didn't I?

(I choose a bottle.)

—This I know from a 007 movie. Sounded good.

—Moore?

(Do my Connery impersonation.)

—Okay, take it. By the way, don't even think of bringing your recorder along.

[Eighty Fahrenheit by the crickets. Door opens.]

MRS. BRODIE: Here you are!

A.: Hello, Mrs. Brodie.

MRS. BRODIE: Please, it's Monique for you. Niamh, how are you?

A.: Sir. Thanks again for taking us on such short notice.

MR. BRODIE: Frank, Mr. Wells. No problem at all. Come in.

MRS. BRODIE: Did you guys walk all the way?

[Crickets fall silent behind the closed door; the interior resonates like a wood instrument.]

A.: Yes, it was a nice stroll. Such a warm autumn.

MRS. BRODIE: It all ends next week.

MR. BRODIE: There are tornado warnings. I must come your way early next week and help you with the boarding.

A.: Boarding?

MR. BRODIE: Panels. On the windows. You've never had tornadoes in your country, have you?

A.: No, that's something we missed back in—

MRS. BRODIE: Oh, darling, your eyes! What happened?

A.: Oh. Uh … It's nothing serious. There's a funny story behind it, actually; I'll tell you later.

MRS. BRODIE: Okay … Frankie, get our guests some refreshments while I check the chicken.

A.: Smells great.

MR. BRODIE: Mary, mother of Jesus! This wine's worth five hundred bucks at least.

A.: *[Hesitates.]* Ah. Well … I'm sure Ambrose meant to drink it in good company.

MR. BRODIE: *[Laughs.]* I bet! Where's that corkscrew? This I have to try. Monny, you gotta check this out.

[A pencil scribbling.]

What's that? Oh, the lady's right; we must let it breathe. First things first: Where is that damned thing …? Here it is. Oh, listen, I haven't told Monique yet, but Mr. Glew just phoned me yesterday. Told me about the land. Now, I really must—

A.: It's my pleasure.

MR. BRODIE: But that's more land than we can use!

A.: Hey, you work it; you own it. That's how it should be.

MR. BRODIE: Well, what with your cousin's gift first and now this, I'm starting to build myself some estate. And our kids aren't really interested in the farm. The girl's working at the Democratic headquarters in Richmond and the boy's in college now, so—

A.: Look, you build an estate big enough and I promise you some second cousin twice removed will just sprout among the cabbages.

MR. BRODIE: [Laughs.] Yeah! You should know! [Pop!—a bottle uncorked.] Ah, there it is.

MRS. BRODIE: Here it comes! Everyone sit down.

[Words of approval lost between chairs being pulled out and cutlery clanging.]

MR. BRODIE: Well, dear, I think our guests would like to say grace?

[A slightly awkward, soft jazz–filled wavering.]

A.: Uh … Sssure … Uh, Niamh, would you like to do the honors? Thanks.

[Guests and hosts sitting upright, hands linking.]

[Blank.]

Amen.

MR. & MRS. B.: Amen.

A.: Thank you, Niamh.

So, apart from the grace incident, so elegantly dodged, the lunch went smooth as silk. The Brodies were the perfect family, Niamh ate like a perfect daughter, I kept trying not to think how strong a tornado should be to compromise our house (and how far it would relocate the Brodies' little Cape Cod–style farm, for that matter), and no other supernatural beings were alluded to until coffee.

It was tricky to bring the subject up. There's no way ghosts can casually wash up in social talk. People who just let slip a reference to the occult in the middle of a serious debate (like, "I read in the *Post* that the global economy will relapse, and so says Saturn in Capricorn") deserve execution.

Fortunately, my burned eyes, which never fail to impress an audience, served as a reminder of an open issue throughout the afternoon. And so, once we'd moved to the coffee table, I nudged the conversation toward Axton House. I first recounted our interview with Curtis Knox last Sunday as a token of my willingness to share any gossip about Ambrose's activities; then, lingering on the motif of recent visits, I just dropped, "By the way, I saw the ghost too."

They stared at me for a while. I don't think they even considered laughing. I added, "Hence my eyes, as you may have noticed."

It was tense. Mr. Brodie even started a sentence switching back to "Mr. Wells," after having agreed to settle on a first-name basis. I cut him off, insisted I was serious—I had seen the ghost and I thought they would be interested.

Once again, Mrs. Brodie's curiosity saved the day:

"What's she like?"

"So you know it's a *she*," I said.

They couldn't retreat now.

I talked about the electrician from town, how he had hinted to me about the Axtons, and how he had refused to give me the whole story, just a name: the Ngara girl. This is the Brodies' version of the story Sam wouldn't tell.

Long before Point Bless grew bigger than a humble market, Axton House was already there, roughly as we know it. It belonged to the Axton family, who might have come among the first settlers in Virginia. Brodie says they were of Dutch ancestry, and boastfully proud of their bloodline. They claimed all land from the present town to Powome River, and the native Indians they took it from were the first to work on their plantation, which soon grew to require slaves from Africa and farther. The Axton patriarchs often traveled themselves as far as Australasia to fetch them.

Even in those brutal times, the Axtons were particularly brutal. They mistreated the slaves and didn't show much more respect for free men. They kicked dust over the poor and engaged in land feuds with the rich. They were feared in the short range, hated from a distance. However, the enormous plantation seemed to run autonomously and the Axtons needed nothing from the prospering community of Point Bless—not even their fear or hatred. They shut themselves away, and the townsfolk chose to think they had banished them. Gossip and isolation were their weapons. The former might not have harmed the Axtons. The latter certainly did.

Charles Robert Axton, said to be the second-to-last male in the family, was born in 1814. He was rumored to be the son of first cousins, and not the first case in the family. Axton himself married his stepsister, who apparently died in childbirth. The child no one saw, though he was rumored to be profoundly retarded or malformed. Perhaps he never existed, and Axton was the last of his kin after all.

By the time Axton took the reins of the plantation, the good days for human exploitation had drifted away. With plenty of free states and cities for the fugitives to take refuge in, and the 1808 act prohibiting the importation of slaves, Axton had trouble refilling his ranks. By then, however, it was common knowledge that the Axtons didn't just own slaves; they were selectively breeding them. When fugitives from the plantation spoke out, not needing to run any farther than Point Bless to find some sympathy, vile secrets were disclosed: They had seen masters picking out men, sterilizing the weak while forcing the strong to copulate with the women. And these fugitives were themselves the offspring of such selection, perpetrated by generations of Axtons in search of the strongest workforce: the perfect slave.

Evil, though, is often pestered by irony. Charles Axton spent his abominable life crossing humans and mixing strains, while his own bloodline of European gentry was slowly extinguishing. The slaves he bred were not only the strongest, but also the most prone to escape. With their numbers dwindling, the twisted fantasy of the family was tumbling down, as was the family itself. Only when Axton failed to produce a boy from a decisive crossing between—some say—a Senegambian man and a remotely Malaysian woman, he realized his failure: The perfect slave would never be born, and the Axtons would perish. Unless one problem sorted the other.

From that failed crossing Axton had obtained a girl. (Mrs. Brodie said, "A beautiful girl"; in Mr. Brodie's version she was described as "hideous"; in any case, a girl carrying the most exotic and therefore freshest genes in her body.) Axton, on the other hand, had become a widower, and the rumored father of a deranged son. (According to this version, the son was virtually a beast, imprisoned in Axton House's attic.) Axton's last bad idea, worthy to top over a century of atrocities, was to have one bloodline save the other. The details are nothing that either Mr. or Mrs. Brodie wishes to taint their Christian home with. In few, brutal words, Axton *fed* the mixed-breed girl to his son, trusting the boy's animal instincts would do the job. She wasn't over eleven. But she'd been bred to be fit, and it showed.

Allegedly, when Axton walked back upstairs to retrieve the girl, he found her cowering in a corner, and his son's broken body sprawled on the attic floor.

Versions split again: Some say Axton killed the girl right on the spot. Others say he tried to do himself what his son failed to do. In both versions, the girl did not survive.

By the time Axton's plan was so catastrophically foiled, the world outside Axton House had long been falling to pieces. During the decade it took for the mixed-breed girl to hardly reach sexual maturity, Axton had been too busy building expectations to pay any attention to his plantation, and most of his slaves were gone. Also, at the time of the gruesome climax of the story, a Civil War had broken out. That was when the last remaining slaves, the oldest of the bunch, fled as well. They didn't go very far; most of them weathered the war in Point Bless (the town saw little fighting). They were not only Africans, but also Native Americans and South Asians. Many local black families descend from them; a few still feature slanted eyes. When they told the whole story, an old woman referred to the last child in their colony as the *Ngara* girl. Nobody knew what that meant or what language it stood for, but it stuck. It might be the name coined by a heterogeneous and multilingual community for a new race with a single representative.

Axton didn't seem to care about the desertions. The rest of his life he was a shadow of his former self. Perhaps he was feeling the accusatory presence of the Ngara girl watching him. In 1865, the federals found him sitting on his ramshackle porch. No one knows exactly what he said to Captain Norton of the Union, but he got shot in the leg right then and there. It had to be amputated. He died in utter poverty and isolation in 1875.

It should be noted that this story was not recited in one go. Mr. and Mrs. Brodie interrupted and contradicted each other several times, and both Niamh and I threw in questions as well. It seemed to me that the Ngara girl legend was clearly common knowledge in Point Bless, but the Brodies had never compared their versions before. It's like the story is alive within the community, but seldom verbalized.

After that, Mr. Brodie concluded, Axton House remained unperturbed for twenty-five years, until an English entrepreneur named Horace Wells, who went on to work as a railway engineer, acquired the land in 1900.

"And that's when the legend of the ghost arose," I supposed.

The Brodies stared at me as if I'd made a major mistake.

"Not at all. The Ngara girl had been seen long before. That's why the house was unperturbed. Horace knew very well what he was getting into."

Mrs. Brodie added, "In a way, I think that's the reason he bought the house."

We all remained silent. Not that I was surprised: I could understand the Wells' way of thinking. Had I had the chance, I would have bought a haunted house too.

In the end, I had only one last question: "Why does the ghost appear to be linked to the bathroom?"

Mr. Brodie allowed himself a chuckle, as if to dissipate the dark mood of the evening. "That was no bathroom back then, son. They used outhouses."

We left at dusk.

EXCERPT FROM JOHN LEEK'S *GHOSTS OF GHOSTS*. CHICAGO, 1980

For years in our profession, a strong current of opinion has discouraged referring to our area of expertise as *ghosts*. Many indeed, perhaps the most respectable of them, rather speak about *entities, agents,* or even more innocuously, *phenomena*. This tendency not only aims to push our bullied field of study closer to the jurisdiction of undisputed sciences by pulling it away from the deprecated realm of folklore, but also seems to admit, through the very imprecision of its terminology, that our science is still young—embryonic, according to Flyte (4)—and that we still face as long a road as *Homo habilis* did when he first grabbed a tool.

However, once we change all taboo words into pseudo-Latin, reformulate all the superstitious gibberish into academic jargon, embrace the scientific method, apply self-criticism, unravel speculation, dismiss demoted disciplines, tear up Kirlian photography, fire the mediums, destroy the hoaxes, expel the madmen, burn the pulp, and return to square one; once the whole corpus of parapsychology is reduced to one bookshelf of serious works on the occult and a handful of respectable students, among which I may not qualify to be, once we have done all this, ghosts will still be there. [. . .]

It is fairly easy to get carried away in our work. Several reasons come to mind. 1) There is so much to prove, and so much recognition awaiting those who prove it. 2) There is so little to start with, and so frail, we feel the urge to back it up with fabricated replicas. 3) There are so few of us, we tend to think we are special. We describe ourselves pedantically as perceptive, receptive, sensitive, open-minded, and other meaningless attributes. 4) There are personal implications. The smallest phenomenon, if proved legitimate, opens the door to staggering possibilities for all humans. Any evidence of anybody's afterlife implies an afterlife for us. 5) There is religion: We need to believe. [. . .]

That notwithstanding, unexplained things are there, waiting to be explained. Call them what you want: entities, agents, phenomena—no term is too vague. Throwing together all contributions from all disciplines into one single container word, they will still amount to nothing but a speck.

Take ghosts from that pile—i.e., *any real evidence (and by real I mean just nonrefuted) of unexplained phenomena ever documented that our spiritual background makes us associate with intelligent beings.* Even narrowed down through the sieve of skepticism to a few cases scattered all over the world—Marbaden, Averoigne, the Areba twins, Skagen 1963, Bells of Thudeney, Bangharh, Chapelizod, Heck House, and a few others—the little pile of evidence remaining still shows some consistencies. This is what humbly, as a scientist, I daresay we know about what, for lack of a better term, we may call *ghosts*. And it fits on one page.

1. There *are* mostly invisible, inaudible, incorporeal entities that can at times be perceived in the same way by different unbiased observers.

2. When unperceived by other means, they have been consistently noticed as cold, humid, and electrically charged. These attributes have been measured.

3. When seen, they appear as vague shadows, as if their bodies were hardly dense enough to deflect light. They are never seen in darkness.

4. When heard, they may sound in frequencies either too low or too high for the human ear. Legitimate recordings exist. Contrary to popular belief, animals have not been proved to be more aware of them than we are.

5. They can speak, and are therefore assumed to have human intelligence.
6. In their presence, wave signals are distorted.
7. They cannot interact with material objects.
8. However, the fact that they are often linked to a particular place (what we call a haunted spot) suggests that they are aware of their surroundings, and of us.
9. There is always an oral background tradition (either previous and genuine or succeeding and fabricated) associating each one of them to a once living person or persons.
10. Not all mean any harm.

(In bed.)

—What now?

—Nothing. The ghost is the least of my concerns.

—So we back to shake books?

—What's the point?

—We got a code to break!

—What for? That code will only lead to more codes, just like the Aeschylus cipher did. That's their little game; they get off on secrecy for secrecy's sake; they're hiding nothing!

—You KNOW that's not true.

—They even *refer* to one another in code! Leonidas, Hector, Prometheus—we don't even know their names!

—*Leonidas = Ambrose; Prometheus = S.W.L.; Sophocles = Edward Cutler (the guy who sent the CD from Ibiza) & Bob's your uncle!*

(He reads carefully.)

—Okay . . . 3 out of 20. Except for Bob. I don't think I have an uncle Bob. Aunt Liza would've told me.

—*We'll find the rest. You just downhearted. Get some sleep.*

AUDIO RECORDING

[A light switches on.]

[Bare feet cross the room. The toilet lid is lifted.]

[Silence for a reasonable lapse to pee.]

[Flush. Steps approach the microphone. A pencil telegraphs a message. A paper is torn. Footsteps exit. Light is switched off.]

A NOTE LEFT IN THE BATHROOM

You and I gonna get along?

ONE WEEK LATER

I look down to Earth. I'm a spit dropping toward the planet.

I can see the curve of the blue canvas far beyond my feet (the highest altitude a pair of Puma training shoes ever reached). And in the blue immensity below, the zygote of an island is growing.

I'm targeting it.

I'm free-falling to an island from a hundred thousand meters, at flesh-tearing speed.

I see it growing larger, yet minuscule in the boundless blue. Shaping into a cyan lagoon, with sand borders, and evergreen arecaceae, and a World War II bunker on one of the corners, all this closing up at the speed of lightning.

I kaboom-land on the rooftop. Thunder.

I wait for the dust to be carried away by the tropical breeze. Ears adjusting to the pressure. The cement is cracked in a twelve-inch radius around me—ground to dust in the epicenter under my rubber soles. Bones resonate like steel. I stand up, legs called to attention and responding, the tingling sensation fading away.

Seagulls squawk. No one noticed me.

VIDEO RECORDING

*[JACK IN: Black shapes crawling over the screen. As the figure
operating the camera moves back, it focuses automatically to
define her in high-angle shot. NIAMH smiles back, self-proud. Her
hair is buzz-cut on the left side, long and violet and untamed on
the right. Behind her, a tiled bathroom with a vaulted ceiling.]*

*[At ground level, A. walks in, stops halfway to the toilet to check
Niamh. She's now plugging in the SOUND: atmosphere noise.
Voices are strongly metallic, hollow.]*

A.:   Oh, good. Peeing in front of a nineteenth-century ghost AND
        a sound recorder wasn't that embarrassing anymore. Good for
        you to keep up the challenge.

NIAMH: *[Turns to him, holding herself to the top of the ladder; gestures
        downward emphatically.]*

A.:   Yes, I know there are other bathrooms, Niamh. *[Turns back to
        the toilet.]* I just can't remember where we put them.

*[SQUEAK. As he checks to his right, the camera pans in that
direction, as pushed by Niamh herself. There's a dog in the tub.]*

        There's a dog in the tub.

*[HELP was chasing a rubber duck floating in the water and foam
of his bath. Now noticing his master's attention, he noisily wades
across and tries to lean out.]*

NIAMH: *[Without turning this time: short, commanding whistle in G
        minor.]*

[Help sits in the water obediently.]

*[Fully satisfied with her overall performance, Niamh jumps off
the ladder. Before she leaves to give him some privacy, a super-*

short whistle to call his partner's attention, then a quick cross sign. Now she exits.]

A.:   *[Looking her way.]* What? Is it Sunday AGAIN?

[No answer is heard, unsurprisingly.]

             [To Help.] Teenagers. It's always church, church, church with them.

[The dog snorts some foam.]

NIAMH'S NOTEPAD

(In church.)

—SUNGLASSES OFF! This is MY God you're talking to!

LETTER

Axton House
Axton Rd.
Point Bless, VA 26969

Dear Aunt Liza,

One in the music room where we spend the evenings playing piano and writing our celebrated epistles to you. One in the mile-spanning library, sentineling the desk we continue to mine from time to time, invariably obtaining frustration and tedium. One in the kitchen where we cook and eat. One in the bathroom, where the ghost was last seen. That's the present distribution of our newly acquired security cameras—a giant leap forward from our EVP recordings. The old smoking room (northwest corner of the second floor, a room where we used to play pool on the rare occasions when we remembered there was a pool table there and could find the room) is now the surveillance center, where the monitors are. And, of course, miles and miles of cable now slither about the corridors and hang down the stairwells.

I still don't know exactly what we're trying to catch. Niamh won't tell. That's so much like Niamh.

Anyway, what with the cameras and the shutters and the reinforcing boards that Mr. Brodie helped us put on the conservatory—there's a tornado watch in the area and even Father Epps gave a warning after the service—the house is looking more and more like a fortress. And we're still due to find the treasure hidden inside.

In fact, we keep checking in at the tower more and more often and looking outward, our skin cracking like ice under the western wind. The cloudscapes are apocalyptic.

NIAMH'S NOTEPAD

(In the tower, watching the storm approach.)

—Weather will never get better after this.

—You think so?

—Sun will never shine again. Winter will follow. This the final airstrike on a very old summer.

(I hold his hand.)

—Still, that winter won't last forever, you know.

—Too far ahead.

—Yeah. That's beyond winter solstice anyway.

—I so curious about that day, like time will end after that.

A.'S DIARY

I don't think we had been offered such a spectacular view of the area since our car trip to Alexandria. Even after we left the tower, we couldn't hide from it. The wind was strenuous. The windows shuddered in their jambs. I could put my hand on the wood paneling and feel it tremble. Downstairs we found Help moaning at the front door. Not even Niamh could coax him into doing his business on some newspapers—he's already used to running all the way across the front yard to the first line of trees, so we let him out. Meanwhile we stood watching reports of an F2 in Appomattox, not three counties from here. Our fascination was slowly turning into . . . I don't know. Something close to fear.

Right then, we heard Help over the skyquake, *barking.* I hadn't heard him bark since we brought him home. I was beginning to think that Niamh was infectious.

We tiptoed outside. Virginia had turned into Mordor. Ice pellets began to ricochet on the gravel. Help was barking menacingly at a car, stopped about thirty meters from the south corner. The car didn't fit. It was white and belonged to this half of the century. No one stepped out of it.

Then the car started again and rolled to the pergola before the conservatory. We ran toward it, Niamh carrying an umbrella she didn't dare open for fear of being Marypoppinsed away.

Just as the driver opened the door, the wind stopped. I felt the air around us come to a standstill. It was like the troposphere was going to plummet to Earth.

And then our guest stood up.

LETTER

[Cont'd.]

Let me write a portrait of Mark Strückner to caption Niamh's picture.

He seems the kind of man this house was built for—even though he was only the butler. For a start, the house does not look too high around him. That's because he stands seven feet. And he doesn't bow often.

He'd be well built for a shorter man, but his height makes him look thin, in the Gothic style the house favors. His cheeks are so caved in, his skull stands like the ruins of an abbey in a Friedrich painting, hollowed out like a dome, deserted by receding gray hair. His blue eyes, as far as I could tell, are tragically sad. His handshake amazingly gentle.

Niamh really liked him from the beginning. That's good enough for me.

AUDIO RECORDING

[Rain pattering in the background. In the foreground, porcelain shivering.]

A.: Do you take milk or sugar?

STRÜCKNER: Uh, sweetener, actually. Wait, there's some in—

A.: No, no, please; you sit down. Niamh, can you get that, please?

STRÜCKNER: It used to be in the second cupboard on the right, above the oven. *[Pause.]*

A.: Is something wrong?

STRÜCKNER: I was … thinking that carpet needs cleaning. Sorry. I'm not used to being a guest in this house.

A.: A guest? Please. You lived here far longer than we have.

STRÜCKNER: That means nothing. It is your house now; I … I did my part. It belongs to you now. The Wells scion. Thank you.

[Stirring.]

You don't look at all like him. I mean that as a good thing.

[Spoon pats the cup.]

A.:   I guess my arrival came as a surprise.

STRÜCKNER: Yes, it did. It did. Although Mr. Wells mentioned he still had some lost relatives in Europe. More often during the last year. But of course, I couldn't imagine you'd turn up and claim the property.

A.:   We didn't. That was Ambrose's doing. And Mr. Glew deserves some credit for finding me. He's been looking for you too.

STRÜCKNER: Yes, I thought so. I...I'm sorry about that. Suddenly the house didn't feel all that hospitable.

A.:   We feared you might've gone back to Europe.

STRÜCKNER: Oh, no. No. I have nothing left in Europe. My whole family lived here. Within these walls. During World War Two, in Germany, John Wells, Ambrose's father, was a cryptographer in charge of deciphering German intelligence, and my father was an informant. He sent my mother and me to Switzerland with her family while he stayed in Germany, resolved to see the Nazis fall. But as the fight neared its end, it became clear that the Reich would take Germany with it, whereas he, as a humble cook gone spy, would be lucky to get a tin medal. So when Wells was discharged in 'forty-four, he took Father under his wing, offering him a good position in this house. Mother and I joined them in 'fifty-two. I was ten. Ambrose was seven.

A.:   You two grew up together.

STRÜCKNER: Despite our differences. I started doing housework soon after my arrival, so we didn't share the playroom much. Still, our fathers served as models; they showed us how servant and master could treat each other with mutual respect and com-radeship; and so we did as I gradually became houseboy, cook's assistant, cook, and butler after my father, whereas Ambrose succeeded John as Mr. Wells. When I say my whole family lived within these walls, I include everyone within these walls.

[Slowly, a teacup alights back on its saucer. Rain persists.]

So when Ambrose ... Mr. Wells passed away, I saw nothing to keep me here. I contacted an agency. There was an opening in Washington. I decided enough people had grown lonely to death in Axton House, and I took it.

A.: You said Ambrose mentioned me more often during the last year?

STRÜCKNER: Yes. Actually, it was like he'd been reminded of his relatives in Europe around May. I remember he got a phone call; the next day he drove to Clayboro to meet somebody about his family, or so I guessed. After that, he spent much time ... arranging things. Like rewriting his will.

A.: So ... he knew.

STRÜCKNER: Knew?

A.: What he was about to do.

STRÜCKNER: I don't ... *[Hesitation.]*

A.: What?

STRÜCKNER: I don't know.

[A most uneventful minute elapses.]

Look ... I don't think he knew what he was about to do, no. He just ... suspected it.

A.: He suspected he would jump out of a window?

STRÜCKNER: Yes.

A.: But a suicide knows what he's doing.

STRÜCKNER: A suicide opens the window in advance.

[...]

[Nothing.]

[Just rain.]

A.:   Whoa.

[Pencil scratching. Expectation.]

STRÜCKNER: Uh … No. No, his father did open the window. *[Muffled.]* God, I'd never thought of that.

A.:   But why? Why do you think he did suspect—

STRÜCKNER: Because he knew he was following his father's path. That's why.

A.:   What, what path?

STRÜCKNER: Everything. His work, his reunions … The obsessive research chasing him into his dreams. The nightmares. The hallucinations.
You know what I'm talking about, don't you?

[Wind whooshing, stirring the downpour.]

A.:   I … I've been having some rough nights.

STRÜCKNER: Waking up screaming?

A.:   A couple times.

STRÜCKNER: Going to the bathroom in the middle of the night and seeing things?

A.:   Okay, okay, I see the pattern. Then why me? She sleeps in the same room and she's okay.

STRÜCKNER: Then it must run in the family. Maybe you are a little like your cousin after all. Sorry to say.

A.:   But I'm not following in his steps; I don't work; I'm not doing research—

[Pencil slashing violently. Pause.]

               Okay, we do research, but not the kind Ambrose did, I'm pretty sure. What did he do?

STRÜCKNER: I don't know.

A.:   What did the Society do?

STRÜCKNER: I don't know.

A.:   What is it all about?

STRÜCKNER: I don't know!

[Zenith reached. The wind weakens. Vertical rain resumes. So do the speakers, quietly.]

A.:   Tell me about the reunions. Whatever you know.

[Tea refill.]

STRÜCKNER: *[Oxygen refill.]* Every year since I remember, since before I arrived, since before my father arrived, the night of December the twenty-first, a large banquet is prepared and the table is laid for twenty people exactly. The food is to be left in a buffet for guests to help themselves, and all bedrooms must be clean and ready for use, including the staff quarters. At exactly six o'clock, all servants are to leave the house.

A.:   Where are they supposed to go?

STRÜCKNER: Anywhere. In the old days, they were paid for the trouble. Now that I'm the only permanent staff they used to send me to the Jefferson in Richmond. They even carried my suitcase to the car and everything. Masters serving the servant.

A.:   So you actually met the twenty?

STRÜCKNER: Yes. In the beginning the servants were supposed to leave before they arrived, but with Ambrose the rule became laxer. Besides, some of them I knew already; they'd come more often.

A.:   I know. Caleb Ford and Curtis Knox. I spoke to Knox two weeks ago.

STRÜCKNER: Mr. Ford was maybe the closest friend of Ambrose's. Their fathers were friends too; they were together in the war. Ford lives a short drive from here, in Clayboro.

A.:   So I heard. He's in Africa now.

STRÜCKNER: Still? Ambrose—uh, Mr. Wells was worried he couldn't find him.

A.:   Sorry, you were saying the servants are gone, and then...?

STRÜCKNER: Oh, yes. Once the twenty are alone, they eat, they drink, and at night or early morning they perform their one and only ritual. Don't ask; I don't know the slightest thing about it.

[Pause for challenging questions; none are posed.]

The next morning they sleep late, then spend the rest of the second day distributing their homework, and they leave early on the third, when I come back. They are allowed to stay longer, but some of them have families to spend Christmas with. *[Beat.]* Well, a few.

A.: What's the homework about? What are they supposed to do?

STRÜCKNER: I never knew. It's what they call research. Though sometimes, by the way John Wells talked about it especially ... it seemed like a hunt to me.

A.: A hunt.

STRÜCKNER: A manhunt, yes.

[Silence.]

Whatever it was, it used to require piles of books, frequent visits to college libraries ... and field trips, of course, until ten years ago, when Mr. Wells was forbidden to travel abroad. Rheumatism. His father suffered from it too.

A.: Where did he travel to?

STRÜCKNER: You name it. His last trip was to China—six months. The year before that, Greenland. The year before that, Brazil. After the doctors banned him from going abroad, he still spent a month in Alaska.

A.: Did he travel alone?

STRÜCKNER: I think each one had his own task; only occasionally would they assist one another. The years without trips were the worst, I think. He could stay up reading till dawn, talking foreign languages on the phone ...

A.: So you think he suffered ... I don't know, occupational stress? Like a yuppie?

STRÜCKNER: *[Quick.]* No.

[Slower.] Well, I don't know. But it's the nature of that occupation... Do yuppies have nightmares? Do yuppies bite their tongues in their sleep? Do they stare at you in the morning like they'd been to hell and back during the night?

[Silence answering the rhetorical question.]

But then, he made it all seem so trivial. "Old men playing old games," he used to say. "Do not worry," he said to me once. "You might think we're studying dark subjects, playing with forbidden things, but we don't interfere in cosmic matters. We just watch from behind the red rope. It's just a bourgeois pastime." That's what he called it. "A bourgeois pastime."

A.: Doesn't sound like he enjoyed it very much.

STRÜCKNER: Sometimes he did. That's the point. A few times he would return from abroad exhausted, but immensely happy, retelling everything he had seen, possibly concealing the most crucial of it, but exultant anyway. And he was happy for the rest of the year, as though he'd passed all his exams. Most other times, though, he worked straight from one December the twenty-first to the next, some years looking just overwhelmed by the problem, others perplexed, others even bored. And then there were bad years. After I came back from Richmond the last time, when I understood that the year of his fiftieth birthday was going to be one of the bad ones... I feared this would happen.

A.: *[Quickly, not allowing the rain to steal another dramatic pause.]* Listen, this Society of his... Do you know if they used code names?

STRÜCKNER: Code names? No. *[Beat.]* No, no, I'm pretty sure they didn't. Although... Well, they did...

A.: It's okay; say it. You're just supposed to be discreet, not deaf.

STRÜCKNER: *[Chuckle.]* Well... they always used a lot of references to Roman and Greek classics. But it's the sentences they used... like "being Archimedes." Or "I wish I were Sophocles." They made it sound like a theater class.

A.:   Did you have a code name?

STRÜCKNER: Me? *[The sound of a smirk.]* Well, yes. Occasionally, Wells would call me "Aeschylus." I don't know why.

A.:   Mr. Strückner, do you know that Ambrose left a message for you on his desk?

[A second's lapse.]

STRÜCKNER: How do you know?

A.:   I saw the envelope. Did you decipher the message inside?

STRÜCKNER: I destroyed the message; how do you know it was encoded? Did Mr. Knox tell you about this?

A.:   No, I know because I saw the envelope, and Aeschylus was the key word. Or wasn't it?

STRÜCKNER: *[Sigh.]* Yes, it was. A simple alphabetical code. Mr. Wells used to exchange notes like that with Mr. Ford; he showed me how it worked.

A.:   So you deciphered it.

STRÜCKNER: Yes, I did.

A.:   But you never followed the instructions.

STRÜCKNER: I couldn't. The message referred me to the safe in his office, but I don't know the combination.

A.:   He didn't mean the safe. The message said, "Check behind the Van Krugge," didn't it? He left a letter for you hidden behind the painting.

STRÜCKNER: Wh—Oh, God.

A.:   Could you go get it, Niamh? Don't worry, sir; Ambrose is to blame. He tended to overcomplicate things.

STRÜCKNER: How stupid of me. That's what Mr. Knox was looking for.

A.:   Uh … this Mr. Knox, was he friends with Ambrose too?

STRÜCKNER: Oh, yes. They met quite regularly. He lives in Lawrenceville. I phoned him the day Ambrose died and he drove here right away.

A.:   Thanks, Niamh. Mr. Strückner, this is … This is Ambrose Wells' letter to you.

[Paper unfolding.]

Uh … We'll take this to the kitchen and leave you with it. Come on.

[Teacups board a tray and the porcelain tremor moves away, along with the footsteps, and both are shut behind a massive door. Only the pattering remains.]

[A couple minutes drop by.]

[Sniffing. Paper crumples delicately beside the voice recorder; in the background, softer than the rain, perhaps higher above, air flows jerkily around a bulky throat lump, muffled behind long-fingered hands.]

[Door opens; A.'s voice approaching.]

A.:   Would you fancy some whiskey, Mr. Strückner? We found a bottle.

STRÜCKNER: No. *[Sniffs hard, for reassurance.]* No, I'm okay.

A.:   I'm sorry, sir. I know you lost much more than an employer.

STRÜCKNER: It's okay. He … *[Sigh.]* Most thought of him as a hermit, on account of the last years. But I think he saw so much more than most men could ever dream of.

[A chair sighs, relieved.]

Well, uh … I think I should be going if I'm to be in Washington for the night.

A.:   Mr. Strückner, there's something I must ask you. You surely have read the bit about the book. We haven't been able to find that book.

STRÜCKNER: That book …

[Paper unfolding, once again …]

I really don't know what he's talking about.

[Anticlimax.]

A.:   Well, it seems there is a book you used to read by a tree.

STRÜCKNER: That I used to read? I don't remember ever reading in the woods.

A.:   It was a children's book. Maybe something you and Ambrose read together...

STRÜCKNER: We never read together.

A.:   Or something you borrowed from the library...

STRÜCKNER: No, no, you don't understand. When I first came here, I didn't speak a word of English. I had been living with my mother in Aarau; I learned English working here. I used to play with Ambrose because... Well, because children just get along, that's why, but we could hardly talk to each other back then, let alone read together.

[An untimely thunder comes rumbling along—one that might have fit better at some other key point in the dialogue.]

A.:   So these letters...

STRÜCKNER: I'm sorry; I don't know what he's talking about. *[Voice grows distant as he stands up again.]* Look, you have both been very kind, but I fear the storm may get worse, so I need to—

A.:   Wouldn't you rather stay for the night and leave tomorrow? I don't think it's safe out there. Your room is just how you left it.

STRÜCKNER: Again, it is very kind of you, but I only have Sundays to myself; I must be back in my new house first thing tomorrow. You know. A butler's job.

A.:   Oh, now that you mention the job... Niamh? I think this belongs to you now, sir.

STRÜCKNER: Oh. *[Chuckle.]* Oh, God.

A.:   As Ambrose wished. I think it's worth some money.

STRÜCKNER: Oh, I know it is. I was there while he was bidding on the phone.

A.:   Yeah, that sounds like him. Whatever it takes to hide an ugly safe.

STRÜCKNER: Thank you. Really, thank you.

A.:   You think you could retire with that?

STRÜCKNER: Well I ... I don't know. *[An insufficient pause to think. Amused:]* God, I don't know. I wouldn't know what to do, really. I've been looking after richer people all my life.

A.: Well ... Whether you retire or not, if you don't care to have rich people around ... Well, you'll always have a room and a job here. And we don't need much looking after; we have surprisingly low hygiene standards.

STRÜCKNER: *[Laughs.]*

A.: What I mean to say is, if you want a job, you'll have one. And if you plan to retire ... Well, this is your family's house as much as mine.

STRÜCKNER: Sir. Please don't take this the wrong way. But the memories I have from this house are ... hard. And ... your eyes tell me you will need some looking after.

A.: I have Niamh. Don't worry about me.

STRÜCKNER: Too late, sir. I worry. It's my job. But I wish you two the best.

A.: Thanks, Mr. Strückner. It's been a pleasure.

STRÜCKNER: Likewise.

[Handshake.]

Miss. A pleasure to meet you.

[Writing. Reading.]

Oh, thank you! That's so sweet of you. Thank you very much.

[All voices walk away from the microphone.]

A.: Please promise if you ever drive by you'll pay us a visit.

STRÜCKNER: I can't promise that I'll wander this far, but if I do, you promise me that I'll find you in good shape.

[Distant voices fade in their own echoes in the hall. A door opens far away. In the immediate surroundings of the microphone, the gale never gets tired.]

[A minute after: A car starts beneath the rain, grinding the gravel, and speeds away.]

[Another minute after: A distant door closes.]

[Footsteps approach, along with a pencil scratching on paper.]

A.:   Yes, I know.

[One pair of footsteps comes closer and plonks down on the sofa, next to the microphone.]

[A few piano notes fall like lazy raindrops. It's Sinéad O'Connor's "John I Love You."]

[A deep breath. Paper unfolds, very slowly.]

    [Muttering.] "That wonderful book of our childhood..."

["I let tears fall like rain / Apple-sized they were / All over her..."]

    "You used to read by a tree..."

["And through all of those times / When you could have died / This is what you find..."]

    A book you used to read...

["There's life outside your mother's garden..."]

    By a tree...

["There's life beyond your wildest dreams..."]

    By...a...tree...

["There hasn't been any explosion / We're not spinning like—"]

SHIT!!!

[Piano stops on an off-tune, quizzical note; rain doesn't. Voice and footsteps stampede away.]

Quick, car keys! Before he reaches the highway!

[Hurried steps out of the room; door opens to the gale, door slams.]

[...]

[Door opens again.]

NIAMH: *[Very loud calling whistle.]*

[Footsteps come closer: Niamh grabs the voice recorder. Much distorted noise accompanying the following sounds: sliding on wooden floor, impatient whistles, a dog sprinting downstairs, the loudest downpour ever, rubber shoes and paws on flooded gravel for about ten seconds, a car door opening and closing, muffling the storm down to a loud surrounding drumroll.]

A.:   Help, in the back. In the back.

[The voice recorder tumbles onto the backseat and crashes somewhere on the car floor. Engine starts. Something fluffy shakes.]

Yeah, good place to do that, Help, thank you.

[The Audi speeds up. Seat belts fastening.]

It's not just a cipher. It's a pun. Hurry up; let's hope he found a roadblock!

[A loud screech; the rain drumroll grows irregular again as gusts of wind alter its pattern.]

[Five minutes of reckless driving follow.]

Roadblock! There he is; he's pulling back!

[Car horn. Noise; doors open; the rain is tumbling down like buildings; wind gusts shouting past. Voices are almost inaudible.]

[A car window lowers.]

A.:   How would you spell "by a tree"?

STRÜCKNER: What?!

A.:   In German! You used to read the book "by a tree" because you spoke German; how would a German spell "by a tree"?!

[Thunder crashing like a train through a mall.]

STRÜCKNER: Uh … "Bei," bee, e, i … Er … "A tree" … I don't know; it'd be pretty close to English!

A.:   What's German for *tree*?

STRÜCKNER: "Baum," but—OH, GOD DAMN—
      Sorry.

A.:   What?

STRÜCKNER: Baum! L. Frank Baum! *The Wonderful Wizard of Oz* is the book that was written by a "tree"!

Actually, L. Frank Baum set fourteen books in the fantasyland of Oz, and he wrote another forty-one novels, many of which are represented in Axton House's library. This we found out in the catalog, immediately after a wordless drive home and a straight march through the front door and into the library, all three of us in our dripping coats—no, all *four* of us in our dripping coats: Help was there too.

It was Niamh's idea that led us to the right book: She went for the one on the highest shelf, which people shorter than Strückner would have missed. She climbed on my shoulders to get it.

It was *The Magical Monarch of Mo*, a 1930 edition with original illustrations by Frank Ver Beck. This I caught only after leafing through it twice. By the third time, when Strückner had joined us on the iron balcony, we noticed the trick: Several groups of pages were glued together on the margins, forming three different pockets. By then we were breathing easily enough to use a letter opener and spare the book some damage. Shaking all the books in the library, in the end, would have produced nothing.

It was at this point, once we had laid three sealed envelopes on the library desk and Niamh was wielding the opener in her hand, that Strückner's sense of butlerdom got over the excitement:

"Well," he said, "curious as I am, we are not supposed to read them."

Niamh and I exchanged looks. I told Strückner he was absolutely right. So we put them in the drawer and I instructed Niamh to post them tomorrow in the morning together with our daily letter to Aunt Liza.

To which she nived in acquiescence.

And, of course, she never carried it out.

Next morning we woke up extra early to wave Strückner good-bye once again. He'd called in the night before, apologizing for the inconvenience, as if being delayed by tornadoes were an unforgivable license.

The postapocalyptic dawn after the storm was astounding. Even by American standards.

As soon as the car disappeared into the graying woods, we raced upstairs and tore open the letters.

LETTER

Axton House
Point Bless, VA

Dr. V. Belknap
402 Lafayette St.
Midburg, VA 26900

Dear Dr. Belknap,

I am truly sorry to inform you that unfortunately I will not be able to continue with our sessions. Health problems forbid me to take the long drive to Midburg anymore, even on a quarterly basis.

Please believe me when I say that I resent terminating our professional (and may I add, on my behalf, friendly) relationship in such an abrupt way. Not only because our sessions, I realize, were more fruitful than my incurable cynicism implied, but because even as an excuse for a day out, I enjoyed them. I enjoyed the long drive, the cozy little café below your office, and above all the sixty minutes of conversation with you. As I travel down the road of life and my body and mind pay the toll, to fix the rapidly wrecking parts becomes less of a priority than it is to appreciate what is left. Therefore I hereby thank you for so efficiently treating my most urgent condition: self-involvement and boredom.

On a personal note, and only if you care to continue our talks on dreams and such, will you allow me to recommend you some literature? Try U. Bianchi's article in the June 1968 issue of *Mind & Beyond* magazine, and if you tolerate his views, check the bibliography—particularly J. Kuttner and I. Dänemarr. I caught you kindly repressing a sneer at these names when I mentioned them, but it is not as a patient in need of comprehension that I quote them now, but as a friend. Take them, if you will, as a memento from your doubtlessly most trivial case.

Yours sincerely,
Ambrose Gabriel Wells

LETTER

2/14/1995

Axton House
Point Bless, VA

Mr. Curtis Knox
120 Vaughan St.
Lawrenceville, VA 23868

Dear Curtis,

By the time this letter reaches you, you will know what became of me better than I do now. I dare to assert so because you are Socrates, and we both know Socrates don't travel much. Other years I chose a different opening—for I have been rewriting this letter every year since 1974, usually around my birthday. (I always trusted that I would not leave in winter, at the beginning of a new campaign. Although I do fear, every once in a while, especially on the nights before the meetings, while Strückner oversees the lodgings, that some year, maybe not this one, hopefully not the next, but some year, it will be so dreadful that we will not last a single night. I never brought that up, but I do think about it. I wonder if you do.)

But I beg your pardon: I digress. As you will surely have guessed, this is not a suicide note. At the time of writing this I do not intend to put an end to my life. I am writing it because I fear that the end may be put.

If so, some issues must be addressed. Our Society must be taken care of. As a Member, I am expected to bring a replacement. As a Host, I am bound to set a new course. As our Historian, you shall be entrusted with my posthumous vote on the fate of the Society. And my vote is this: *Dissolve it.*

Yes, I know what you are thinking: I am a hypocrite. Indeed I am. I have been for twenty-one years. Every February I pen an anxious caveat about our activities and I exhort you not to celebrate another meeting. And yet, once the meeting approaches and my letter goes unread, I say go on, *encore!,* one more year! Simply put, I want you all to end this game only because I can't play anymore.

It is true, Curtis. I am a lousy loser. But since I know you are not callous enough to just dismiss a letter from the dead, I might as well try to justify my stand.

First, I am a Wells. As you well know, my position grants me a few privileges. As the Host, I call the meetings. Members report to me. The Archives lie with me. My grandfather Horace was among the first players. Were it not for him, this fellowship would have no reason to exist; we would not meet; we would sleep at night; we would live peacefully in ignorance. A Wells began this game; a Wells may be given the chance to end it.

Second, I am childless. Which leads you all into a position the Society has historically avoided: a succession debate. Nobody challenged my grandfather when he willed the reins to his son. And when my father forgot to write a will, nobody objected to Stillwall becoming my teacher and putting the reins in my hands. (Have you considered, by the way, that my father, who actually committed suicide, never left a note? Have you considered that his act too was an attempt to dissolve the Society?)

Third, I am dead. And here is what my father failed to make you all see. He probably felt as I feel now, the same way we all feel in bad years. But he took his own life. So the Game didn't do it, we all thought.

Well, not this time, Curtis. The Game has taken *my* life. The Game is responsible. As it was for Spears, Lutz, Dagenais . . . Must I go on?

All this you can transmit to the Members for discussion. You can borrow the red notebook in the left top drawer in the study on the third floor for their contact details, together with my key to the Archives, which are yours to do with as you see fit. I have always admired your oratory, Curtis; I am sure the debate will result in the Society taking the course you support, no matter what it is. However, the Key to the continuity of the Society I am entrusting to the Secretary. This is only to ensure that there will *be* a debate.

I know I am not posing any problem that the nineteen of you cannot overcome. New situations call for new measures, and our Society has wonderful improvisation skills. We are not bound by laws carved in stone, after all. It's just a bourgeois pastime.

Good-bye, my friend.

Yours truthfully,
Ambrose Gabriel Wells

[To Caleb Ford in Clayboro, Virginia]

```
Q H T B A G L I L I O G N E D W
R B R N U I E Y Y D U D X P Q N
Q E O X I P G P I T A E E D D X
M O T D V P T I A B P R T O N E
O P N L L K P B P X Y E X K C P
R B C E Q H L A M C R N O R Q N
Y E Z C D E B C A E P H O D N R
W G L Z Q R U O I Z L X L I R K
A E T L Y D O D Y D I L M K B U
T E C L Q O O E R B R Z A E C P
Y D N L N O L I W O Y I G B T Q
Y D O T C P V Y B L G O O V C E
D B N P O E R B L H D M X A B L
L Z E G T H N L H S U H D Y Y D
B Y F O H L G U I L N R G B M O
T E O P D Z B T A E Y D I L Q O
```

(Breakfast at Gordon's.)

—So? What do you make of it?

—Did you sleep at all?

—Couple hours.

—You can't go on this way.

—Can we focus on the letters?

(. . . I can't.)

—Look, I gather Dr. Belknap is a therapist. He has nothing to do with the sect or whatever. So, Knox.

—Ambrose trusted him, but not quite.

—He transmitted his last will to him, but saved the baton, as you put it, for Caleb. "The Secretary."

—& ciphered it.

(We check the cipher.)

—So what is this optical illusion?

—It's not like the Aeschylus note—too long.

—Strückner said Caleb's father was in the war with Ambrose's father; maybe they're both into cryptography. This might be a more advanced level. What's more advanced than a substitution code?

—*Everything.*

—Yup. I feared that. Okay. I'll look into it.

—*I will. You go to sleep.*

DREAM JOURNAL

I'm sleeping in the park and the policemen come and speak to me and prod me with their truncheons. I can't understand them. Suddenly I stop a truncheon going for my arm. I foresee the other truncheon's due trajectory. I duck and kick the aggressor in advance.

I knock them out in under five seconds. I look at their bodies on the snow, astonished. I look at my hands.

I look at my hand. There's a Rubik's cube.

I look at my hand. There's a grenade, and the pin's off.

I look at my hand. I hold two fives.

I look at my hand: It pines for the window, fingers clutch the sunrays, but they fail. I fall. And the monster thrusts the pitchfork through me and I wake with the sound of my splintered ribs.

The main challenge we face on "resetting parapsychology," as Bach put it, is how not to repeat the same mistakes. We have agreed on a new tool, the scientific method. But this new cement will soon degrade if contaminated by two of the most hazardous agents to science: egotism and its bigger brother, anthropocentrism. [. . .] Quoting Ernest Bach again (10), "The legitimate questions for parapsychology to attempt an answer are: *Do ghosts exist?*, which is due to challenge any open mind, and, *What are they?*, which is bound to interest any real scientist. The wrong question is, *What do ghosts want with us?* [. . .]"

Not even I think myself ready to claim not to be taking this ghost business *personally*. Here's a piece of why. During the years-long process of writing this book, many colleagues have been kind enough to read the manuscript and share their feelings. A strong majority complained that my ten points on *what we know about ghosts* are too scant, the result of too severe a purge. However, one valuable piece of feedback came from a late good friend of mine whom we will call Jonathan—a pure psychologist, a "para-free" one, who took interest in the supernatural only at an amateur level. On reading those ten pivotal statements, this genuinely scientific man immediately signaled the fifth item ("[ghosts] speak, and are therefore assumed to have human intelligence"), and remarked, "This is a logical fallacy. Parrots speak, and they do not have human intelligence."

What a beautiful way to exemplify how anthropocentrism leads to speculation! We don't know what ghosts are, but given a clean slate, we compare them to ourselves. We hear voices: We assume they're human. We see shapes: We try to outline a person out of them. (Of course, the outline looks more like a blot, and that's why we made up that ghosts wear loose gowns or blankets.) Surely the use of aseptic terminology such as *paranormal phenomena* is meant to dehumanize ghosts, but as soon as we lower our guard, we are humanizing them again. We are tainted by the old notion of ghosts as lost souls, rejections from hell, but this is not part of our selected evidence: It is folklore and religion, a different corpus of knowledge that scientists must put aside.

Others might think of Jonathan's input as destructive. Personally, I thank him for it. I owe him my growing skepticism and puzzlement, which are not bad things; gullibility is. Jonathan was not prejudiced, and knowledge found him at rest: He never chased ghosts, but toward the end of his life, he saw one. He told me the day after, and he was perfectly at peace with it. One week later he died of cardiac arrest caused by pancreatic cancer.

VIDEO RECORDING

BATHROOM MON NOV-20-1995 15:33:03

[Light is switched on, and for a couple of seconds it throbs and ebbs and eddies inside the left lightbulb over the sink like a disoriented glowworm. A. looks up, waiting for it to stabilize. A gentle drone settles in.]

[A. turns on the faucet and rinses his face. He lets his wet face drip, arms on each side of the sink, water running. He looks to his left, toward the bathtub. His breathing stops.]

[The clock keeps counting empty seconds.]

[His eyes anchored somewhere between him and the tub curtain, he feels the faucet and turns off the water.]

[He checks the camera. Then back at the nothing before him.]

A.:   You don't care much for hiding anymore, do you?

Niamh's forecast was right: After the storm washed away, it left a new sky and a new earth behind. The former is silver-gray at its brightest, and cawing; the latter is just cold. The woods are petrified. Tall, balding birches stand Strückneresquely, mimicking the Gothic style of the house, just as the house used to mimic the environment. The grounds are yet snowless, but also . . . everythingless. Bare naked.

November has settled.

It's funny how as night falls and Axton House darkens into a black lifeless silhouette that would cause Shaggy and Scooby-Doo to poop their pants and flee, we inside find it glowing with a welcoming scent of lit fireplaces and yellow wood. It feels like home under this new light—a light born of the very house to shelter us from winter. It feels cozy and protecting and soft, like a Russian dacha or a bungalow in the Alps. There is warmth in the paneling and the thick carpets. There is warmth in Niamh sitting by the fire, chin propped on her knees, cheeks ripening like peaches, brittle body inside an undershirt in a T-shirt in a flannel shirt in a cardigan, slowly peeling off layers as the heat sinks in, and you always wish to be somewhere there, between two layers, never in the core, but close.

LIBRARY MON NOV-20-1995 17:43:43

NIAMH and A. at the paper-ridden desk. She is skimming through a red notebook. He is examining a rather large, four-sided key in his hand.

A.: Okay, so we have the key to the archives, but not the lock. *[Flips the key in his hand.]* The keyhole must look like a cross. That's not easy to miss.

[They swap the objects.]

A.:   *[Riffling the notebook.]* And this is cool, but it doesn't give us the code names. So we have a list of names and a list of code names, but no way to link them. Except for the three we have. What were the initials in the Prometheus letter?

NIAMH: *[Lounging with her feet on the table, she scribbles three letters on a Post-it.]*

A.:   *[Reads.]* "S.W.L." *[Turns some pages.]* That's Silas W. Long, from someplace called ... *[Frowning.]* "Butt, Montana?" *[Wondering, he shows her the page.]*

NIAMH: *[Amused, lips a word for him.]*

A.:   Butte. Butte, Montana. Thanks. Oh, and we now know that Curtis Knox is Socrates. That makes four solved. Four out of twenty. That's some progress. I think.

NIAMH: *[Starts writing on her own pad.]*

A.:   *[Reading the letter in his hands.]* "Socrates don't travel much." What does that mean?

NIAMH: *[Shows pad.]*

A.:   *[After reading, standing up.]* I don't know. *[Searches through the desk.]* Where's the ledger page with the code names?

[Niamh retrieves it from the paper underbrush and hands it to him.]

Thanks. *[Checks. Leans on the table.]* Well, I didn't have much of a classical education, but ... Leonidas was a hero of the Battle of Thermopylae against the Persians. And Hector is the guy defending Troy in the Iliad. Then Archimedes, Sophocles, those are pretty obvious.

NIAMH: *[She just shrugs.]*

A.:   *[Staring at her.]* You don't know who Archimedes was?

NIAMH: *[She scribbles for a few seconds, punctuates, then shows.]*

A.:   *[Reading.]* "Guy who ran naked crying eureka." Yes, that'd be him. He had discovered something important, hence the streaking outburst.

NIAMH: *[Bends in a silent laugh.]*

A.: *[Oblivious.]* So he was a physicist of sorts. And Sophocles was a playwright. Now he is some guy named Edward Cutler, the one in that telegram from Ibiza. Then Zosimos … This I looked up the other day in the Britannica; he must be Zosimos of Panopolis, an alchemist, but that's way after the classical period. Socrates, aka Curtis Knox, is a philosopher, of course … And then we enter a dark area, because I don't know what these are. Dioskuri, Anchises, Elpenor … Phoenix rings a bell … This Alexandros could mean Alexander the Great … The last ones make some sense again, but they're from mythology, not history: Chronos, Prometheus …
Actually, this last part looks like a ranking: Chronos is … well, he's time, a notion, a primordial figure; Prometheus is a titan; Heracles is a demigod; and Zeus is a god. THE god. The king of gods.

NIAMH: *[Writing.]*

A.: *[Still on the ledger page.]* That's funny, because if they're ranked in ascending order, Ambrose, as Leonidas, was right at the bottom.

NIAMH: *[Shows notepad.]*

A.: *[After reading.]* Yeah, I have that effect on women. *[Sighs. Props himself on the desk.]* Doing research with you is incredibly tiring, you know? I have to do all the talking and you're like the funny sidekick.

[Tosses the ledger page back into the chaos.]

Well, I think that's all we can get from the letters, so … should we post them?

NIAMH: *[Shakes her head.]*

A.: Yeah. Thought so. So much for granting a dead man's wishes.

*

Ultimately we decided not to post any of them. The cipher is evidently the most important, but its intended recipient is absent and there is no way to contact him. So there is no harm in holding on to it awhile longer.

The one for Knox we could post, I guess, but we don't like him very much.

And then there's Dr. Belknap.

MAN:	Dr. Belknap's office.
A.:	Hello?
MAN:	Hello, sir.
A.:	Oh, hi. Sorry, I wasn't receiving you well. I'd like to make an appointment.
MAN:	Could I have your name, sir?
A.:	Uh … Wells.
MAN:	Is this your first visit, Mr. Wells?
A.:	Yes, Dr. Belknap has been highly recommended.
MAN:	Good to hear. May I have your address and phone number?
A.:	Number one Axton Road, Point Bless, Ponopah, two-six-nine-six-nine. Phone number seven-five-five, nine-six-three, four thousand.
MAN:	*[Keying in the background.]* Okay, let's see … Does Wednesday the thirteenth suit you?
A.:	Well, it's kind of an emergency. I'd hoped to see him sooner.
MAN:	Her.
A.:	What?
MAN:	Dr. Vanessa Belknap is a woman, sir.
A.:	Oh.
MAN:	You know, if you have an emergency, maybe this is not the first place to call. Who recommended us to you?

A.:   Well, Wells. Ambrose Wells.

MAN: Oh, Mr. Wells! How is he doing?

A.:   He's dead.

[An abrupt blip of silence.]

      I fear I've got the same thing. That's why it's an emergency.

MAN: Could you hold on for a minute, please?

[Button press. Baroque chamber music.]

A.:   Niamh? Niamh, are you on the phone?

NIAMH: *[Short whistle in F.]*

A.:   Are you recording this?

NIAMH: *[Short whistle in F.]*

A.:   In the name of the lost eighteen minutes of the Watergate tapes, could you tell me why?

NIAMH: *[Two notes, dropping.]*

A.:   No, of course you couldn't.

*

In the end they squeezed me in for tomorrow at three.

EXCERPT FROM JOHN LEEK'S *GHOSTS OF GHOSTS*

Ironic as it may sound, if we are to relinquish any preconceived ideas on the nature of ghosts, anthropocentrism might not be completely off topic. Many critical parapsychologists (a seldom used denomination that grants the bearer the disdain of both para-psychologists and everybody else) do justify the human nature of ghosts, although differing from spiritualists on one crucial point: They don't treat ghosts as once living humans, but as human creations. [...]

M. Cassel (16) is regarded as the champion of this theory, which states that what we call supernatural phenomena could altogether be a general misperception, a trick of our mind, which does not make them less real phenomena (just as conscience, dreams or *déjà vus* are real occurrences whose objectivity relies only on the agreement that we all subjectively experience them). [...] Leon Karnach (17) does not discard the physical evidence (neither does Cassel), but favors the scenario of observers being the triggers. In his words, "Assuming that the reach of the human mind is still unknown, a man causing lights to flicker with his mind, even unconsciously, is still more plausible than a deceased man's mind causing the same effect." In the end, parapsychology derives from *psychology*, which in turn comes from the Greek word ψυχή (*psyche*), meaning *soul* or, in modern times, *mind*. The subjective nature of our field of study seems undeniable. [...]

All of the above taken into account, ghosts as a subjective experience—i.e., *human perception of real supernatural phenomena*— may be summarized in another set of few, tentative statements. I will not number these; numbers tend to make statements look falsely irrevocable.

First of all, accounts show that ghosts have been perceived in a haunted area by unbiased observers not knowing an iota about the existing folklore. Their testimony is logically deemed more conclusive than that of people who knew the legend before perceiving the ghost, and thus expected to perceive it. Their perception, however, may still be triggered by the presence of aesthetic conditioners or topoi, from whose influence virtually nobody is free. For instance, an old, desolated castle predisposes the visitor to be aware of moving shadows.

On the other hand, the legend of a haunting always predates the haunting. Folklore always relates ghosts to specific people who were in life, to say the least, remarkable. This, according to Karnach (17), reaffirms the subjective theory: *In absence of anyone else, it is the living who judge whether someone was remarkable or not.** We notice the ghosts because we noticed the living first.

Also, once you notice, they notice that you notice. (18, 19). [. . .]

Health effects are inconclusive, but reports are consistent enough to grant them some significance. Exposition to several haunted spots (Heck House, Vine House, Chillingham, Provnorsk) has been associated by independent sources with acute migraine, hallucination, epilepsy, eye/ear/nose hemorrhage, and at least two cases of intracranial hemorrhage. (20, 21)

People who are about to die seem more prone to notice. (22, 23)

---

* The emphasized passage was underscored in pencil in Axton House's copy.

In the stone-barked grove, the blindfolded girl in the turquoise dress stands listening. Her blindfoldless twin is watching from a short distance. They were playing hide-and-seek when the hiding sister was assaulted, a scream snatched out of her mouth by the coarse hand of the hideous man who holds her captive. None of the three dares to utter another sound. The whole forest lies still.

The blindfolded seeker has noticed. She's already alert. She staggers toward them, or in their general direction, not in a straight line, but in a long arc, away from her twin at first, turning, spinning, arms radaring the environment, turquoise dress waltzing around her. Her footfalls are the only sound in the world. And now she's approaching.

She orbits toward them like a silent planet.

The hideous man is paralyzed. The hider does not attempt a further sound.

Nor does the seeker.

Her stretched fingers just miss them for a couple of inches.

The hideous man wishes he could stop giving off smell, or heat, or whatever.

Then the seeker stops spinning, facing slightly off their way.

She kneels down. She grabs a stone. As big as her fist. She throws it and breaks the hideous man's nose.

The hobo in the park knocks down the policemen.

A hotel blows up in the horizon of ramshackle rooftops beyond the handshake.

The gas tank in the desert explodes.

Puma shoes hit the island, cracking the cement.

The grenade throbs in my hand. People scampering away. I throw the thing over the cars. Over the bridge. Into the river. And it all ends in a humble splish.

I lay a long word on the Scrabble board. Greek letters on the tiles.

Pull the tubes out of my arm.

Kiss the redhead under the blanket.

Her lips caress the red poppy.

And I figure out how to finish the Rubik's cube in five movements. I execute the vision. The white side is sorted. Everything is sorted. I look up at the girl in lingerie and magenta blush, and she smiles at me.

EXCERPT FROM UMBERTO BIANCHI:
"WHAT DREAMS ARE MADE OF," *MIND & BEYOND*, JUNE 1968

[. . .] It was 1906 Nobel laureate Camillo Golgi who inadvertently directed scientific interest to a field previously worked only by occultists (Jacques Sandoz, *Conversation des âmes*, 1728) or mediums (Salomon Percevaux, allegedly dead from brain stroke during a public exhibition of telekinesis in 1846). Golgi's reticular theory, which views the brain as a continuous network of cells communicating via electrical impulses, revived some curiosity about the idea of thought transmission, not among doctors, but engineers and physicists: Tesla's 1922 experiment with seals is a good example. Even after Golgi's theory lost favor to Ramón y Cajal's neuron doctrine, it still inspired some achievements in the study of brain-body connections (Furshban & Potter, 1957). However, these studies hold no interest to a new school of German scientists who seek something even more ambitious: the brain-mind connection—or, as Humphrey Bogart put it, "the stuff that dreams are made of."

Despite its mystic connotations, these researchers' quest is purely a physiological problem. Bergemaier, Kuttner, Dänemarr, they are all neurologists, not psychologists. The contents of the mind are for Jung's successors to study; what these men and women are searching for is the physical support of those contents.

Electricity seemed an elegant solution: a form of energy, impalpable and ephemeral, just like thoughts. Konrad Bergemaier (b. Mainz 1899), one of the earliest advocates of this school, seemed to be on the right track when, in 1927, he managed to transmit the sensations of cold and warmth between two individuals. Unfortunately, the oversimplification of this principle in the hands of Nazi scientists led into the dead alley of wire-based telepathy, culminating with the human experiments in the forties that brought shame to the discipline. And still, Dr. Eva Ruff's work on prisoners in Dachau shows how a wrong theory may lead to atrocious accomplishments.

Nevertheless, Bergemaier's true disciples are far from discouraged, and even now new methods are being applied to old ideas with remarkable results. Jan Kuttner's work with animals is quickly assimilating the techniques of mainstream neurology. In his words, "The electric nature of thought seems to be the right principle, but our predecessors omitted the biochemical support." This omission is now being mended. In East Germany, Karl Hannemann started replacing the old copper wire, first with animal collagen, next with the sophisticated gel developed by W. Opfstau that provided the breakthrough of 1967, in which two subjects shared a mental image (a rampant horse). Isaak Dänemarr (ironically, a subject of Ruff's experiments) expects to be able to "project" thoughts on photographic paper.

Should these researchers succeed, they will not only clean the name of a deprecated science. They will "transmit ideas, fantasies or dreams, not by the mediation of a word or a drawing, which is a mere suggestion, but keeping the substance of which ideas are made" (Bergemaier, *Nachwirkungen*, 1955). They might implant or remove ideas. They might record dreams. It will be the dawn of electric memories.

A.'S DIARY

I think we discovered the place from which Wells and his Society drew the inspiration for their fashion statement. It must be Midburg, Virginia.

The town is a two-hour drive from Point Bless, but the landscape is as different as one coast is from another. Point Bless feels southern; Midburg is pure North, Northernly old, New England style. Narrow streets look narrower thanks to trees meeting overhead, laying an elegant carpet of autumn leaves on the cobblestones. Redbrick buildings gaze incurious behind wrought-iron railings. Engines do not eclipse birds. Everyone looks like a librarian and none pay any notice to our conspicuous car.

I can tell why Ambrose chose a therapist this far from Axton House: He felt at home here, among other men with hats and civilized pigeons.

We hardly drove a hundred kilometers, but judging by the cityscape alone we could have crossed several state lines.

Which we might have done, actually. Apparently I slept most of the way.

We located Dr. Belknap's office by the café below referenced in Ambrose's letter: dark green awnings and a flock of small round tables behind the rain-sprinkled windows. It had to be here.

It was two forty-five p.m.—in time for my first therapy session.

A.:   Well, I don't know.

[Continued sound of scribbling in the background.]

I guess it all started in football training. Football meaning soccer, of course. There was this kid. He wasn't very good either, but he was eager to play, didn't feel awkward like I felt. I guess I wanted to be like him. One evening the coach got mad at us for some reason, maybe because he'd waved me across the field and I'd waved back while we were supposed to be defending. They had us running around the premises for hours. And I'm pretty sure he slowed down for me. So, anyway, when we got to the locker room, everybody else was gone. And ... it'd been raining, so we were wet. So we took our clothes off. And ... we watched each other. And I remember the sound of the rain. And the silence of the lambs. I do remember those lambs.

[Pencil scratching on paper like a stressed cat.]

Are you writing all this?

[Writing ceases.]

What … What the fuck—is that supposed to be me? *[Scoff, slapping.]* I am emptying my soul for you and you're doodling a—Why do I have wings? Wait, those are my ears?

[Door opens.]

DR. BELKNAP: Mr. Wells?

A.: Oh! Hi.

DR. BELKNAP: *[High heels coming over.]* I am Dr. Vanessa Belknap. I am very sorry for your loss.

A.: Thank you. Uh, this is my friend, Niamh Connell. We were just…

DR. BELKNAP: Fooling around on my couch?

A.: Er … yes. Wow, you're good. I already feel like you're X-raying me.

DR. BELKNAP: *[High heels coming closer.]* I'll take that as a compliment. Is that yours?

A.: Niamh, your Walkman's on the doctor's desk.

[A hand gropes the microphone. STOP.]

*

[REC. The following fragment sounds muffled.]

DR. BELKNAP: … version, which of course I am not allowed to discuss.

A.: Why not?

DR. BELKNAP: Because of my work ethics. I am bound by medical confidentiality.

A.: Yes, but Ambrose Wells is dead. Isn't it like in Masonic law?

DR. BELKNAP: I beg your pardon?

A.: You know, you're not allowed to say that another person is a Mason until the other person is dead.

[An awkward blank.]

DR. BELKNAP: You know, I happen to be a Freemason and this is the first time I ever heard about that rule.

A.:   *[In due time.]* Oh. Well, so … can't you tell me what you talked about, in a general way?

DR. BELKNAP: What you talk about with a therapist.

A.:   I'm not even sure what a therapist does, to tell the truth.

DR. BELKNAP: Their best. *[Leaning back on a leather chair.]* I'm not sure Ambrose needed a therapist, actually. I guess he appreciated my listening.

A.:   He was fond of you. That much I know.

DR. BELKNAP: Good. The feeling was mutual.

A.:   Was there something between you?

DR. BELKNAP: *[Leaning forward.]* Mr. Wells, you do not seem to trust my professionalism.

A.:   With all due respect, I'm seeing you right after the only other patient of yours I know of jumped out of a window. That's giving you some credit.

[Blank.]

Okay, since I can't pull anything from you, I'll push in. Did he tell about his research?

About his being Leonidas?

About his dreams?

[Longer gap.]

Did he tell you how they'd pluck his eye out every night?

DR. BELKNAP: How do you know that?

A.:   I don't know; how should I know?

DR. BELKNAP: Did he keep a diary?

A.:   Did he?

DR. BELKNAP: How else would you know what he dreamed?

A.:   Perhaps I dreamed it myself.

DR. BELKNAP: Are you implying that you and a man you never met are sharing dreams?

A.: Is that the craziest thing ever said in this room?

[Slower.]

DR. BELKNAP: It's funny you suggest it. Your cousin used to talk about that.

A.: About what? Sharing dreams?

DR. BELKNAP: Something like that.

A.: Is this covered by medical confidentiality too?

[A sigh of resignation.]

DR. BELKNAP: Mr. Wells sometimes showed interest in conducted telepathy. Oh, it's … How to put it softly? It's a debunked science, like phrenology, a supposedly scientific approach to telepathy. It was widely disregarded in the nineteenth century until some questionable doctors in Germany, grossly misreading Golgi, interpreted that since thoughts are nothing but electric impulses, and electricity can be conducted through wires, thoughts can be conducted through wires.

A.: Yeah, I read something about it. Nazi experiments and stuff.

DR. BELKNAP: Yes, well, some of them resumed the work after the Nazis, hopefully using more ethical methods. Some people claimed to have gotten results in East Germany.

A.: Guy named Dänemarr? With a double R?

DR. BELKNAP: Very good. He intended to record dreams. Yeah, sounds pretty cool, doesn't it? As far as I know, he's still trying.

A.: So tell me about Ambrose's dreams.

DR. BELKNAP: I can't. Medical confidentiality.

A.: Okay, then tell me about mine; they seem to be the same.

DR. BELKNAP: Are you requesting a therapy session, Mr. Wells? Because in that case, you might start by sharing your real name.

[Blank.]

A.: Niamh, why don't you go to the café downstairs for some cake?

[...]

Please go. I'll come later. Hey. Don't forget your Walkman.

CASE NOTES FROM DR. VANESSA BELKNAP*

Case file #0262
Name: #############   Sex: Male
DOB: 6/25/1972   DOE: 11/21/1995 (23 years old)
Address: Axton House, Axton Rd., Point Bless, VA 26969
Phone: (755) 963-4000

OVERVIEW ON ARRIVAL: Patient is a newcomer to the U.S. after inheriting a large piece of real estate from his unacquainted second cousin twice removed Ambrose G. Wells from Point Bless (no loss grief). He avoids talking about his BG. Doesn't mention any family, except for an aunt Liza. Probable only child or more likely far youngest. He lives now with an "intimate friend" or "associate" (female, about 17, Irish, mute, acquired condition) with whom he shares a house big enough for six families. Their relationship is challenging: Body language says mutual interest, no sex. He likely feels guilty or unworthy, compensates by means of paternal care. She feels rejected and can't express her feelings (due to disability), which he takes advantage of. *(Note: I didn't get whether Liza is his aunt or hers.)*

He first approached me to inform that Ambrose G. Wells of Point Bless (cf #0178) "defenestrated" in September this year. Despite his lack of grief, he manifested deep interest in his ancestor's profile. In the course of the conversation he mentioned a recurring dream of Ambrose W., whom he claims to have never met. (Later in the session he said it was his own dream.)

---

* This is a transcription from Dr. Belknap's file. Her handwritten notations are included in italics.

SESSION 1

1995 NOVEMBER 21, 3:30 TO 4 P.M.

Icebreak by questions on BG and relationship with friend Niamh. Admits dependency. She drives and takes care of the dog. He avoids talking about his homeland. Idealized vision of the U.S. through movies and TV. *X-Files* fan.

On his second night in Axton H. wakes up, goes to bathroom, sees "a shadow against the tub curtain." The lights glow brighter and explode. Doesn't remember how he got to bed again. In the morning he had severe subconjunctival hemorrhage (*Note: Right eye isn't healed*). House is rumored home to the ghost of a slave girl dead in the Civil War. (*Note: Ambrose G. Wells lived in the same house and confirmed the ghost story. He claimed to have seen a shadow in the bathroom on his last session, April '95.*)

Prompted on belief in ghosts, claims he "wants to believe." He has felt the "presence" in the bathroom several times. Yesterday saw "her" again in a "stronger" way. He shrugs at my pointing out that he's only begun to distinguish the shape of the ghost *after* being told how it would look.

Suffers very vivid dreams. (*Note: He never says nightmares.*) Relates the eye one as cued: He is tied down to an operating table in a basement in Africa with a blood-splattered surgeon and a black army officer. They pull his eye out. Extreme pain. Then he gets free and kills both. (*Note: He narrated the dream combining first and third person.*) Prompted, he "just knows" it's Africa. Queried, he knows somebody who is in Africa now.

Prompted, not all dreams are that bad; "these are the least enjoyable." Asked for an enjoyable one: He sits in a car in a traffic jam and he's solving a Rubik's cube. (*Note: first person all the time.*) The driver is a girl in underwear, "spit-in-your-facingly beautiful." Queried, "I don't touch her." Queried, he has other dreams like that: He's walking on a snowed roof and sneaks into a bedroom, inside a red-haired girl's bed and feels "her breath in my face." He remarks that, in that dream, he is a girl too. (*Note: Explore possible issue of repressed sexuality.*) He asks, "Am I not supposed to dream what I live?" We discuss dreams. I demystify Freud for him. We track the sources for the dreams. Revelation: He sleeps with Niamh. They never touch. "We keep each other company."

Switches topic to Ambrose Wells. Prompted, he denies that Ambrose killed himself. "Something happened" to Ambrose, and he fears the same "might happen" to him. He denies black thoughts and sleepwalking. (*Note: Niamh would know.*)

I ask why he guessed that his cousin had the same dreams: "It seems the kind of stuff that would make you jump out of a window."

(*Note: Ambrose G. Wells (cf #0178) reported an extremely close and gruesome nightmare about a surgeon who pulled his eye out in his last visit, April '95. He also mentioned the black army officer and hinted at the violent outcome. Probable extraordinary case of subconscious suggestion triggered by something in the house. Ambrose mentioned other dreams along the same line: knocking out two policemen, and stumbling in a dark house running away from a man carrying a pitchfork. The notes from that same session quote Ambrose on his father's suicide: "Everything seems to be laid as a path for you to follow, like <u>when you just see the solution to a Rubik's cube.</u>"*)

PROVISIONAL DIAGNOSIS: Inhibited loss trauma, paranoia, delusion, pathological fantasy. MORE THAN HALF OF HIS STORY ISN'T TRUE.

BATHROOM WED NOV-22-1995 01:33:03

Lights wink ON.

> [A. leans over the sink, breathing hard. He doesn't touch the faucet.]

> [In frame comes the top hemisphere of NIAMH's demishaved skull. She stands by the door.]

A.:   It's okay, Niamh; sorry I woke you. Go to bed.

> [His eyes return to the drain hole. Nothing moves.]

> [Not looking.] Go to bed, Niamh.

> [Niamh withdraws. The door closes.]

> [A. pulls his shirt off and turns around, trying to inspect his back. He turns around again. Presses three fingers on his sternum.]

> [The light in the bulb drones brighter for a couple of seconds. A. checks the bathtub.]

Shut up.

DREAM JOURNAL

The baby stirs, head pressed on the Latina's bosom, and I hope my heartbeat won't disturb her sleep, while my other hand is aiming the shotgun at the countermen behind the windows, hands up in the air. With imprudent flies buzzing dumbly through the path planned for the slug.

I pull the tubes out of my arm. A tiny Styx of blood trickles down my skin. Green industrial tiles.

The Chinese student sits at the piano, playing the keys one at a time and writing ideograms on a notebook.

And the four notes run deep under an ultraviolet water mass of dancers, sparkling with white smiles and white bra straps. And I am torpedoed toward the surface along a shaft of sunlight, and spit out of the warping sea, out into a tempest of chrome clouds, and the surfboard under my feet knifes a vaulting amphitheater-shaped wave of a billion tons of salt water curling overhead, and I feel I'm *God*.

(Then there's the eyeball, and then the pitchfork again.)

MUSIC ROOM WED NOV-22-1995 10:57:38

A. lies cuddled on the sofa.

> [HELP trots in, straight to the breathing bulk. He clambers onto
> the sofa and sniffs the body. Head tilted, he stares at A., gently
> pokes him with his paw. A. doesn't move.]

> [Exit Help through the ballroom door.]

*

LIBRARY WED NOV-22-1995 10:59:01

NIAMH sits on the desk, the ciphered letter in front of her. With a pencil,
she encircles groups of letters, as in a word-seek puzzle.

> [HELP straggles in from the gallery, sits by Niamh's desk
> expectantly.]

12:51:13

> [Niamh flings the pencil at a bookcase in frustration.]

> [Help swiftly retrieves the pencil with his mouth and offers it to
> his mistress.]

NIAMH'S NOTEPAD

(At Gordon's for lunch, over the cipher.)

—I think it's a grille.

—What's a grille?

—Like in Mysteries of Old Peking?

(I pluck holes in a napkin & lay it over the cipher.)

—I see: The letters showing through spell the message. So Caleb must have a perforated card to read this.

—& Ambrose too.

—Isn't it a big giveaway? To have a perforated card lying around?

(Shrug.)

—And besides, the cipher is short as it is. If only a few letters count, how long is the real message? Three words?

—Strückner didn't need more.

—No, I guess not.

—You think I wrong.

—No, I don't think you're wrong. Maybe it is a grille. All I'm saying is, Ambrose wouldn't have a perforated card sitting in his desk. In any of them. For a start, we would've found it.

—So he destroyed it?

—No, because it's not a single-use device either. Caleb needs the same grille to read it, so it's something they both have, or know. Maybe it's not a physical object, but more like a rule. Like, read every five letters, or three letters forward and two down, or as a knight moves in chess. Check the puzzle section in the newspaper; there might be more.

(I find a story in the newspaper. Show him.)

—Did we know THIS?

AN ARTICLE IN THE *SOUTH VIRGINIA COURANT,* NOVEMBER 22, 1995

Extended Rwandan Genocide Kills 100 a Month
By Meredith Cohen—Associated Press

KIGALI—About one hundred Rwandan Tutsis a month are still killed by Hutu refugees settled in bordering eastern Zaire, from where they make incursions into Rwanda and threaten to tumble the young government.

Despite the end of the hundred-days genocide with the rise to power of the left-wing Rwandan Patriotic Front (RPF) in July 1994, ethnic tensions have not decreased between the Hutu majority and the decimated Tutsis under the appeasing government of new Rwandan president Pasteur Bizimungu.

Génocidaires who fled the country, supposedly fearing retaliations, are now settled in massive refugee camps in eastern Zaire. From there they continue to launch attacks on the Tutsi population in the province of South Kivu and lead violent incursions into Rwandan territory.

"[Zairian dictator] Mobutu is not only permitting and support-ing these attacks, but plotting to weaken our new state and eventually conquer it," denounced Henri Umutoni, spokesman for the Kigali government.

The Rwandan genocide of 1994, perpetrated by members of the FAR (Forces Armées Rwandaises) together with extremist Hutu militias (Interahamwe), killed half a million to one million Tutsis and moderate Hutus across the country.

LETTER

Axton House
1 Axton Rd.
Point Bless, VA 26969

Dear Aunt Liza,

Sorry about our silence. I just realised A. hasn't written any letters in the last 2 days. I hardly see him writing now. He reads & naps most of the day. Nights getting a little too hard. We drove to Midburg yesterday to see Ambrose's psychotherapist. I didn't like her very much. He did. Paid for a session & everything. Hasn't made things better so far. She said she a Mason. Are there Mason women?

He left me to crack the cipher letter to Caleb (he told you about the cipher, right?) & he just reads what Ambrose's letters & Dr Belknap (that's her name) talked about: German madmen trying to transmit thoughts thru wires & stuff—conductive telepathy, Dr B. said. He found the literature in the library, but most of it in German. I wish again Strückner were here. I liked him a lot. He could help me look after him. He won't let me help him. He wakes me up at night dreaming & I don't dare to wake him because he gets so angry at me, like I interrupted. He doesn't get any rest & then he just falls asleep around the house & his right eye is still red brimmed & he doesn't want me to take pictures. I told him to change beds & he said I should *move to the 2nd floor! You should tell him something. He'd listen to you.*

  I miss you a lot. I wish you were here.

Love,
Niamh

A.'S DIARY

Of course it's excruciating to have an eye pulled out and be forked on the ground every night. It's fucking agony.

But I long for the rest. I want the proud look of the woman in lingerie driving. I want the peace of the Arab reader dying. I want the peach-fuzz warmth beneath the redhead's blanket, and to hear her love in the dark.

DREAM JOURNAL

Waves ripple gently through the waist-tall grass, tingling the red paper flowers afloat, breaking tenderly on my torso and hers, a colorless shirt knotted over her navel.

I pick one big clunky poppy and give it to her, and she takes it between two fingers to her face, but the breeze disassembles the petals as soon as her fluffy lips touch it. There's something wrong with her. In the way her normal-girl skin glows under the sun like a burned Polaroid.

I sit reading a magazine under the clopping of wind-chiming kitchenware. My stall is an insect among mammoth skyscrapers. At the counter, before a bowl of noodles, the yuppie just dropped his chopsticks.

The book falls out of my hand.

I fall. And the monster comes behind me yielding his pitchfork, and I just flinch, hoping it won't hurt this time, but it always does.

SECURITY VIDEOTAPE: RAY'S HARDWARE AND ELECTRONICS

1995-11-23 THU 10:01

A girl with one shaven temple exposing loads of metal on her ear is browsing through the back shelves. The WOMAN in the down vest and wool hat comes behind the counter.

WOMAN: Oh, there you are.
NIAMH: *[Waves a hand at her, continues checking boxes.]*
WOMAN: *[Calling inside.]* Sam, it's the girl from Axton House again!
            [To NIAMH.] Haven't seen your brother for a while; how's he
            doing?
NIAMH: *[Just nods.]*

> *[SAM, under a baseball cap and holding a mug of coffee, joins the
> woman.]*

SAM: Hi, there! Buying ourselves a new toy, are we?
NIAMH: *[Flashes a quick grin in his direction.]*

> *[She finally chooses a box, approaches the counter, starts check-
> ing her wallet. Sam slips the box toward the woman.]*

SAM: So how's that security kit we got you?
NIAMH: *[One hand raises a thumb while the other one produces a bunch
            of notes.]*
SAM: Yeah, had it myself for six months now. Full color, sound, one
            tape a day …
WOMAN: *[On the cash register.]* Two hundred ninety-five, dear.
NIAMH: *[Starts counting money on the table.]*
SAM: *[Inspecting the goods.]* Another camera? Girl, I'm looking
            forward to seeing that film you're doing. Gonna be some
            blockbuster.
WOMAN: *[Taking the money.]* Thank you very much.
SAM: Will there be any ghosts in it?

[Niamh stops; stares at the man.]

[An extremely indecisive second lingers by, pondering whether to elapse or not, and finally does.]

SAM: *[Handing her the goods.]* Just kidding.
NIAMH: *[She takes the box, smiling, waves at them, and starts to leave.]*
WOMAN: Good-bye. Say hi to your brother!
SAM: *[Together.]* Have fun!

[They wait, following her off frame until the doorbell is heard twice.]

WOMAN: *[Now cold.]* You're an asshole.
SAM: I was being nice!

HANDHELD CAMERA

An aquarelle blur of indecisive objects is laboriously morphing into Virginia, with a big house in the foreground with a conservatory and breeze breathing on the mike. Then the country sways lightly and the camera motions forward with a crunching sound of Converse-trodden gravel, and casually zooms into the arthropod vine crawling down the windows, and the many broken slats on the rotten wooden shutters, but the image quality is too bad to capture the beauty of its ugliness. So the camera keeps gliding across the field of hungover rain puddles toward the verdant wall at the end of the garden, then swerves right into the desert backyard of the once cheerful house that gazes down at the camera like a grumpy grandmother flash-smiling just for the album's sake, until the camera turns again onto the magnetic green form of the box hedge forming the outer wall of the maze, and it is ensnared toward the gate in the middle, closing in, until it spies the flakes of white paint peeling off the iron archway supporting the hedge transom overhead.

And inside, the camera checks the two passageways on the left and the two on the right, and a myriad dead leaves and insect carcasses down below where Niamh's imitation Chuck high-tops meet the floor as they step in frame for the first time and walk, choosing the first passage on the right.

There a tunnel of green walls runs into a long dead end, but the camera follows the blind road anyway, hoping to discover a gap in one of the walls, which actually happens, and there it turns left around the wall, panning into another green passageway, and it crabs along it, indistinct leaves flowing past, swarming, rubber footfalls accelerating; then it takes a right turn before the end, checks the right side, then chooses left, then turns right again, then it slows down as it dollies forward. Then a U-turn to the left. Then the camera tilts down, mike closing into the breakfast sound of ground leaves, the zigzagging right and left and right too quick for the autofocus, and finally into a square where the camera reveres the frozen sculpture in the middle.

It is Ariadne, sitting against a sky of television static, her marble skin blackened by mold between her lips, and fingers winding a ball of petrified yarn. [Stop.]

Look up at the iron archway of the gate. The camera tilts down. A gentle-veined hand comes into view, macramé bracelets dangling around the delicate wrist, and that hand grabs a twig and draws an arrow on the gravel, pointing left. Then the Chucks follow the arrow, run all the length of a long passageway. They take a right turn at the end, and the camera wonders at the many gaps opening onto each side. It looks down again, and the twig draws a left arrow. The Chucks follow the arrow. [Stop.]

One Chuck wipes the arrow. The twig, like a Baba Yaga's forefinger, scrapes a new arrow on the sweet putrid ground, pointing in the opposite direction. The Chucks follow it, run across another green tunnel, and stop at the new path on the left. The twig draws an arrow pointing at it. [Stop.]

The Chuck wipes the arrow, then pivots a hundred and eighty degrees, runs forward to the next dead end. [Stop.]

The twig draws an arrow somewhere. [Stop.]

The Chuck wipes a different arrow, turns around. [Stop.]

The camera looks upward, pining for some other color. [Stop.]

Heavy breathing through the nose saturates the mike. [Stop.]

A notepad lies on the floor, a section of an unfinished labyrinth penciled on the top page, behind the miniature wall of umber leaves in sharp focus, their crisp borders nibbled by sugar grain–size insects. The parallel walls of a green unfocused corridor run into oblivion. Then Niamh whistles, overloading the mike. When the sound waves settle, a magpie is heard fluttering in fear of a train engine.

The silence slowly ebbs in again, like the shadow of a ripe black rain cloud coming from the north. Niamh whistles again. The silence is not held back much longer.

Niamh jumps into the frame, running forward, reaching the spot in the passage where Help comes crashing through the left green wall, and she hugs the dog, kisses his head, and Help licks her face in return, and he follows Niamh delightedly as she runs toward the camera again, which has time to spot the dirt on the Chucks' tips like mold on Ariadne's lips before being grabbed, and it just confusedly records the final moments in the maze as Help and Niamh crawl back into the hole where— [Stop.]

VIDEO RECORDING

LIBRARY THU NOV-23-1995 13:02:26

NIAMH sitting on the floor, petting HELP, listening to A.'s rambling.

A.: But I told you, and you know it by heart! It's right, right, left, right, ahead, right, and you reach the center!

NIAMH: *[Slaps her notepad on the floor, writes wrathfully. Then shows.]*

A.: *[After reading.]* So you want to map the whole maze. Why?

[Niamh stands up, strides to the desk, grabs the ciphered message to Caleb. With her finger, she draws an imaginary path through the letters.]

A.:   *[Realizing.]* Oh! *[Later, softer.]* Oh.
               [Looking more perplexed than keen.] Okay. Good idea.

NIAMH: *[Writes.]*

[For long.]

[Then shows.]

A.:   Yeah, I see what you mean. And having a map of your own maze on your desk is hardly a telltale.

[She relaxes. Looks up at him as though waiting for instructions.]

               Okay, so you should … take an aerial shot. Can you see the maze from the tower?

NIAMH: *[Shakes her head.]*

A.:   No. We could strap a camera onto a pigeon; they did that in World War One.

NIAMH: *[Writes. Then shows.]*

A.:   Jesus, Niamh, I told you it's a good idea; what do you want me to do, jerk off to it?

[After an ellipsis, Niamh turns around in a snit, stomps out through the west door.]

[Help follows shortly after.]

               [On the dog leaving.] Yeah, sure, take your mother's side.

HANDHELD CAMERA

A wide Novembral sky fills the screen, its bottom rim cracked by the phalanxes of distant trees like the edges of a very old mirror. The obnoxious wind blows into the mike. A flapping scarf is heard every now and then.

The camera booms up as it is lifted, and it sees a column of brick, with a rope tied around it, and then it dollies back to prove that the column of brick is actually a chimney, as tall as the cameraman, sprouting from the roof on the very edge of the steeper rafter, which falls at an approximate sixty-degree angle. Slack rope swings in the wind, stretching from the distant chimney ahead, and the camera pans east, where the gentler pitch of the upper slope allows it to see the whole roof, a field of blue slate punctured by colorless chimneys and a silhouetted tower at the far end. And meanwhile the rope is dropped around the base of a lightning rod, and Niamh's hand pulls the rope gently, forcing the hemp to rasp on the metal with a hoarse sawing sound, peeling the rust off, and the camera turns around, and not two inches away from the white tip of the Chuck the lower slope plummets to the void. [Stop.]

The camera sits lower now, fixed on the western stratus veiling the sky, Niamh's scarf occasionally whipping the lens, rocked by the ululating wind; and then, like a roller coaster reaching the highest summit and looking down into the deepest fall, the camera peers over the edge of the upper slope of the roof. It sits next to the pair of Chucks at the end of trim legs in striped leggings, wiggling excitedly.

The shoes in the end slowly creep down the blue shingles that now fill the high-angle shot as—

CLANG—the whole sled composed of legs and Chucks and scarf and the camera slides down at high velocity in an oblique line, runs onto the spine of a dormer window, ski-jumps off it, the empty sky filling the frame for a fraction of a second, and then it lands back on the roof and slides farther until Niamh's heels hit the ledge of the building's wall, protruding an inch above the drain at the bottom of the slope, and miraculously the shoes and the legs and the scarf and the camera stop.

And the broken lightning rod comes clanging behind, doesn't stop, tumbles over the edge, and is heard bouncing on the ground, far away.

＊

MUSIC ROOM THU NOV-23-1995 14:46:08

[A. stops writing on a CLANGING noise. He opens the French doors and calls outside.]

A.:   Niamh, are you doing anything stupid?

＊

The air stays jaw-dropped. The camera is picked up and raised, and it gazes over the edge like Simba the lion king on the monkey's hands, and it takes in the bleared birches in the back, and an emerald-shiny maze. Zoom in.

＊

(In the foyer, me carrying a lightning rod.)

—Were you on the roof just now?

(Nod.)

—All alone?

(Nod.)

—Wow. Good job.

MUSIC ROOM THU NOV-23-1995 22:37:15

The fireplace is roaring. Dirty dishes on the floor. A., NIAMH, and HELP lie prone on the carpet, watching *E.R.*

A.:   Oh, c'mon. *X-Files* is so much better than this. Scully is in love with Mulder and we don't need piano-music scenes to know. It's just there. It's in the way she says, "Mulder, you're out of your mind"; her eyes are saying, "I'd fuck the soul out of you." That's sexual tension. Not this. This is emotional porn.

[Sips from his Cherry Coke.]

Scully is all the romance subplot I need.

[They stay watching.]

KITCHEN FRI NOV-24-1995 05:13:14

Lights yawningly flicker ON.

(The kitchen: stainless Streamline Moderne and silvery appliances aligned side by side with wooden beams and paneled windows and a redbrick oven.)

> *[A. walks in from the hall. He opens the fridge. Checks a glass in the dish rack. He pours himself some milk, standing by the counter.]*
>
> *[The lights flicker again. A. looks up.]*
>
> *[The lights glow brighter.]*

A.: *[Pissed.]* Now what?

> *[Droning brightness saturates all whites in the image, swelling in a luminous aura like icy embers.]*
>
> *[A fluorescent tube at the back of the room explodes in splashing sparks and smashes onto the counter. A. turns in that direction as the video fills with blazing white and the audio burns with a deafening buzz. He blocks his ears, shouts.]*

What the fuck is wrong with you?!

> *[The image is burned completely white—the last thing remaining a hazy human stain. Not where A. was standing.]*
>
> *[The tubes go off like gunshots.]*
>
> *[Light and noise recede, leaving behind a puddle of milk and glass and A. lying on the floor, unconscious.]*

05:20:00

> *[Nothing else happens.]*

Axton House
1 Axton Rd.
Point Bless, VA 26969

Dear Aunt Liza,

*[...] The doctor came by at 9am, long after the paramedics
left. He remained halfway out thru the exam. Dr checked
his eyes, & I hadn't seen them all this time because he'd
hardly opened them, but now they're completely red, the
whole white part bloodied & flowing onto the irises & when
he began to speak he choked & spurted blood thru his mouth
& nose. & dr said we couldn't keep him on the sofa so we
moved him to his bedroom because dr said he seemed blind
& needed to be in a room he was familiar with. So he's back
to the damn bedroom & there the dr checked the glass cuts
in his soles & all the while he seemed OK, but then while I
spoke to the dr outside we heard him scream "Ah, fuck" & he
was up like in a seizure, & I had to soothe him down & put
him to bed again. & the dr said he'd give him sleeping drugs
because he wouldn't stop rubbing his eyes & the scarlet rim
was turning up again & it looks hot as embers under his eyes,
& I asked whether he'd dream with the pills & asked if he
could have something to inhibit REM, because I remembered*

the Prometheus letter where they said there are tablets for that, & he said OK but warned me that those pills will just make him calm, not rested, & gave me a prescription, which I'll get when I post this if he's better, & meanwhile he fed him a regular hypnotic. I don't want to leave him alone but this would take ages to explain to the Brodies & Help is very little help now. & I don't know what else to do but I'm fucking scared so I'm posting this urgent & hope you get in touch before it gets worse.

*

BEDROOM FRI NOV-24-1995 11:23:04

The angle is not high as in other rooms, suggesting the camera is resting on a piece of furniture, zoomed on the rumpled bed in the far end. A. and NIAMH seem to slumber on it, she over the quilt, he under it.

HELP is lying down on the carpet. Everything's quiet.

11:24:04

[A. springs up, silence shattered; everyone jumps out of their sleep.]

[He clutches his chest, mouth closed tight, nostrils wolfing down oxygen. Then he checks under his shirt.]

[All this while, Niamh watches him as though she were scared to touch him. When she reaches for him, he flinches at first, then checks that it's her, then stands on guard, as if waiting for another blow.]

[She grabs her notepad and pencil.]

—Can I do something?

(*He squints.*)

—I can't read.

—CAN I DO SOMETHING?

—Did you call 911?

(*Nod.*)

—How the silent fuck did you do that?

MUSIC ROOM FRI NOV-24-1995 06:35:50

Morning creeps into the quiet room through the French door shutters.

06:36:44

> [*NIAMH storms in, jumping over the piano chair, straight to the phone. She presses three buttons. HELP comes galloping after her, while she waits nervously for an answer. At the pressing of the hands-free button, the calling tone is heard; she releases the phone and starts tampering frantically with the voice recorder she's carrying, always glimpsing toward the door she just came through.*]

> [*Someone answers the phone.*]

OPERATOR: Nine-one-one, what's your emergency?

[Niamh is speed-operating the voice recorder.]

Hello?

[She presses a button and places the device near the phone. A.'s recorded voice sounds, a piece of broken Muzak in the background.]

A. (REC):   Help. Help, come here!

[Help, called to attention, barks at the recorder.]

OPERATOR: Sir? Sir, can you tell me what your emergency is?

[Niamh just keyed in some command; she presses play again. Help is still barking.]

A. (REC):   *[In a completely unconnected tone.]* Number one Axton Road, Point Bless, Ponopah, two-six-nine-six-nine.

[Help keeps yapping at the device, frantic.]

OPERATOR: Hello? Sir, do you know that making prank calls to nine-one-one is a federal crime?

[Desperate, she clutches her face, fingernails wishing to tear her eyes out … Then she puts those same fingers in her mouth and whistles loudly, "Help!" while Help continues to yap desperately at the phone. She presses some button on the voice recorder, turns up the volume.]

A. (REC):   *[Fortissimo.]* HELP! HELP, COME HERE!
OPERATOR: Jesus … Okay, I'm contacting your local police; this better not be a joke.

[Niamh falls to her knees, released from pathos. Bewildered, Help clambers onto the table, sniffing for a clue to what just happened.]

*

[Cont'd.]

Point Bless police know us already; they know I mute, so they took it seriously.

Now it's 3 pm. He been in & out for the last hours; the dreams do wake him up, but the Starnox gets him again in a few seconds. I'm buying Hypnogog now. I also moved the bathroom camera to the bedroom so I can watch him from downstairs.

Please do something, I beg you.

Love,
Niamh

DREAM JOURNAL

That woman in the poppy field kissing the disassembling flower *she's a ghost too.**

---

* This entry appears written in an extremely sloppy hand.

*

The Chucks are steadied against the wall at the end of the steep roof, and a dead lightning rod lies down below, in the sandy backyard. The camera dismisses it and pans back up to the maze, whose inner walls describe an inverted labyrinth of elevated paths.

VIDEO RECORDING

BEDROOM FRI NOV-24-1995 16:32:44

A banker's lamp in the foreground illuminates the shot, whereas twilight in the window on the right contributes little but a splash of purple. NIAMH sits at the table, directly under the electric light, equipped with set triangle and ruler, busy on a drawing modeled after what she sees on the screen of her handheld camera.

In the background, A. is a mere hill in the stormed bedscape.

> *[Niamh operates the camera, eyes fixed on the screen. She presses play. The sound track is too low to hear, except for a clank at some point. At which Niamh smiles a private smile.]*

16:33:01

> *[The bedscape quakes. Niamh runs over there and reaches A. as he bursts out of the sheets, holding on to her arm.]*

> *[He stares a paranoid sort of stare. His blind hands spider up Niamh's arm, reaching her shoulder. There he looks up, meeting her half-haired head.]*

*

(He sounds high. His eyes are beyond crimson, but he sees.)

—Do you know what I'd like to buy?

(Shake.)

—A Rubik's cube. You ever had one?

(Shake.)

—Don't you think it'd be fun?

(Nod. He relaxes, lies down again.)

—Do I look bad?

—WHY?

—You look at me like I look bad.

—YOU'VE LOOKED BETTER.

—I'm sorry. I want to look good to you. I always try.

(Falls asleep.)

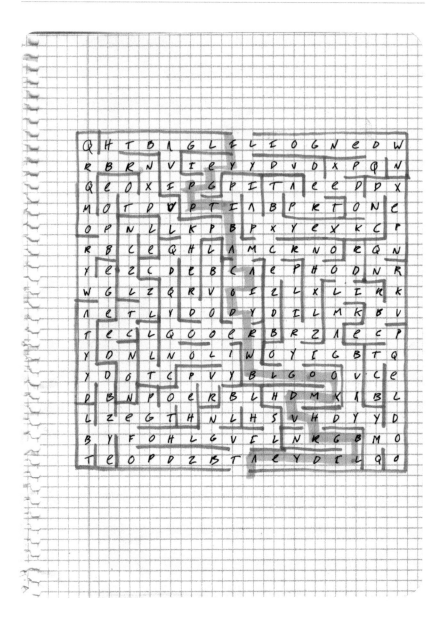

VIDEO RECORDING

BEDROOM FRI NOV-24-1995 21:43:20

It's dark, but the door's been left open and the hallway lights are on. The bed curtain on that side is pulled closed to shield the sleeper from the yellow glow.

21:43:45

[A. wakes up with a snort, hand snatching at his chest as though trying to pry his own heart out. He stares at his clutching hand, whole body throbbing violently.]

[...]

[Slowly, his heartbeat steadies.]

[He looks up. Seems to focus on some point at the right side of the camera, by the door to the dressing room.]

A.: [Impatient.] What?!

[No answer. A. keeps staring.]

Get out.

[...]

I SAID GET THE FUCK OUT! YOU HEAR ME?! OUT!

The smoking room is all mahogany and green and watched by stuffed animal heads over the glowing hearth behind the pool table, littered with large curling sheets of old tracing paper, onto which the same labyrinth design has been penciled over and over again, just as in the one laid on the foreground over a handwritten copy of the ciphered letter on the bureau à gradin *that Niamh has turned into her new workstation, lit by the green-shaded banker's lamp from the bedroom. Her attention is turned to the four small monitors stacked in twos on the VCR, and more specifically to the one monitor showing a man sitting up on a bed, telling somebody to get the fuck out.*

And then Niamh turns a dial and the monitor is muted, but the scream-ing is still heard in the distance, from another room on another floor, far away. And she buries her face in her hands and a sob shakes her diminutive chest, but no sound comes out of it, and her body and clothes tremble with every aftershock of that big sob, tears streaming down her left cheek, her left profile turned to the camera. The bald one.

BEDROOM SAT NOV-25-1995 07:07:52

Dawn is slowly corroding the shutters.

07:08:00

> *[A violent shock blows away the sheets; NIAMH rises in terror, one hand on her chest, the other on her back, breathing as loudly as anything she's ever done.]*

> *[A. stirs despondently. He barely sits up. Niamh feels her spine, checks under her football shirt. They exchange looks. Her mouth's still open.]*

A.:   *[Curious.]* Did you feel that?

TELEGRAM

From: Niamh Connell
Point Bless, Ponopah, VA

NEED HELP NOW STOP LAST NIGHT WAS HORRIBLE STOP
I AM LOSING HIM STOP FIND A SOLUTION PLEASE!

DREAM JOURNAL

I'm beyond return. I know this. I can barely see this page; red stains ebb into my field of view, chasing my writing, closing on the word I'm penning. But I close my eyes and I can see the exact shape of the golden Arab letters on the spine of the book the reader is holding before his brown hand loses its grip and the volume drops onto the carpet as his head gently tilts toward the arched window whence the watery music comes. I can't read Niamh's lips anymore, but the moment I lie down I see the woman in lingerie at the wheel, shining a soul-melting smile at me after I solve the Rubik's cube, and I pride myself on such a goddess showing pride in me. I can't feel Niamh's warmth anymore, but I feel the redhead's breath under the blanket gently drying my ice-cold limbs, her hair caressing me to sleep. And I sleep more than I'm awake. I belong more to her than I belong here. Soon Niamh and Axton House will cease to exist, and there will be the Puma shoes falling toward the speck of sand in the ocean, the snowing cities, the poppy field. I'll be no longer myself. I'll be the hobo in the park, the surfer in the tempest, the dying reader, the piano student, the tomboy in the redhead's bed. I'll be the skeleton playing poker. I'll be the monster holding the pitchfork.

And the sad truth is, I want to be all those people. I'd sooner die forked a thousand times in that house than wake up to a world without monsters or goddesses. I'd rather play the monster myself.

VIDEO RECORDING

BEDROOM SAT NOV-25-1995 11:21:58

The bedroom is in twilight. A gleam of sun slips between the shutters. HELP lies at the bed's foot.

> *[An ear on Help's head rises. Then his whole head, turning to the twitching bulk under the sheets.]*

TELEGRAM

From: Aunt Liza
London, United Kingdom

WHAT IS THE CANOPY MADE OF?

VIDEO RECORDING

BEDROOM SAT NOV-25-1995 11:22:10

> *[A shock wave sweeps away the bedclothes. HELP sets off, barking away. A. convulses in bed; a powerful, rasping, bleeding scream finally breaks through the block in his throat.]*

TELEGRAM

From: Niamh Connell
Point Bless, Ponopah, VA

BRASS!

VIDEO RECORDING

BEDROOM SAT NOV-25-1995 11:22:17

[HELP barks frantically, watching A. sit up in a spasm and strive against the elastic band that ties him onto the bed.]

TELEGRAM

From: Aunt Liza
London, United Kingdom

DESTROY IT NOW.

VIDEO RECORDING

BEDROOM SAT NOV-25-1995 11:22:24

[The canopy and the whole bed tremble under the last flash inside A.'s brain, the one that makes the elastic band finally snap. Shouting for life, HELP crying for help, A. rolls off the bed, bounces onto his feet, and crashes through the window.]

PART II

Backyard Palace

ABOVE-GROUND POOLS
GAZEBOS, PERGOLAS
OUTDOOR FURNITURE
1236 East Hway. Clayboro 26960
Tel. (755) 963 4881 Fax (755) 963 4998

PURCHASE & INSTALLATION NOTICE

INVOICE NO.
474VN-21#38#

SHIPPING ADDRESS
1 AXTON RD. POINT BLESS 26969
SOLD TO
NIAMH S. CONNELL

QTY.	ITEM	PRICE
1 (ONE)	TANGANIKA 76IN. ABOVE-GROUND POOL KIT SIZE XL (16' X 32' X 76IN.)	$4,795.00
1 (ONE)	SAND FILTER	$399.95
1 (ONE)	ATTACHABLE LADDER	$229.95
1 (ONE)	CLOWNFISH FLOATING CHLORINATOR	$0.00

TOTAL $5424,90

11-17-95

CUSTOMER'S SIGNATURE   DEALER'S SEAL (ON PAYMENT)

Customer Copy

[. . .] It was Help who gave the alarm: The fall was too soft. The rain-water closed over me as soon as I crashed through, waking up. Before I could even guess where I was, icy tentacles were clinging to my limbs, injecting lead into my muscles, forbidding any attempt for a stroke.

It took just ten seconds for Niamh to sprint outside, climb over the plastic pool, plunge inside fully clothed, grab my body, and pull my head out of the water. And when she did, the immersion must have washed most of the blood off my eyes, because I could see distinctly the blue walls of the pool and the stone north flank of Axton House and Niamh's face, atoms away from mine, eyelashes beaded with dew, eyelids in ultrahigh resolution over her closed eyes as we clinched and her frozen purple lips kissed mine out of pure exhaustion.

And then the barking stopped because Help jumped or fell (most likely fell) from the bedroom windowsill. And we had to fish him out.

We ran inside, all soaked, teeth chattering (I didn't know dogs could chatter their teeth), leaving a trail of swollen floorboards from the foyer to the music room, where we lit a fire, dropped our clothes, and Niamh changed into new ones before popping upstairs for some of mine. (See the advantages of littering a three-story house with random pieces of clothing.)

(By the fire.)

—Good job, Niamh. Brilliant fucking job.

(Hug.)

—How your eyes?

—I see quite well. How do they look?

—Better than an hour ago.

—Good.

—I telegrammed Aunt Liza—told me to destroy the bed.

—The bed's not wrong. It's not *meant* to be wrong. So what's up with it?

*

We inspected the bed closely. We described it to you already: It's made of carved wood with a brass canopy dressed in salmon silk, big enough to have its own zip code. It took four arms to pull it a few inches off the wall. We removed the sheets, checked the mattress, crawled beneath with a flashlight. There's nothing wrong with it. Yes, I know you're skipping forward to the paragraph introduced by an adversative conjunction, so here it goes.

But. Niamh had a second flash of brilliance for the day and brought up the voltmeter the electrician left behind two weeks ago. She scanned the canopy. On touching the brass frame, there was a distinct crackle. We moved the bed, which required titanic strength, and checked the wall behind it. There are no wires visible, but on the left corner we found a disused outlet of sorts, a copper pipe. I think it's a gas conduit; the house has run on electricity for decades, but the electrician said the plumbing had never been replaced; I guess the gas line wasn't either. Niamh read the exposed section of the pipe; it was four or five volts above a hundred and twenty.

*

—What is right below this room?

—Library?

—But the library has no windows. What's the window beneath this one?

—Playroom?

*

The north wing on the second floor is mostly terra incognita. As I said, the library takes up most of this floor and we cut through it to connect the hall stairs in the west with the gallery in the east. The south side is an updated complex of two bedrooms and a bathroom (one of the rooms was Strückner's). The north side comprises, from the stairs, the smoking room where we keep the CCTV monitors, a nursery or playroom, a small bedroom meant for a nanny, a bigger bedroom for a child or a teenager, and the east gallery again.

Our bedroom must lie above both the nursery and the library. We counted steps to the windows on the third and the second floor to find out. We found some measuring tape and wrote down the distances. We started knocking on the walls, Niamh in the nursery, me in the library, pulling out the scores of books from the immovable shelves that make the perimeter of the room.

No use. We couldn't hear each other. There was a hidden room between.

*

—Let me get an axe & tear the whole thing down.

—Whoa, you're violent today. What about being worthy of the mystery?

—Fuck the mystery—I almost lost you to it!

*

In the end Niamh settled for emptying the bookcases.

Strabo's *Geography* offered some resistance.

Niamh felt behind the volume; she found a latch. She pulled it.
Some locking mechanism clacked awake behind the shelf. The bookcases are separated by pilasters holding lamps; the pilaster to our
left had opened a crack. We pulled it; this allowed for the bookshelf
to swing open. I wondered who built this secret entrance: Axton, or
maybe the Wells? If it was Axton, then yet another reason for the Wells
to buy this house; if it was the Wells . . . Well, what a cool family we are.

The secret room is narrow and long, fitting between the library and the
nursery. A scroll cabinet rots on one side, a desolated workbench on
the other. Even by Axton House standards they looked old.

Even before we found the light switch, we sensed the treasure.
Perhaps it was a reflection in the dark, like that on a crystal object, for
it was a crystal object. Perhaps it was this feeling I got, like when you're
outdoors and the air stops flowing, and you look up and find the perfect thundercloud overhead. For it seemed a thundercloud trapped in a
crystal ball.

Curiosity beat caution, and I touched it.

I recalled how Dr. Belknap scornfully referred to conductive
telepathy as a "debunked science." She said that Dänemarr and his
predecessors were "still trying" to record dreams. I wanted to grab that
crystal ball and drive all the way to Midburg just to prove her wrong.
For they had done it: a device to record thoughts. And every dream
creature that has haunted me since my first night in Axton House,
every face, every letter, every sharp thing and weatherpiece, lay waiting
in that crystal ball to coup-de-grâce me, and as soon as the fore-atom
of my fingertip collided with its empty surface they crossed over and
sprang at me: the hobo who knocked down the policemen, the kid who
threw the grenade, the Chinese student at the piano and the deejay in
Ibiza, the cook in his noodle stall, the dying reader and the chirping
fountain, the bank robber with her baby and flies stupidly crossing the
shells' due trajectory, the twins in the grove, the tomboy on the roof,

the ghost in the tropic, the surfer in the tempest, the torture victim retaliating, the poppy kisser, the Greek Scrabble player, the handshaker before the explosion, the pitchfork murderer, the intubated patient, the skeleton, the meteor woman and her Puma shoes hitting the roof of the bunker on an island in an ocean of nowhere, and after Niamh had jerked me away and flung me across the room, many milliseconds later, as she knelt down and mouthed, *What's wrong,* I still saw lingering on her concerned face the cherished smile of the goddess in lingerie at the wheel, looking at the Rubik's cube in my hand, proud of me, because finally, all by myself, I had figured it out.

*

—*So now what?*

—I don't know.

—*I say we bury it.*

—That might be a little too drastic.

—*NEVER too drastic.*

—The most important thing is to keep it isolated. Take photographs for Aunt Liza; then put it back in the box. Then put that box in a box, and that box in a box . . .

—*& down in the cellar.*

—And keep your gloves on while you handle it.

*

A few other objects of interest were found (Polaroids attached). The most conspicuous of them is a heavy iron bar resembling a large hex key or a screwdriver of unknown purpose. Among the scrolls there were blueprints of Axton House, ranging from Axton times to the 1960s. The secret room is a contribution from Horace in 1901. (I understand that the blueprints were kept here only because keeping them anywhere else would disclose this room.)

The crystal ball, by the way, was found on the corner of the bench. It had rolled out of a cardboard box of foam peanuts fallen off a tumbled shelf, all the way to the north wall, where it made contact with the copper pipe climbing along the naked brick. The rest is speculation.

*

—*What else?*

—Well, that large hex key is a new thread. That's two keys already, and no locks. We should find them. What about the cipher?

—*I mapped the maze & tried to apply the pattern on the cipher & failed. I don't think it's a grille.*

—I thought so.

—*You never said that!*

—I was busy jumping out windows.

—*You should look into it.*

—We will. Together. Tomorrow morning we'll find some cryptography manuals in the library and get it done.

—*Afternoon.*

—Why?

—*SUNDAY.*

—Oh, again? C'mon! I just nearly killed myself!

—*The more reason!*

*

So. We're back to not missing you. But thank you. A lot.

Love you,
A. & N.

P.S.: We kissed!

ONE WEEK LATER

(In church.)

—Is it just me or are these readings getting longer every Sunday?

—*Shut up & listen. This concerns you.*

—No, it doesn't. I'm not a Thessalonian.

—Don't giggle. We don't giggle in church.

Last night it snowed.

This morning we woke to the bluest sky in weeks. Niamh dug out her Canadian Dharma Bum Barbie outfit, including earflap hat to cover her as-of-last-night trim-cut temples, and we followed Help to the woods. The trees stand like colossal skeletons, their branches clutching the air, basking under a most inefficient sun. And yet now, in their winter austerity, they look more alive than ever. Just like the lichen and moss on the ridges and canyons in their bark, these gigantic birches stand like microscopic organisms on the crust of a rock in space, reaching toward the light.

Axton House remains gray and detached and gloomy. We call it home, though. Whether it likes it or not.

KITCHEN SUN DEC-3-1995 13:39:22

THE ROAR OF AN ENGINE outside fills the sound track. THE DOG'S BARKING meritoriously manages to be overheard, though.

> [A. goes to the phone on the wall, dials a number on the earpiece keypad as he wanders toward the counter.]

> [Enter a MAN through the open back door: bulky coat, heavy-duty boots.]

MAN: Hey, could you tell me where I can wash my hands?
A.:   [Checks the man's palms.] Uh … Well, a tank of sulfuric acid comes to mind, but try the sink.

> [On the phone:]

Oh, hi, Mrs. Brodie? *[…]* Yeah, it's me.

[The man starts washing his hands in the sink. His eyes quickly fall on the camera in the southeast corner. He smiles a wide, dumb, scar-split smile.]

[Covering his other ear.] Yeah, I know, there's a lot of noise—I have a snowplow clearing the driveway. *[…]* I don't know, some guys who work on Sundays. Would you like me to send them your way later?

[The man dries his hands on his coat and leaves with a nod to A. In the doorway, he bumps into NIAMH, pulling HELP by his collar. Help keeps barking in the man's direction; Niamh frowns at him as she walks past him.]

Okay. So, I was calling to confirm that appointment with your husband. *[…]* Sure, I'll wait.

[Niamh lets Help go; the dog scampers out through the south door. She toes off her snow boots and heads for the cereal cupboard. A. is now observing her. Both sides and the back of her head are shaved, while a big snarl of curly hair brims over the top. She pours herself a mouthful of Lucky Charms straight from the box.]

Hey. What's wrong?

[Niamh shrugs, her cereal-stuffed face clearly showing something is wrong.]

What? What is it?

[The ENGINE is fading off as the snowplow rolls away from the house. Niamh writes on her notepad; shows.]

> [Reads; then, confused.] He's "checking you out"? Who? The little one with the scar?

NIAMH: [Mimes: "big gorilla-framed one with a mustache."]

A.: Oh. Right. [Awkward.] Uh … should I go and beat him up or something?

NIAMH: [Scoffs. Then she waves the whole thing away.]

A.: Okay. Sorry. Wish I could do something. Must be the snags of being hot.

[Niamh stops halfway to the south door, turns on her feet. A. is now distracted by some papers.]

[She quietly approaches the counter again, staring. A. notices.]

> Uh … I mean, hot in a punk-haired, flat-chested, manga-heroine kind of way.

[He tries to read her as that sinks in, but she just stands unfazed, a germinal nive on her lips.]

[She writes something; he tries to look away, acting impatient, holding on to the earpiece, until she shows. He reads.]

> What—no, I'm not, Niamh; I'm being objective; you are, uh … worth checking out. I just try not to act too Nabokov about it. [On the phone.] Oh, yeah, Mr. Brodie?

[Niamh drops her shoulders in defeat. Then starts writing again.]

> Yes, I just talked to Glew; he said it's no problem to come by today. So he'll be bringing the deeds at four. Is that all right with you?

[She stops writing, shows him the page challengingly.]

[As he reads, on the phone.] Yeah. Okay. *[Then, comprehending.]*
Uh … Wait a minute. *[Puts a hand over the mouthpiece.]* No,
Niamh, "we" did nothing—you did! I had been unconscious the
second before!

*[She glares at him for a very long time that the video time stamp
clearly misreads as only three seconds.]*

*[Then she turns around and strides out, leaving him alone. The
ENGINE is inaudible now.]*

*[A. looks away in contempt, then speaks on the phone
again.]*

> Yeah, Mr. Brodie? Sorry about that. *[…]* Okay, four o'clock it is.
> Thank you. See you.

[He hangs up and exits, chasing her.]

*

MUSIC ROOM SUN DEC-3-1995 13:41:01

[NIAMH walks in from the foyer, under the camera.]

A.:   *[Off.]* Niamh!

*[She stops and turns around by the piano, facing the camera,
hurt. A. comes up to her, stops a few feet away.]*

> Look, I'm … *[Leaves that unfinished. Sighs.]* Niamh, do you want
> to talk?

NIAMH: *[Turns her head away a little, swallowing a lump in her throat.
Shows her empty hands like a piece of blatant evidence as she
lips a silent scream: "YES!"]*

[She leaves through the west double doors.]

[A. doesn't follow this time.]

[The yellowish halo of the wall lamp flickers shyly behind its stained glass shades. A. notices, looks up.]

A.:   *[Scornful, at the ceiling.]* Oh, sorry; did I make you upset too?

[A brief chance for an answer: nothing else happens. The lights remain silent.]

[A. exits, grumbling.]

Damn; these women are gonna kill me.

A.'S DIARY

[Cont'd.]

I don't know. Maybe she's got too much time for herself. Last week was pretty quiet now that I've cut down on window jumping. Which was positive, I guess—I could use the time to restore my health, and she deserved the vacation.

But it's been seven days now. The most action she's got this past week was when we went to the movies in Clayboro to see *Jumanji* and she ate her weight in popcorn. She needs to be busy again. After all, she's here to protect me—so said Aunt Liza. So I'd better return to putting my life in danger soon.

I could also allow her to buy a computer—she's been collecting pamphlets for some time. Much to Ambrose Wells' chagrin, Axton House may end up joining the digital era after all. I fear that with Niamh's technology frenzy and her recent hobby of running across the first floor crashing through doors like a rhino while I cry, "Stampede!" our demesne is going to be hard to recognize by winter solstice.

But hey, even Ambrose's Society seems to be catching up with the twentieth century. I mean, that fax from Los Angeles we received when Niamh plugged the thing in the other day? Who would've told that old telegraph user Ambrose had a fax machine? Wake up and smell the nineties.

*

NM 2121 Horizon Avenue
Los Angeles, CA 90067
NAMACORP (932) 444-4948 FAX: 444-6002

October 30, 1995

From: Tyche
To: Leonidas

Dear Leonidas,

I quit.

I tried calling on the phone, but I didn't get an
answer. I hope it's because your fax is finally
connected.

Anyway, I am eager to see you again next December,
as usual.

All best,

*

(By the way, according to General Leonidas' Little Red Notebook, where the contact details of his friends are listed, this "Tyche" must be Ken Matsuo, who apparently is also the "*ma*" in Namacorp.)

VIDEO RECORDING

MUSIC ROOM SUN DEC-3-1995 16:23:27

MR. BRODIE is overlooking the papers that GLEW is leafing through on the table. By the piano, A. is pouring three glasses of bourbon.

MR. BRODIE: Anyway, if you could get that paperwork ready, that would be great.

GLEW: I don't see any problem. *[Handing Brodie his pen.]* Now, if you would please sign here…

[Mr. Brodie signs both copies.]

    [Takes one copy, hands Glew the other one.] Mr. Brodie, as of now you are the rightful owner of Axton Creek.

A.:   *[Coming over with the glasses.]* Hey, old Axton would be happy to hear that.

MR. BRODIE: *[Chortles.]* Well, hopefully I won't keep it for too long. If we manage to sell it before Christmas, I'd like to take the missus on holidays for a change—see some of the country.

A.:   Well, cheers to that.

GLEW: Hear, hear.

[They drink.]

    [To A.] What about you? Do you and Miss Connell have any plans for Christmas?

A.:   Well, not much. I figured we'd stay home. *[Checking Brodie, complicitly.]* I hear it's when the action begins around here anyway.

MR. BRODIE: *[Chuckles.]*

A.:   No, seriously, I haven't given it much thought. We've been pretty busy these days.

GLEW: Busy? *[Amused.]* Busy doing what?

A.:   Well, you know … being an eccentric millionaire and all that. Do you think that having a pool installed in winter just happens? You have to come up with that kind of stuff; it isn't easy!

[And they all laughed.]

EXCERPT FROM SAMUEL MANDALAY'S *ARS CRYPTOGRAPHICA*

Despite bearing the name of its main advocate, the Scottish polymath Lyon Playfair (1818–1898), the Playfair cipher was devised by prolific inventor Charles Wheatstone (1802–1875) in 1854. It is the most famous and widely used digraph substitution code, and for a brief period in the Victorian era it became the standard of encryption. The second Anglo-Boer war (1899–1902) saw its first application in the military, and it was still resorted to as late as World War II. Its popularity is due to its almost optimal use/crack ratio for a manual code (§ 2.7.1): the Playfair cipher is easy to learn, and the encrypting and decrypting processes are very quick, whereas an attack may well verge on the limits of human patience.

In the computer age, as with any fast manual encryption method, the use of Playfair is heavily discouraged to conceal strategic information, since new algorithms can easily crack it by brute force, the patience issue being nonexistent. Nevertheless, handicraft fans, cryptography purists, or people lacking sophisticated resources continue to choose Playfair for everyday purposes, delighting in its elegance and almost guaranteed safety against any human adversary, no matter how brute.

To use a Playfair cipher, sender and receiver must have agreed on a key word and a few specific details regarding variants. We will stick to British Playfair, the one employed by the Empire in World War I. Nothing but paper and pencil is needed.

The keyword is used to fill the first squares of a 5×5 grid, which is then completed with the remaining letters of the alphabet. In order to fit the 26 letters in 25 squares, *i* and *j* are treated as one. (A variant omits *q* instead, but the *ij* solution is better.) To encrypt a message, dismiss any punctuation or spaces, and break the plain text into blocks of two letters, using some nonsense monograph (usually *x*) to split any pair of the same letter. Find these digraphs in the square and replace them with the two letters at the opposite corners of the diagonals they form.

Let us see an example. Again we used our favorite key word, Mozambique, which fills the first squares of a 5×5 grid. (Of course, we omitted the second *m*: One instance is enough.) We now fill up the rest of the grid in alphabetical order. Notice we skip *j*, for *i* is already represented.

M	O	Z	A	B
I	Q	U	E	C
D	F	G	H	K
L	N	P	R	S
T	V	W	X	Y

Now, for our message, a sample of Legrand's famous encrypted treasure map in "The Gold-Bug":

A good glass in the bishop's hostel in the devil's seat.

Remove all punctuation and proceed to break the text into pairs of letters. The second pair would be the *oo* from the word "good," but we want to avoid pairs of the same letter, so break this one by adding a dummy (*x*), and continue normally. This is the result:

AG OX OD GL AS SI NT HE BI SH OP SH OS TE LI NT HE DE
VI LS SE AT

Had we obtained an odd letter in the end, another *x* would have been added.

Now for the encryption: Take the first digraph, *ag,* and check their position in the grid. Imagine them as the diagonally opposite corners of a rectangle. Take the opposite corners of this rectangle: *z* and *h*. That's our first digraph encrypted: *ag* = *zh*.

Next comes the digraph *ox*. The opposite corners of this rectangle are *av*. Always respect the order: the first encrypted letter is the one on the same row (not column) as the first clear letter. (Remember: in the West, we read in rows, not columns.) So *ox* = *av*.

Let us skip forward to the digraph *he*. These letters fall in the same column of the grid, so the new rule is: Pick the letters below each one of them. Thus *he* = *rh*.

Farther on, the digraph *ls* falls in the same row of the grid. The rule here is: Pick the letters on the right of each one. Thus *l* becomes *n*, and *s* has no letter on its right, so we wrap to the left to find *l*. Thus *ls* = *nl*.

When rendering the encrypted message, avoid presenting it in two-letter blocks in order to hide the digraphic nature of the code. Here is the encrypted message:

ZHAVMFDPBRLCLVRHMCRKZNRKBNXITDLVRHHITQNLRCMX

Use the reverse process to decipher. Remember to change key words often.

[Cont'd.]

So Playfair it is. That bit about "handicraft fans and cryptography purists" was a big hint—it has "Wells" written all over it. But there's a more definitive proof. I've been staring at that cipher for a week: The only letter that doesn't appear in it is *J*.

Sadly, I'm afraid that, despite our efforts so far to abide by Ambrose's rules and be worthy of his secrets, I won't be able to properly solve this puzzle. I may have to work around it: crack the cipher. Which, if I succeed, will give me a reason for pride. The manual says that cracking a Playfair "verges on the limits of human patience." I can see why: I've been on it for two hours this evening and the gallery is already carpeted with five-by-five grids and scribbled nonsense in digraphs.

So yes, I smell a thrilling week ahead.

MUSIC ROOM MON DEC-4-1995 01:34:59

The room is in the dark. In a pool of light from the TV screen at the far end, A. lies on the floor, writing in his diary. NIAMH is cuddled up on the sofa, sleeping in fetal position. HELP is taking good care of the leftover pizza.

APPLAUSE and the closing tune of *Late Night with Conan O'Brien*.

> [*A. stands up, slips the diary in his pocket. He stretches, then turns to Help.*]

A.: Wake me up when Beakman's on.
[*To Niamh.*] Niamh. Come on; it's past your bedtime.

> [*She doesn't move.*]

Niamh?

> [*Nothing. He crouches next to her, leans a hand on her side.*]

Look, Niamh, I'm sorry, I... [*Sighs.*] Maybe... Would you rather sleep alone?

> [*Without opening her eyes, she suddenly stretches both her arms toward him.*]

Yeah, I thought so.

[He takes her in his arms, hers fastening around his neck, and he sets out on the long trip to the bedroom.]

[Halfway to the north door, mumbling:]

Stupid three-fucking-story house of doom.

[Niamh scoffs as they enter the dark area toward the door.]

SECURITY VIDEOTAPE: POINT BLESS POST OFFICE

1995-12-04 MON 09:31

NO AUDIO.

[A GIRL looks right at the camera. Metal loops shine in her exposed ears; a tangled skein of long hair on top of her head faints down in a cascade of delicate curls, which she blows off her face twice in twenty seconds.]

[The EMPLOYEE comes up to the window, hands over a large envelope. The Mohawked girl takes it, bows slightly, and capers away Pippilongstockingwise.]

13—EXT—SHERIFF'S OFFICE—DAY

    [MULDER storms out of the sheriff's office, miffed;
    SCULLY catches up with him.]

                  SCULLY
    Mulder!
    [Reaching him.]
    Mulder, I know what you're thinking, and it's
    crazy.

                  MULDER
    [Turns, angry.]
    Why? Why is it so hard to believe? Premonition in
    dreams has been attested since—

                  SCULLY
    In supermarket tabloids! Mulder, dreams are just a
    by-product of the subconscious mind, which has its
    own awareness, but not the gift of precognition.

                  MULDER
    Then how do you explain this?
    [Hands the file to her.]

                  *

MUSIC ROOM MON DEC-4-1995 10:44:29

A. stands facing NIAMH, an arm extended to her, an open envelope in his hand. Their eyes are locked on each other.

                  *

SCULLY
[Off guard now, soothing.]
You're reversing causality. Dreams don't trigger
events—events trigger dreams; our experiences feed
our minds.

MULDER
Okay, how was his mind fed this? How can he dream
about an event happening halfway around the world?

*

10:44:53

Same stance. Niamh fishes her notepad from inside her pullover and
writes.

*

—Canada not that far.

LETTER

Axton House
1 Axton Rd.
Point Bless, VA 26969

Dear Aunt Liza,

[. . .] There is no sender's address on the package, but the stamps are
postmarked somewhere in Ontario. It contains no written messages,

just photographs, but it's safe to assume that it follows the telegram we received on Wednesday 29.

I'll be attaching photocopies of some of the photographs. The postcard with the New England–like estate is labeled on the back as Sexton Hall, in Alder Parish, Sudbury. I think I recognize the trees on the left.

In the second picture, the twin girls dressed as fairies in a school play, they have red hair in the original.

In the third one, the family at the wedding, the couple is irrelevant. The same twins stand on the front row left, next to the Saint Bernard. The ones in turquoise dresses.

A TELEGRAM

From: Daniel Vasquez
Alder Parish, Ontario, Canada

FOUND! STOP PICTURES ON THE WAY STOP NAMES
IN DECEMBER STOP DIOSKURI

*

This is the second telegram we've received from a Society member. (Who am I kidding—it's the second telegram I've received in my life.)

Anyway, the first one arrived shortly before Ambrose's death, from some Edward Cutler (aka Sophocles) in Ibiza. I just reread it; it features a similar structure: "Found! Thank you. I look forward to our next reunion." It too announced he was sending a CD (the one I forbade Niamh to play again, because every time she does we literally drop whatever is in our hands, and even Help gets so overjoyed he pees on the carpet). Then there's the letter from Prometheus (aka Silas W. Long), dated November first, which began with a straightforward, "I give up." And finally, the fax from Tyche in Los Angeles, announcing his surrender as well. Can you feel your spider sense tingling here?

Ambrose wrote to Knox, "As the Host, I call the meetings. Members report to me. The Archives lie with me." These telegrams and letters are definitely the members reporting.

Strückner said that during the December meeting each member was assigned a task. I'd say Edward "Sophocles" Cutler and Daniel "Dioskuri" Vasquez completed theirs. Silas "Prometheus" Long failed.

Then there's that ledger page with the twenty code names. It was titled, "1994 Quest Status Report." Number 4, Sophocles, was marked as "Found!" (The folder containing the CD and Long's telegram was labeled 4.) Numbers 7 (Cybele) and 15 (Alexandros) were "Found!" too. Thus there should be two other numbered folders somewhere in the house.

We delved into Ambrose's desks again, this time knowing what to look for. We found number 7, Cybele. It contained, among other things, a copy of a Mexican police file with a mug shot.

Her name is Amelia Ramos. She's the woman holding the baby and the shotgun in my dream journal.

VIDEO RECORDING

KITCHEN MON DEC-4-1995 16:39:03

NIAMH staring at A., A. staring down at the papers and photographs sprawled over the counter, dumbfounded.

[Niamh writes on her notepad, shows it to him.]

I believe you.

[A. smirks.]

A.:   You believe these people are hunting down their dreams?

[He sighs.]

Well, thank you … But, I mean, you're a Catholic. You'd believe anything.

[She mouths a silent holler, then slaps some papers in his direction.]

[Laughing.] Sorry! Sorry! I had to say it!

[THE PHONE RINGS. Both glance at the alien device on the wall.]

[RING.]

[They exchange looks.]

[RING.]

Okay, I'll get it.

[On the fourth RING, he picks up.]

Hello, Wells residence. *[…]* Uh, no, sir, he's not at home; can I take a message for you? *[…]* No, sir.

NIAMH: *[Approaching, she writes hastily.]*

A.: I'm Jones. *[Reading from Niamh's notepad.]* I'm the new … "vailit."

NIAMH: *[Silently shouts the noun at him.]*

A.: *[Reading her lips.]* Valet! I'm the new valet. *[…]* As you wish, sir; I'll take note of your call. You're welcome, sir. Good-bye.

[He hangs up.]

That went well, right?

NIAMH: *[She writes again, then shows.]*

A.: Too British? How's that?

NIAMH: *[Mouths a word for him, wildly overacting.]*

A.:   *[Reading her lips.]* Jones. *[Again.]* Johns. *[Again.]* Jawns.
           Jaaawns.
NIAMH: *[Thumbs up.]*

LETTER

[Cont'd.]

The thing is I don't need people to believe me. I need a Scully to confront me. And Niamh can't do that job anymore—she's clearly blinded by my sexy delusional blathering.

I could turn to you, but I'd really need someone who spoke to me in more than three lines per letter or one letter every two weeks.

It's okay. I know just the right person.

Kisses,
A.

NEUE WISSENSCHAFT: **And why crystal balls?**

ISAAK DÄNEMARR: Why not?

NW: **Well, it seems to stir up undesirable connections.**

ID: I see. I don't know; I haven't given much thought to the design. At this point I'm too focused on functional aspects to pay any attention to aesthetics. The ball is just a containment unit.

NW: **Like a roll of film.**

ID: More like a computer disk.

NW: **What is the difference?**

ID: The film actually contains the little pictures on it. Whether you use a projector or just look with your naked eye, you see them. The disk contains digitized information, ones and zeros. Without a computer to process it, it is useless.

NW: **So, what kind of computer do we need here?**

ID: A human brain.

NW: **Please expand. What is inside the ball?**

ID: Broadly speaking, it is a scale model of a neural network. Of course, by scale I mean larger-than-life. It contains a kind of rough synthetic protoplasm based on Opfstau and Hannemann's collagen; I call it neuroplasm. This is a chemical compound coagulated into a kind of flexible foamy tissue with microscopic pores, which acts like the brain as conceived by the reticular theory.

NW: **Just for clarity—are we talking living tissue here?**

ID: Well . . . organic.

NW: **Living?**

ID: Kind of.

[Against a background of coffee stirrers and speakers.]

A.: Morning, Doc.

DR. BELKNAP: Morning. Morning. Thank you for coming this far.

A.: It's okay. Niamh likes to drive. And I like the place.

DR. BELKNAP: Ambrose used to like it too. Are you sure you don't want to take this upstairs?

A.: No. I don't need therapy anymore. I told you, I have her.

[A slight demur.]

DR. BELKNAP: Okay. Let's get straight to the point. I read the bibliography you recommended. It's . . . eldritch, for lack of a better word.

A.: I don't know what eldritch means, so I think it's a great word.

WAITER: Morning, Doctor.

DR. BELKNAP: Hi, Justin. Coffee, please.

A.: Were you aware that these things existed?

DR. BELKNAP: Crystal balls? Containing dreams? I am not fully aware of their existence now.

A.: But you read Bianchi's article.

DR. BELKNAP: I haven't seen the artifact. Did you bring it?

A.: No.

DR. BELKNAP: Do you have it?

A.: Yes. In a box, inside a box, inside a box, in the basement. With

other boxes. I never understood that penchant among treasure keepers and ancient civilizations of putting the golden
idol on an altar in an empty room. It's like telling Indiana
Jones, "Hi, here's our most prized possession, ready for you
to steal."

DR. BELKNAP: Like where Ambrose used to keep it?

A.: Used to keep that one. There are others.

DR. BELKNAP: Where?

A.: In a vault. We found it last week.

HANDHELD CAMERA*

*The camera follows A. with the map, all echoing footsteps against the sun-
light crawling through the western windows high on the wall. They U-turn
around the young wooden wine racks, where oak kegs digest their contents
and torn spiderwebs swing sadly from the bottles, and pace toward the
darker nave of the basement, where old junk comes to live, and a puddle of
leaked water at the far end reflects the sunlight and draws waving lines on
the ceiling, and the basement is green-blue and cold like an indoor swimming pool trespassed at night.*

*A. stops by a cluster of retired furniture and discarded paintings on the
south wall, checks the map again, drops it to curl into a scroll on the floor.
He pushes a large canvas aside, dragging or tumbling other minor framed
things propped in front, and the circle of stainless steel behind it eclipses
out. The camera zooms in to check the Startrekish lock in the center of
the vault door—a minimal disk of the same shiny material, with a cruciform keyhole in which A. fits a four-sided key. The vault clacks open with
a hydraulic wheeze; A. reaches for the side, pulls, and swings the massive
door open wider. He checks the camera in a close-up, a slightly reddened
eye like mist before the tempest.*

*A. steps into the open mouth, camera following, watching its step,
Chuck high-tops going over the high steel sill, and the image fades to black.*

---

* This video is date-stamped November 28.

A light switch snaps. Crystal balls shine at the camera, their som-
ber surfaces untroubled but for a sticky label apiece, each one nested in
its square compartment of the shelves covering the curved wall inside the
cast-iron-ribbed vault, filled with ancient file cabinets of wood-faced draw-
ers on black iron frames, each of them marked with a handmade label in
a tin frame.

A sort of flat-topped birdbath stands in the center like an empty altar.

AUDIO RECORDING

DR. BELKNAP: How did you know there was a vault?

A.:   We knew Ambrose kept some archives somewhere. Plus we had the blueprints; they gave away the vault.

[Spoon dances in a coffee cup.]

DR. BELKNAP: And you claim that by removing this crystal ball from the room, the dreams stopped.

A.:   No; I keep dreaming the same stuff. Mostly. But now it's really dreams. They lost power. It's like … it's my brain re-creating the same scenes. Not my brain being fed the scenes.

[Background conversations.]

You don't believe me. C'mon. Say I'm mad; we're not in therapy anymore.

DR. BELKNAP: No, I won't say that. It's just … hard to imagine.

A.:   Well, you're a psychologist—

DR. BELKNAP: Psychotherapist.

A.:   Whatever; you must know how it works. An artifact contain-ing … raw feelings, unprocessed sights and sounds and pains that the brain interprets—is that too crazy?

DR. BELKNAP: No. It has existed for thousands of years. It's called a book.

AN INTERVIEW IN *NEUE WISSENSCHAFT*, MAY 1981—PART TWO

NEUE WISSENSCHAFT: So you can record dreams in this.

ISAAK DÄNEMARR: Well, it is far from a refined prototype—but yes, I
have been able to record and replay. Loose images, at least.

NW: Like your mentor Karl Hannemann's rampant horse?

ID: Much more than Professor Hannemann's horse. Bigger notions.
Complex ideas. Even complex strings of ideas.

NW: For instance?

ID: Well, it is hard to manage wakeful thoughts, because the stream
of consciousness tends to wander. But, for instance, I can make
somebody listen to music, and record what images the music
evokes in him.

NW: Are we talking just video or audio?

ID: Video, audio, smell, flavor, touch . . . (*Smiles.*) You must not
think in terms of screens or speakers; I can't play these thoughts
on a TV. I tried that. They play on your brain.

NW: This is better than cinema!

ID: Indeed. Although it is only good for short subjects now.

NW: What is the capacity of one of these crystal balls? In hours
of sleep.

ID: Seconds. It is hard to tell; so far I am hardly able to replay
anything outside the last ten seconds recorded. All the previous
material is lost. The protoplasm is reshaped. Overwritten, in
computer terms.

NW: Do you mean that thoughts do take up room?

ID: Undoubtedly, yes. However, the human brain is a flexible
container, to some extent. It does not require new brain cells
to store new ideas thrown at you. It associates old ideas to new
ones. But the ball can't do that; it can't organize information or
browse through it, so it stays with the last thing it's fed. About
ten seconds.

NW: Nevertheless, you are able to record a man's thoughts in a ball.

ID: Yes.

NW: And transmit the thoughts from a ball to another man?

ID: Yes.

NW: **Can you copy one ball into another?**

ID: Yes.

NW: **This is amazing.**

ID: Thank you.

[DR. BELKNAP and A. arguing, voices overlapping.]

DR. BELKNAP: When I say "elephant," you picture an elephant in your mind; your brain makes the elephant, triggered by just three syllables.

A.: No, you should see the elephant I'm seeing, okay? If I tell you, "They plucked my eye out," and you picture it, and try to feel the pain, and concentrate on that hot spot you feel behind your eyeball, you won't feel even half of what that crystal ball makes you feel. These conductive telepathists or whatever explicitly rejected words. They said they're just a suggestion. The ball has everything in it. The stab of your optic nerve snapping, like a hair pulled out. The speed of a body dropping to Earth from the stratosphere. The temperature inside a girl's bed.

DR. BELKNAP: You sleep in a girl's bed!

A.: Another girl's bed!

[Postclimax silence. Pencil scribbling. An empty second.]

Yeah, sure. Waiter? Can we have another slice of raspberry pie here? Thanks. *[Shift; now quieter.]* This is real; it's not confusing like dreams. You know, like in dreams, when you're talking to your grandmother and suddenly she becomes the mailman? Or how you try to read but letters just get scrambled? Well, it doesn't happen here. The edges are not blurry; everything is perfectly defined.

[A dish arrives. It slides on the table toward the microphone.]

DR. BELKNAP: I'd still like to see that ball. But… for the time being, I believe you.

A.:   *[At his quietest.]* Really? Then you're less of a skeptic than I am.

DR. BELKNAP: Well, I did my own research on this Dänemarr. *[Foraging inside a handbag.]* I thought you'd like to see this. Do you have access to the Internet?

A.:   We're working on it.

DR. BELKNAP: This address links to an interview with Dänemarr from a German magazine. It was part of a series on science exchanges between the two Germanies in the eighties. The West seemed impressed enough.

A.:   Cool. Thank you very much.

DR. BELKNAP: How is everything else?

A.:   Fine. Fine, I told you on the phone. No fever, no rough nights…

DR. BELKNAP: The ghost?

A.:   No news. Although the ghost was a whole different matter, I think. It's unrelated to all this.

DR. BELKNAP: I revised your cousin's file too. Since… I am no longer your therapist, I think you should know that in April he claimed to have seen a ghost. In the bathtub.

A.:   Oh.

DR. BELKNAP: A strong coincidence.

A.:   Not really. People who are about to die often see them.

The Lone Cypress at Monterey Bay (17 Miles Drive)

1438X

Nov 30, 1995

Dear Ambrose,

I hereby quit my quest
for this year.
In the future, I respectfully
suggest to restrict the Game
to missions on land only.
I'll be seeing you soon—
yours truly, E. Kingston—

Wish you were here!

Printed in Thailand

Ambrose Wells
Axton House
1, Axton Rd.
Point Bless, VA 26969

BEDROOM WED DEC-6-1995 11:37:21

The view of the bed is blocked by boxes and waves of bubble wrap. In the foreground, NIAMH is plugging in the computer.

⋆

GALLERY WED DEC-6-1995 11:37:26

The south windows on the right multiply themselves toward the far end of the room. The camera lies low. An undergrowth of scribbled paper sheets, many of them showing five-by-five alignments of letters, pervades the checkered floor. In a very narrow clearing sit a notebook, Mandalay's *Ars Cryptographica,* half a bottle of Yoo-hoo, and A. in lotus, holding a baseball bat behind his neck.

> *[HELP barks somewhere. A. unfolds his legs, comes to the window, and looks out.]*

A.:　　　　　*[Mildly concerned.]* Ooh, fuck.

> *[Turns around, only to be confronted with his maelstromic workspace.]*

LETTER

Axton House
1 Axton Rd.
Point Bless, VA 26969

Dear Aunt Liza,

[. . .] It was Curtis Knox.

We served tea in the dining room—the music room wasn't clean enough. It was awkward in the beginning. He probably didn't want to talk to us, and Niamh didn't want to talk to him: She's convinced he was behind that break-in we had in early November. I had almost forgotten about that—it happened four weeks and a window jump ago—but to Niamh, he still was the intruder she saw running away into the night. She was tense.

I dismissed her ten minutes into the conversation. See, I still refuse to believe him capable of entering a house through a window. I can imagine him taking off his waistcoat and rolling his sleeves up if the situation requires it (by the way, he sported an unseasonal tan), but not in order to commit a crime. And even if he'd been behind the burglary in some way, he was now willing to give diplomacy another chance. He would surely not pull out a gun and demand anything. He'd pay somebody else to do that.

So Niamh left us to resume setting up the computer upstairs while we discussed the tea set, the weather, and how the Internet was bound to change our lives, among other frivolities. I expected Knox to be a sort of computer skeptic; he isn't. I commented then that I was surprised that Ambrose never adopted this technology.

"Ambrose?" he said. "Why would he of all people be interested in the Internet?"

"Well, for a start, he'd save a lot in long-distance calls," I said.

That was the "frivolities over" signal. Knox leaned forward, left the cup and the saucer on the table, and his voice went three degrees Britisher.

"As a matter of fact," he began, "that is somehow related to the motive of my visit."

About two minutes of zigzagging preamble followed, which I failed to memorize.

"The thing is that for some time I've been waiting for some . . . let's say message from Ambrose Wells in the event of his death."

I feigned shock and leaned forward to show how Japanesemonsterly interested I was. "Please continue."

"I mean, of course, as a result of a disposition in his will, a commission, a covenant, if you wish."

"I see," I said, while mentally tracing back the string of mutual lies that had brought us here. "Of course," I lied forward, "Ambrose's death came as a shock to us all."

"You didn't even know he existed."

"And so I was beshocked the most. I mean, maybe he hadn't enough time to arrange everything."

"I am pretty confident this was taken care of."

"Really? When was the last time you guys met?" I asked, for lack of a better question.

"June the twentieth," he answered. "Still, this was a long-running business."

"Business," I repeated. "What kind of business?"

"Well, uh . . . studies he left unfinished and that he surely arranged for someone to continue."

"Just to make sure—are we talking Mason stuff?"

I really loved this reaction shot. He would have needed to pull a very big gun at me now to take him seriously.

"Mason or whatever," I clarified. "I understand Ambrose was part of a circle of scholars who did some kind of research."

"Indeed, he was, yes," he cut to the chase. "The research is the least of my concerns, of course; given the nature of his demise, I cannot pretend his mind wasn't troubled by far more serious matters than our silly work," he said, and he almost chuckled before realizing how inappropriate that would be.

"Oh, so you're in the group too."

"Well, yes, but unlike me—and this is the point that was worrying me—Ambrose's position in the group entitled him to certain . . ." The following word took him time to get out. ". . . privileges . . . that he was bound to pass on to somebody else."

"What kind of privileges?"

"Well, a special set of responsibilities, together with the possession of . . . certain tokens."

"Like a crystal ball?"

(Yeah, well, I had to say it. We couldn't be sitting there all day.)

A minute or so flew by, Knox staring at me all the while as he reformulated his strategy. Finally he said, "You found it."

"Yes." I improvised a lie based on truth. "We found a message from Ambrose regarding this . . . 'Society.' I guess you guys were still part of his concerns after all. I guessed, too, that this Society was the reason for your last visit."

"You never told me."

"Well, I'm telling you now. This message was addressed to the person he had designated to resume his functions."

"Do you still have it?"

"No, the person to whom it was addressed has it. Caleb Ford."

If that came as a harsh surprise, his flinching wasn't that obvious.

"Ambrose had an address for him in Kigali," I resumed.

"In Africa?" he asked. He said it in the exact pitch of Michael Palin in *The Meaning of Life:* "'A tiger, in Africa?'"

"We're still waiting for an answer."

"But Kigali is just an anchor point. He could be anywhere in the Great Lakes area."

"I understand, but what am I supposed to do?"

"Are you aware of what's happening in that region?"

"Uh . . . Well, we don't watch CNN, but—"

"There is a civil war going on! There are genocidal raids!"

"What is your point, Mr. Knox?"

He made sure to breathe before this one.

"I'm saying, and I am deeply sorry to do so, that Ford is probably dead."

He didn't seem much sorry. Barely concerned, at most.

And yet, once I brushed aside his body language and actually listened to his theory, I was the one affected. It had never come to my mind, but the scenario was not implausible. Ford hadn't contacted anyone since April. There were some calls to Rwanda in the phone bills

I examined weeks ago, but most of them were brief—probably a message left at a hotel, and nothing else. And then there was this notion of what a hotel in present-day Rwanda must look like. Is there a reception counter and a bell? Is the paint on the walls coming off? Is there a man in a suit behind the counter, or a child on drugs wielding an AK-47?

"You see," Knox interrupted, "it's been eight months without news from Caleb Ford. I'm afraid we must assume the worst." He looked down for a second, succeeding to at least appear honest. "In all modesty I think I knew Ambrose Wells enough to know that he would have thought of me as the second in line."

"He never considered that eventuality."

"Still, if you consider it yourself, I think you will agree that the most sensible thing to do is to give me what Ambrose meant to give Caleb."

"We don't know if Caleb is dead. If he were, we would have been told. Until we find out what happened to him, as long as he's not declared dead, I'm abiding by Wells' instructions."

"It's Africa. There will not be a death certificate."

"As far as I know, there is a stable Rwandan government right now. There are authorities; they can identify a body."

"There must be a million bodies lying between Kigali and Zaire!"

"Is Caleb Ford white?"

"Yes."

"Then his body will stand out."

He rose from his chair. "Oh, this is outrageous!"

"Careful. You're talking about Uncle Ambrose's will."

"Oh, now he's 'Uncle Ambrose'? What happened to 'second cousin twice removed'?"

"He gave me this house! I'd call him 'Daddy Cool' if he wanted me to!"

We exchanged a couple more lines, but none as good as that one, so I'll cut it short. Knox left promising he would get in touch with Glew, the lawyer, to make me see reason. I can imagine what Glew will tell him, though. Provided that the message to Caleb was signed without witnesses, and thus not legally binding, Ambrose's will prevails, and it says I inherit Axton House *and all of its contents.* And the crystal ball was found inside Axton House.

The question is, why does he want *that* crystal ball? As far as we know, it's nothing but a recording device; there are many more in the basement. What makes this one special?

Or even better: *Which ball was he talking about?*

On the other hand, if Caleb is dead, this puzzle we are trying to solve might turn unsolvable. Ambrose surely never counted on this eventuality. Maybe he suspected that Caleb was in trouble by September, but not when he wrote the letters in February, including the ciphered one to Caleb. The chain might be completely broken.

Our only hope then is to break the code once and for all, and hope that the ciphered letter will give us some real clues. Like what does that large hex key we found open, what do the crystal balls really contain, and what happens in this house on the winter solstice? Otherwise, we are stuck.

But let's not despair. We still have puzzles to think through.

VIDEO RECORDING

BEDROOM WED DEC-6-1995 23:01:15

NIAMH and A. sitting at the computer, thinking.

Deeply.

For very long.

A.: *[Suddenly, his chin dispensing with the support of his right hand, he snaps his fingers.]* Use the rubber chicken with a pulley in the middle.

[Niamh does some clicking. They stare at the screen, expectant.]

[Ecstasy ensues.]

Yaaay! I'm a mighty pirate!

Honestly, I think I tried every conceivable key word.

The first and most obvious option was *Caleb Ford* (or *Caleb* or *Ford*), in the same fashion as the Aeschylus message, which used the recipient's name as the key. But after trying and failing I realized what a foolish choice it would have been, since anyone intercepting the letter (like ourselves) would know Caleb's name from the envelope.

Still, we tried other easy solutions, just to put them out of the way: *Ambrose, Wells,* and *Axton House.*

Of course, just as Strückner's code name was Aeschylus, Caleb must have a code name too. We learned all the code names in the Society from that ledger page; we just don't know which one is Caleb. So I tried them all: *Leonidas, Hector, Archimedes, Sophocles, Zosimos, Socrates, Cybele, Dioskuri, Anchises, Elpenor, Coroebus, Phoenix, Amphiaraus, Tyche, Alexandros, Asterion, Chronos, Prometheus, Heracles,* and *Zeus.* All failed.

I also tried *society, twenty, crystal sphere, crystal ball, dream, nightmare, ghost,* and *Ngara.* Oh, and *Belknap.* Hey, who knows.

And I even tried *redhead, pitchfork, eyeball, grenade, surf, Rubik's cube,* and *Puma shoes.* To no avail.

So, enough with the niceties: It has to be cracked.

★

—How?

—Well, according to the manual, all we need to attack the cipher is a breach. A string of clear text.

—Which you don't have.

—No, but we know what to expect. Sort of. There was another letter, the one for Knox, written probably on the same day, to be read on the same occasion, not ciphered. That should give us some ideas.

(Meditating.)

—Letters begin with the date. First word = February?

*

I spent most of Monday putting that theory to the test. It failed. By midnight I'd hit several dead ends. I entertained the possibility that February had been abbreviated to Feb., but this line of attack seemed flawed anyway. The fact is that Playfair does not offer a standard way to encrypt numbers, so if the date is there, it must have been spelled out. And the message is only 256 characters long; if you begin with "February the fifteenth, nineteen ninety-five," you've almost run out of space before even getting to the subject.

Of course, Ambrose might have skipped the date. In that case, the letter would be headed by the sender's address: "Axton House." That path took me half of Tuesday before I stalled.

And I also tried assuming the first words were "Dear Caleb." There went the other half of Tuesday.

*

—I don't think it begins like a conventional letter: He's bound to keep it brief.

—It still could end like one. He must have signed it.

—So the last word is Wells?

—Or Ambrose? A.G.W.?

*

I actually tried all three. Plus *Leonidas,* Ambrose's code name.
And thus I wasted Wednesday.

VIDEO RECORDING

`GALLERY THU DEC-7-1995 11:04:25`

An autumn carpet of white and sepia paper sheets lies over the gallery like war propaganda from an enemy fighter.

Defeated A. sits under the dreary windows, bouncing a baseball against the opposite wall while studying the cipher in his free hand.

Five-by-five grids multiply across the papers strewn around the room.

HELP watches the baseball in its endless cycle out of A.'s hand, off the wall, onto the floor, back into his hand.

NIAMH is playing "Cockles and Mussels" on a harmonica.

> *[Niamh pockets her instrument, fishes for her notepad and pencil.]*

A.:   Don't bother suggesting anything; I'm not listening to you. *[Throws the ball.]* Face it: This is not your field. Just stand there and be cute.

NIAMH: *[Voiceless snigger.]*

[A. loses the ball. Help immediately catches it and offers it to his master, tail wagging. A. ignores the dog and stands up.]

A.:   Okay, which words are bound to appear in this letter? This is Ambrose to his best friend, Caleb, speaking from the grave; which words is he likely to use?

[Niamh starts writing at once; he starts pacing around, carelessly stepping over the papers.]

       "Dead." "Society," I guess. "Secret."
NIAMH: *[Shows notepad.]*
A.:   *[Reading.]* "Crystal sphere," yeah, good. Also, "friend." He has reason to get emotional; he did with Knox. "Love."
NIAMH: *[Shows a new word.]*
A.:   "Sorry," yes, not bad. But none of those words helps; look.

[He retrieves the cipher, shows it to her.]

       Check the first line; see how it begins. This digraph, L I, is repeated.

       QH TB AG LI LI OG NE DW . . .

       Every digraph in Playfair is encoded in the same way, so this word also contains a series of two letters repeated, like ... "coconut." Think of words like that.

[Niamh seems to consider it, but she soon shrugs off the question. A. resumes his wandering.]

       It's right in the beginning; how do you begin? You don't put the date, nor the address; you don't say, "Dear Caleb"; you just go straight to the point.

NIAMH:	*[Starts scribbling.]*
A.:	"Come at once." Or, "I need you."
NIAMH:	*[Delivers her line.]*
A.:	*[Stopping to read.]* "I am dead." Okay, maybe not that blunt. *[Resumes.]* "If I am dead…" *[Stops, points at Niamh.]* No, "If you read this… then I am dead."
NIAMH:	*[Lips something for him.]*
A.:	Right, "If you're reading this." "If you are…"

[EPIPHANY.]

"If you are… ARE, RE… reading this!" *[Frantic.]* That's it! That's how it begins!

∗

The sentence is likely to go on, "I am dead / will have died," whatever; but the string *if you are reading this* is long enough: We have eight pairs to start with.

```
if yo ua re re ad in gt hi s?
QH TB AG LI LI OG NE DW RB RN
```

We know each digraph has been encoded using the same five-by-five grid of letters (which we must reconstruct), following these rules:

1) If both letters fell in the same row in the grid, Ambrose picked those on the right of each one. (Horizontal rule.)

2) If both letters fell in the same column, he picked those below each one. (Vertical rule.)

3) If they didn't share a row nor a column, he picked the letters diagonally opposite them. (Diagonal rule.)

Now, one property of the diagonal rule is that it encodes every two letters into two different letters. So it can't produce pair #3 in our list, *ua* = *ag*. This one must have followed either the horizontal rule or the vertical rule, meaning that all three, *u, a,* and *g,* shared either a row or a column in the grid. Same goes for pair #6, *in* = *ne.*

Another property of the diagonal rule is that it always places the first half of both plain and encoded digraph in the same row. An example: pair #5, *ad* = *og,* follows the diagonal rule.* This means that *a* and *o* share a row, and so do *d* and *g.* This way, #5 proves that *a* and *g* do not share a row; pair #3 cannot follow the horizontal rule then; it must follow the vertical one. That gives us a piece of the grid.

```
                        u
       PIECE I          a  │  o
                        g  │  d
```

(There could be other columns between these two—hence the line—but that's not important at this stage.)

Similarly, pair #4 (*re* = *li*), which is diagonally encoded too, proves that *i* and *e* don't share a column. Therefore, pair #6 follows the horizontal rule, and thus it gives us a second piece of the grid.

```
                     r              l
       PIECE II    ─────────────────────
                     i      n      e
```

Let's now shuffle the first piece of the grid with pair #7 (*gt* = *dw*). This will locate new letters *t* and *w* relative to *g* and *d.*

IF PAIR #7 IS HORIZONTAL: IF PAIR #7 IS DIAGONAL:

```
 u                                  u
 a   o                              a  │  o
 g   d │ t   w                      g  │  d
                                  ─────────
                                    w  │  t
```

---

* Quick proof: If it didn't, all letters in pairs #3 and #5, *u a g d o,* would make up a whole column/row. That would make pair #7 impossible.

(It can't be vertical, because that would require g and d to share a column, and we already know they don't.)

Let's go further: If we shuffle it with pair #2 ($yo = tb$), letters y and b fit only in the second scenario. (The first one is discarded because pair #2 would not abide by any rule: o and t must share either a row or a column.)

```
PIECE I        u
               a │ o │ b
               g │ d
              ───────┼────────
               w │ t │ y
```

Now let's shuffle the second piece with pair #8 ($hi = rb$). This will place letters h and b relative to i and r.

IF PAIR #8 IS HORIZONTAL: IF PAIR #8 IS DIAGONAL:

```
 h
 r            l          h     r           l
─────────────────       ─────────────────────
 i    n    e            b    i    n    e
 b
```

Combining this with pair #1 ($if = qh$), only the first scenario applies. (The second doesn't, because i and h don't share a row or a column.)

```
            f │ h
              │ r          l
PIECE II    ──┼───────────────
            q │ i    n    e
              │ b
```

We can now merge these two pieces together using their only common letter: b. This is tricky because of the lines: Only letters with no lines between them are truly stuck together, so we don't know in which order they fall. But we do know the five letters comprising the b column: b, h, i, r, y. Which one is right below b? It can't be y (piece I shows clearly a gap between b and y); it can't be i (it's above b); it can't be r (it's below h); therefore it's h.

q		i	n	e
		b		
f		h		
		r		1
		y		

Since letters *i, n, e* are known to be stuck together, but they don't follow the alphabet, it is safe to assume that they are part of the key word, so we put that row on top. And the letter *q* is in the key word too. And *q* is usually followed by *u*. In our drafts, though, *u* carries along *a* and *g*. So:

q	u	i	n	e
	a	b		
f	g	h		
		r		1
		y		

And that's enough to solve the key word.

NIAMH'S NOTEPAD

—There's this thing that's been bugging me since I talked to Knox yesterday. I asked him when was the last time he saw Wells alive, and he answered June the twentieth. Just like that. Month and day. How come he remembered the exact date?

—*Birthday?*

—Maybe. But there's a cooler answer.

—*Summer solstice!*

—Exactly. I think the Society used to hold another regular meeting—one with Ambrose's nearest colleagues, Ford and Knox. This year Ford was in Africa, so only Knox attended. However, if you hold regular meetings every solstice, and need to call an emergency meeting in between . . . What is there between solstices?

—*Equinox.*

—Which means unscheduled meeting, red alert. *Equinox* is the key word.

e	q	u	i	n
o	x	a	b	c
d	f	g	h	k
l	m	p	r	s
t	v	w	y	z

LETTER (DECIPHERED)

IF YOU ARE READING THIS, I QUIT THE GAME. I ENCOURAGE YOU TO FOLLOW MY EXAMPLE, IN A LESS DRAMATIC FASHION IF POSSIBLE. IT IS NOT A BOURGEOIS PASTIME ANYMORE. SHOULD THE OTHERS FAIL TO SEE THIS, YOU AS THE SECRETARY HAVE THE LAST WORD. AXTON HOUSE, THIRD FLOOR, STUDY DESK, RIGHT THIRD DRAWER. I SHALL TALK TO YOU THERE.

LETTER

Axton House
1 Axton Rd.
Point Bless, VA 26969

Dear Aunt Liza,

We're fucked. [. . .]

A blank paper. That's the thing most resembling a message you'll find in the right third drawer of the desk in the study on the third floor.

We searched the entire room—which, by the way, is a rather dark, maroon-colored, seldom-explored chamber decorated with sordid illustrations à la Gustave Doré. It holds the last of Ambrose's workspaces, the one devoted to his personal affairs. We browsed through it once weeks ago, looking for the red notebook with the twenty's names.

And that's the point. All this encryption, all this secrecy, just to make us look into a drawer that wasn't even locked?

Obviously Ambrose trusted that no one stumbling upon what is hidden in this desk would deem it vital information. Certainly nobody did after his departure. Strückner had his own cipher to worry about. Had Glew, the lawyer, been looking for legal documents here, he would have dismissed it as what it seems: a blank paper, barely concealed under an old phone book, next to a family album, a deck of cards, and a stock of staples and paper clips, somehow containing a piece of information worth of all this conspiranoia.

EXCERPT FROM SAMUEL MANDALAY'S *ARS CRYPTOGRAPHICA*

As much as computer algorithms are called to open a new era in cryptography—and will surely not disappoint us—machine ciphers still have one obstacle to overcome: They are conspicuous. Algorithm-generated code can hardly be camouflaged or disguised as plain text, and whenever there is visible code, it will stoke the enemy's curiosity.

What traditional methods (even the most childish of them) still do better than computers is to comply with the third of Sir Francis Bacon's rules: hiding the code—not only the information. Acrostics, Cardan grilles, invisible ink, and other techniques have been used since ancient history to conceal even the existence of a message to be concealed. Secret texts can be camouflaged within longer texts, or the environment. There is an infinite number of writing patterns hidden everywhere around us. It is human imagination that finds new ways, not artificial intelligence.

Consequently, computers cannot yet guarantee the simultaneous application of the RIB principles of cryptography (randomness, invisibility, brevity: § 4.1.1). As long as we adhere to these rules, our man-made ciphers will remain a challenge for both human and mechanical attackers.

VIDEO RECORDING

KITCHEN THU DEC-7-1995 18:11:45

Several objects gathered on the table: The blank paper presides; a saucer of sliced lemon, a knife, some cotton balls, a hair dryer, and NIAMH sit around it.

A., on a stool, is now taking a lemon slice. He squeezes a few drops onto a pinch of cotton. Then, leaning close enough to sniff the paper, he rubs the cotton over the top. Niamh gently applies heat with the hair dryer.

> *[They sit back, as though yielding room for whatever emerges from the paper.]*

[Suspense.]

[Bordering on boredom.]

A.:   Aw, fuck this.

[He squeezes half a lemon with his hand, squirting juice all over the paper and half the counter, then sweeps a few cotton balls over it, Niamh providing heat at maximum power all the while.]

[She turns off the dryer. He releases the paper onto the table, hoping it has learned the lesson.]

[It hasn't.]

[WALL PHONE RINGS. They exchange looks.]

[RING. She nives. A. reaches for it.]

    [Grumpy.] How come you can call an ambulance but can't tell somebody to fuck off?

[Picks up on the third RING.]

    Yeah?

[He stares at the receiver. Then, to Niamh.]

    They hung up.

[He does the same. Niamh just finished writing; she shows.]

*

—They calling more & more often.

—I noticed. It just adds pressure.

—?

—Because winter solstice is coming. And we're nowhere close to finding what's supposed to happen in this house. We're probably behind schedule. And members begin to wonder if everything's all right.

—*So? If we don't find out in time, they won't come. Nothing will happen.*

—I'm beginning to fear that something will happen anyway. With a crystal ball, or some other evil thing hidden around. What if it's due to happen at the winter solstice—and we're not ready?

*

[Both stay silent for a second.]

[Or two.]

A.:   *[Suddenly.]* Okay, let's see what the Internet has to say about this: ways to bring up invisible ink. Go!

[Niamh jumps off the counter and out.]

*

[Cont'd.]

We tried iodine. Actually, we tried Betadine; it was supposed to do the trick. Only it didn't.

We tried ammonia vapor—filled a bucket in the coal room with two bottles of ammonia and poured in some bleach to bring the fumes up, to no avail. Then Help peeked inside the room without wearing a mask and he threw up.

We tried ultraviolet light: took the car, drove to Clayboro, had a beer, told a barman that I'd been taken to a disco in the vicinity recently that featured UV lights and couldn't remember where it was, collected the names of three spots between Clayboro and Virginia Beach, drove another forty miles for the closest one, paid the tickets, elbowed our way to the stage, checked the paper, swore our brains out, had two shots, and left. People really liked Niamh's hair.

I don't know. I have theories, but I don't feel like writing them down. But hey, you feel free to jump in anytime. I mean, you don't have to wait until I'm throwing myself out of a window; your input is always welcome.

You should get yourself an e-mail account; it would improve our communications. When you have it, notify me at theycallmemister wells@lycos.com. We miss you here in the twenty-first century.

Kisses,
A.

(At Gordon's.)

—Maybe we're barking up the wrong tree.

(He stares at my line for a while.)

—I have no idea what that means, but I do think we're trying to extract an answer from something that can't give it to us.

—Maybe there was a real message & they took it.

—But why just leave it in an unlocked drawer?

—False bottom?

—No, we checked that. I'm not hungry; have my toast. Oh, you had it already. Good for you.

—Maybe Ambrose not all that smart.

—If there was a real message and they took it, what's that blank paper doing there?

—Where else would you keep a blank paper?

KITCHEN FRI DEC-8-1995 09:39:25

[RING.]

[HELP diligently trots over to the wall phone.]

[RING.]

[He stares up at the apparatus, head tilted.]

[RING.]

[He dismisses the phone, goes to his water bowl.]

[RING.]

[Lap, lap, lap.]

[No ring.]

*

`MUSIC ROOM FRI DEC-8-1995 16:24:53`

Rain spattering on the windows, and the gentle slapping of playing cards on the coffee table as NIAMH sets up a game of solitaire.

> [A. walks in from the south, passes her without a word, lies down
> on the couch at the end of the room, next to where HELP lies
> curled up by the fire.]
>
> [The game goes on.]

16:25:30

[A. moves his hands from his chest to under his head.]

[NIAMH places the last ace remaining in the foundations of her game.]

16:26:04

[The Earth continues to rotate.]

16:26:05

[A. catapults himself up from the sofa, jumps over HELP, crosses
the room in three strides, and crashes against the coffee table,
paralyzing NIAMH with one extended, expectation-creating
hand.]

A.:   Tell me. You. Didn't. Shuffle. Those. Cards.

NIAMH: [Terrorized, shakes her head.]

A.:   [Insanely, Jack Nicholsonianly calm.] Good. Now, put them back
           in the exact order they came.

[Niamh gazes at the cards on the table. She takes an ace back
from the foundation, hesitates ... places it in one of the tableau
columns. Then takes another one ...]

[... Consults A., impotently.]

A.:   [Sinking his face into his palm.] Ssshit.

[Niamh stares at him, then at the cards on the table, extremely
worried. Then, by chance, at the camera.]

[She shakes A.'s arm.]

16:44:48

[NIAMH has just finished piling up the cards. A. is now standing.]

A.:   Okay, now listen. The blank paper was a red herring. It makes sense. It's a progression. Each code is harder than the previous. First was the Aeschylus cipher: basic level, meant for Strückner to get. Then it was the "book by a tree" riddle, a personalized code. The third was a Playfair: professional code used in World War Two. And last, invisible code, one you can't even see. Only it wasn't the blank paper; that's still too conspicuous. The Playfair just said "right third drawer." And the manual says, "There are infinite writing patterns around us." Like a deck of cards. A deck is fifty-two cards without the jokers, which makes twenty-six black and twenty-six red. Twenty-six are the letters in the alphabet; that is the pattern: A deck contains two alphabets, enough to conceal a short message!

NIAMH: *[Stenopadding.]*

—You turn me SO on when you do that.

A.:   *[After reading, amused.]* I know. Take a long shower later; now listen.

[Sniggering, she grabs a blank paper (THE blank paper, most likely), as A. skips through the cards.]

Okay, I was thinking black alphabet and red alphabet, but that would require too much guesswork without stating an order for the suits. So it's probably black for one half of the alphabet, and red for the other. And ... the ace of spades usually comes on top in a new deck, so let's say blacks are the first half, from A to M, and reds are from N to Z.

[Niamh is already composing a table of equivalences.]

Now, the first card in the deck as we found it is the queen of spades. That is … the letter L. Next is the three of hearts, which is N, 0 … P. "L-P." Next is nine of clubs, that is … J?

NIAMH: *[Double whistle warning, busy writing.]*

A.: No, I. Next is the king of hearts: Z. "L-P-I-Z."

[Niamh looks up at him for reassurance.]

It's okay; this is just landfill; you can't just throw away the cards you don't need. Ten of clubs … Three of clubs … King of spades …

*

Q♠	3♥	9♣	K♥	10♣	3♣	K♠	9♦	6♠
5♦	7♠	10♥	8♣	Joker	10♠	A♠	K♣	5♠
6♦	6♥	A♣	3♠	5♥	5♣	4♠	6♣	2♥
8♦	A♥	7♥	2♠	4♦	9♥	Joker	J♣	2♦
9♠	A♦	J♥	8♠	2♣	Q♥	7♦	7♣	8♥
Q♣	K♦	10♦	3♦	J♠	Q♦	4♣	J♦	4♥

L P I Z J C M V F R G W H [joker] J A M E S S A C R E D F O U N T B Q V [joker] K O I N X H B Y T G U L Z W P K Y D X Q

*

[Both focusing on the ex–blank sheet; even HELP seems involved.]

A.: There it is; the jokers mark where the message starts and ends. It's the only part that makes sense. *[Frowns.]* Some.

[Grabs the paper for a zoom-in.]

James, sacred, fount... B-Q-V. What does this mean?

[NIAMH suddenly explodes, chair pawing the ground like a mad horse; she frantically writes in her notepad; shows.]

A.:   *[Reads.]* "Henry James' *Sacred Fount*." Is that a book?
NIAMH: *[Nods.]*
A.:   How come you know that?
NIAMH: *[Stares.]*
A.:   *[Back to his paper.]* Okay, then maybe B-Q-V didn't stand for letters; must be the card numbers themselves. Two, four, nine. That must be the page!

[Niamh bounces onto the table and dashes out, scampering the papers on her way.]

A.:   *[Speaker voice.]* JUMANJI!

[They all dash out for the library.]

PAGE 249 FROM HENRY JAMES' *THE SACRED FOUNT**

Dear Caleb,

I always find great comfort in the words of that *sifu* in Yunnan who told us that the best place to hide a leaf is in a forest. And whenever I flick through these pages in particular I am further reassured that this letter is well hidden, for no one in his sane mind would read beyond page one hundred of James' extravaganza. I know it is safe for us to talk

---

* The page was sewn inside the book, printed in the same type as the rest.

here. It is overdramatic too, but this is what the Society was created for: to put some drama into our lives.

Unfortunately, in every story some characters must fall along the way. If you are reading these lines, my friend, you are the hero to our story, and I am the character whose death will serve as an example. Hopefully one you will not ignore, as I did with Spears, Dagenais, or Wells Sr.

I don't have many regrets. We led fascinating lives, all of us. The places we visited, the people we met, the things we *saw,* they are all well above what the average man will witness. We paid the toll too: All of us suffer sleep disorders; seventeen underwent therapy at some moment; many have panic attacks; a few have had seizures. These scars will not wash away, but neither will the experience.

I am not advising you all to throw it away. I am just telling you, do not let it consume the rest of your lives. They have been enriched and consumed enough. What further enlightenment can you expect? For three generations my family has participated in this magic, gazed at it with awe and fear, and I, at fifty, stand not an inch closer to understanding it than my grandfather stood when this gift first fell upon him. It will never cease to surprise you if you live for a thousand years. It will never acknowledge you either. There is no end to this trip. You all might as well stop now; take some rest; meet before Christmas and share the good memories. May the Society live long and peaceful years.

The Wells' heirloom is yours to dispose of. Strabo guards last year, and the key to the present. The past is for our Historian to look after; the present, only you know where to find.

There are no instructions for you, Caleb. Just these words of mine, written in good faith. The dead cannot give orders; they can only whisper.

It has been a pleasure to live this adventure together. Farewell, my friend.

Ambrose G. Wells

(After like 5 minutes.)

—What IS Strabo?

—He was a Greek geographer of the first century. The book in the library that you pull to reveal the secret room was a volume of Strabo's *Geography*, but we already knew that.

—SO?!

—So . . . nothing. This is it.

*

GALLERY FRI DEC-8-1995 17:30:23

The many windows cry gentle raindrops. HELP, NIAMH, and A. sit on the Playfair-strewn floor, waiting for page 249 of Henry James' *The Sacred Fount* to say something else.

*

—All these clues led NOWHERE?

—Well, they led to the secret room in the library, but we blew that surprise already. We didn't follow the steps properly.

—Who the Historian?

—Curtis Knox. Those are the ranks in the Society: Ambrose is the host; Caleb's the secretary; Knox is the historian.

—"Past & present"?

—When the host died, he split the legacy between secretary and historian. He did it because he wanted to end the Society: A divided empire is harder to perpetuate. "Last year" is the crystal ball we found in the secret room. It belongs in the archives, which means the vault in the basement, where the other crystal balls are, which are the past, which is for Knox. But we've been there too. It's useless; it's a nightmare catalog. The key to the present must be that sort of hex key we found in the secret room, but we don't know where the lock is. Caleb does.

—*Then we wait for Caleb?*

—I'm beginning to think Knox was right, Niamh. Caleb never made it out of Africa.

LETTER

Axton House
1 Axton Rd.
Point Bless, VA 26969

Dear Aunt Liza,

[...] So, we're back to fucked again.

As usual, I am open to any suggestions from you. I mean, if you happen to be interested. Not like all this is any of your business or anything.

Kisses,
A.

VIDEO RECORDING

GALLERY FRI DEC-8-1995 18:06:29

HELP leans his head on his mistress' calf, sharing the depression. An idle right hand of NIAMH scratches him gently, while the left hand holds open *The Sacred Fount* for one of her eyes to read for the nth time. (The other one is hidden by the tuft of hair cascading down her face.)

Meanwhile, A.'s visual line has long ago spiral-plunged like a wounded F-16 into the marsh of wasted paper covering the whole breadth of the windowed gallery: dozens and dozens of paper sheets with five-by-five grids, consonant-infested paragraphs, and speculative maps of a labyrinth.

Raindrops peek through the Gothic windows.

   [A. fishes out a paper. One of the labyrinth maps.]

A.:   Niamh ... Did you draw this maze?
NIAMH: *[Nods.]*
A.:   *[Finger stabbing the drawing.]* How does one get here?

HANDHELD CAMERA

Torn shreds of clouds hover ghostly in front of the eye of the camera, between the moving figures and the electric green corridors of the maze. A., in a red jacket, marches ahead, camera peeking over his arm to spy the hand-drawn map, while Help trots past them, eager to explore, unceremoniously crossing the gate and sniffing the hedge. The red jacket reaches a gap, points left, and then follows his own finger, camera tailing him, and the mist keeps receding as they advance, and a cautious whistle, very close to the mike, alerts Help not to wander around, and so the red jacket, the camera, the quadruped, and the green-walled street all transcur in silence, cleaving the obliterating fog, but the camera fears, and then confirms, by glancing over its scarfed shoulder, that the fog only feigns to allow them, for it lurks behind them and it veils the yards they previously walked, like the Red Sea closing after Moses and his people. And at a new intersection the red jacket points to his left, and follows, and shortly after it takes a left, and they all enter a cul-de-sac. Where the man consults the map, and the camera waits, and the dog sniffs and reclaims by urination the land they have conquered.

"It's supposed to be on the other side of this wall," says A.

We flung Niamh's scarf over the hedge and tied one end around a bough. Then we trekked around, keeping the same wall to our right. After what seemed like miles, we met the scarf again—the tied end. So there is a closed area within the maze.

We still have to figure out which entryway the Society used to take. There must be a narrow clearing between two trees somewhere to let people in and out, but Help suggested it was faster to just crawl.

The closed section turned out to be disappointingly close to the rest: more oppressive green walls and a single corridor. The passage meanders between the foliage, flooded with fog always skulking a corner ahead.

We zigzagged our way, generally heading to the west. It looked shorter on the map. By the end, the lane becomes a U-turn and stops in a dead end, but the wall in that U-turn conceals more than trees. A small part of the hedge has been cropped out, but not up to the top, so as not to make the gap visible from the sky. And in that gap sits another weathered statue, one with the appeal of having been less looked at: a man with a bull's head.

There's no inscription on the pedestal. You can't walk around the statue, but you can complete the U-turn to see its back. This is where our hearts jumped: at the discovery of an inconspicuous, hexagonal hole between the minotaur's shoulder blades.

This was the perfect reward to our faith. And to our bringing that large hex key we found in the secret room.

Niamh fitted it into the hole. A latch clacked somewhere within the marble torso. She turned the key a quarter to the right. Gears were set in motion inside the monster's skeleton. Stone grumbled.

When we ran to the front again, a narrow crack had opened in the pedestal. Spider silk and mold kept it sealed. We removed the heavy slab, dropped it onto the ground. An object lurked inside the pedestal.

Niamh touched it.

The millisecond after, she'd been thrown like an overdressed mannequin against the hedge behind her, the upper half of her body actually crashing through the foliage.

I pulled her up; her limbs were shaking. She gazed at me in shock through the billion shadows lingering in her pupils.

I used my own jacket to make the treasure roll out—by this time I'd guessed it was a crystal ball. The electric shock, though, was unexplained. Niamh told me she hadn't actually felt electricity; her hand didn't hurt; she'd just felt a spasm. We didn't need to keep Help away from it—he doesn't like it.

I wrapped the ball in my jacket and we returned home.

HANDHELD CAMERA

The man sticks closer to the camera now, too close to come into focus, and the fog is closing in too, revealing but five yards ahead the green passage-way. Then Help rushes past the camera, fading into the mist, and by the time the pitter-patter of paws on sallow leaves should fade away, he bursts into riotous barks.

Then the man says, "Fuck," and both he and the camera speed up forward, taking a right in the maze foyer, glancing outside the gate, where finally the hedge disappears, and the fog recedes, and the barking continues, and the dull Gothic house can be seen in the distance, as well as the naked backyard, and a white car parked right in front, and a Victorian man standing by, aiming a revolver at the camera.

*

A freezing drizzle chose to join us.

It was really an uncomfortable situation, standing there, both parties obviously unwilling to shoot or be shot. There was only Help's barking to distract us from the awkwardness.

"Drop what you're holding," the man said at long last.

"It might break."

"No, it won't."

I dropped it, together with the jacket, which I was really yearning for under the rain.

"Maybe we should talk," I suggested.

"Where is Ambrose?" he asked. His mustache twitched on his uttering the name.

I chin-pointed to Axton House.

"He jumped out of the bedroom window in September."

His visage upgraded a new level in tension. He was blond and blue eyed, with a youthful yet weary look to his face.

I added, "I really think we should talk, Mr. Ford."

KITCHEN SAT DEC-9-1995 11:14:01

Tea is ready. A service for three is laid on a tray on the counter.

NIAMH feeds HELP biscuits.

A. checks the clock, arms folded, leaning on the sink.

We left him in the music room, reading page 249 of *The Sacred Fount* by the fire while we made tea. We owed him that, at least: a letter from the dead, plus five minutes alone to mourn him.

We returned clearing our throats (those of us who can) to give him time to pull himself together, which he visibly did. He had this sort of childish face where sadness seems to leave a deeper print. At first, he'd struck me as a naive yet courageous Dr. Watson type. Now, he'd just learned that his Sherlock Holmes was gone.

I asked casually, "So, how was Africa?"

"Hell on Earth. Thanks for asking," he answered.

(Later I learned he'd spent eight weeks in an understaffed, under-walled embassy, waiting for repatriation.)

A spoon fell clinking off Niamh's hand while she served the tea. I asked her if she was okay. She started to walk out, tried to lean on the piano, failed, and crashed very gently onto the floor, her idle hand inadvertently playing a dramatic cue.

I ran to her, talked to her, but she hardly tried to keep her eyes open.

"She'll be all right," said Caleb from the rocking chair he'd settled down in. "She just needs to sleep. She touched it, didn't she?"

"How is that relevant? How does it cause you to doze off?"

"It's not the Eye that causes it; it's a brain mechanism of self-defense. She has seen so much, her brain is exhausted."

"She said she hadn't seen anything."

"It's quite the opposite. She just channeled such a formidable quantity of information so quickly, she didn't notice. But her short-term memory is full over capacity. Her brain must shut down and go into REM sleep, so it can clean up. Just lay her on the sofa; she'll have some unquiet dreams."

She was completely passed out at this point, so I carried her to the sofa. Help sat next to her and didn't move for the whole conversation; one of the longest I've had in my life.

"How did you know where the Eye was from this?" Caleb asked, alluding to James' book.

"We didn't. Niamh drew a map of the maze; we noticed a closed section. We broke in."

"What about the key?"

"It was in the secret room."

"How did you find the secret room?"

"Same way: mapping the floor."

"How unorthodox," was his comment.

"Well, I find your protocols a little over-the-top. You people go to great lengths to hide dreams."

"Excuse me?"

For the first time I looked up from Niamh's face. "Dream recordings. What you keep in those crystal balls. Spheres. *Eyes*," I tried.

He glanced at me once again, his mustache retracting with a mixture of interest and skepticism I was growing accustomed to.

"You two did a lot of work," he remarked, "and yet I don't think you grasped half of it."

"Please enlighten me. I am genuinely interested."

He skipped his turn there.

"On the other hand, I could just find out myself," I thought aloud. "If there's one thing I have, it's time."

"Not that much," he pointed out.

"Oh, you mean till the solstice meeting? Well, if I'm not allowed to know what it is, I don't see why it should take place in my house. Maybe you should get a new manor. And new artifacts."

"But this letter bequeaths the artifacts to me."

"An unsealed letter with no witnesses and no legal value."

"Ambrose meant for me to have them."

"Ambrose meant for you to arrive before I did. Ambrose meant Strückner to interpret instructions correctly. Come to think of it, he never planned this legacy business so well. Now I am the owner of Axton House and all of its contents. That includes the keys, the archive in the basement, and the crystal balls."

"Not that one," said he, pointing at what sat on its own chair, still shrouded in my jacket.

Niamh came splashing out of her coma like a harpooned dolphin. I rushed to soothe her down, to dissuade her from trying to scream.

Ten seconds later she fainted back to sleep while I was holding her shoulders. Caleb appeared utterly unmoved. I studied him a second time. It was hard to picture him in a war zone in Africa. I saw him like one of those characters in Westerns—probably the town's clockmaker or some paper pusher working for the railroad company: someone who wears tweed in the desert and whom people poke fun at because he keeps his fingernails clean. I bet he kept them clean in Rwanda. And yet, despite his round face and soft manners, there were those deep lines around his blue eyes that confirmed it: *I was there.*

"Okay, I give up," I said. "Please tell me. What makes that sphere so different?"

He hurriedly began to answer, then stopped himself at the first syllable. He mentally rewrote it, then dismissed it. He tried a new strategy, thought for an alternative route. It eluded him. I kept my most receptive face on all the while.

Then he remembered his briefcase—the only thing he'd retrieved from his car after returning his revolver to the glove compartment. He laid it on his lap, unzipped it, took out a folder. There was a Post-it on the cover, numbered "12." He browsed through its contents, then decided to share a picture.

"Are you acquainted with this man?"

It was a black, trim-haired male in a cheesy driver's license picture, with a limestone wall as a background.

"No."

He nodded understandingly, taking the photo from me, and gave me a four-by-six black-and-white picture in exchange. "How about the one on the right?"

I saw two white men on a pier. The one on the right. *The surgeon in the blood-drenched coat forces the pincers between the eyeball and the socket.*

I flinched and covered my right eye in a knee-jerk response.

"I see you know him."

I think I stammered for the first time in my life since puberty. "How the fuck . . . ?"

"He was a South African of Boer ancestry; became a doctor in Bloemfontein. In the early eighties he joined a community of young Afrikaners who meant to settle in the north. Actually they ended up living off African hospitality and stocking up on shaman drugs. He somehow ended up in Rwanda with permanent psychosis. Took advantage of the genocide last year to perform some creative surgery."

I sit up and grab the surgeon's skull and shove his face into a rack of syringes, needles up.

"Did that really happen?"

"I saw his corpse. The doctor's, that is. I never found the victim's body, but I don't think he lived much longer after that. Phoenixes rarely grasp any more than some extra minutes."

I feel the breeze through my fingers inside the cavity. I shoot my way along the corridor, guerrillas with Kalashnikovs splattering their useless brains on the walls.

"This is impossible."

"I presume you have other folders like this," he said.

"Yes." My mind was unfocused, distracted by atrocious memories of soldiers burned alive. "Numbers 4 and 7. And we think 15 is here somewhere, but we didn't find it."

"15 was pretty early this year; it must be filed already," was his speak-of-the-weather comment. "Number 4 was the techno musician, right? Catchy. So Cutler found her?"

"He sent a CD." I kept rubbing my eyes, trying to sweep off the confusion. "Number 7," I stuttered, "she was a Mexican woman, holding a baby. Somebody sent a police file. A woman looking just like her."

"Not just like her. It must be her."

I looked down at Niamh—she was twitching on my lap.

"What's happened to her?" I asked again. "What did she see inside that sphere?"

"Nothing. You don't look inside it. It looks outside. It's an eye."

And he pointed to, and I looked at, the hideous thing we'd retrieved from the minotaur, lurking from its hideout under my jacket.

"I always tend to give things more credit when I read them in print," he said, standing up. "Allow me; Ambrose has some good bibliography on the subject."

EXCERPT FROM G. L. BURGESS' *RELICS OF A BIGGER WORLD.* NEW YORK, 1957

Nonetheless, as Berkeley put it, "History, not only myth, defies materialism." The past described in ancient chronicles is populated by ideas, not objects or subjects. It is speculation to vouch for the existence of such objects between allusions in books. That all-seeing mirror that the Byzantine historian George Hamartolos believed to be in possession of Alexander the Great may or may not be the same one that Herodotus and Dio Chrysostom attributed to Gaumata the Magian. Or Gaumata's mirror might actually be the "omnivident window" atop the Tower of Rulers near Erzurum, said by Pliny the Elder (*Natural History*, xxx.103) to overlook the whole universe "without shrinking." (This tower, incidentally, might be the one that Galland places in Ethiopia.) In 1666, Borellus (*Alchemy*, XIII) borrowed from Pliny the adjective *omnividens* to describe a crystal ball in the unidentified palace of Amber, inside which "the reflections of all living creatures in the universe dwell." Here the Frenchman might have been quoting Zosimos of Panopolis, who claimed to have seen such an object in a Scythian temple; or Abulfeda, who placed it in Amr, Iberia, and averred it was "the eye of a pagan god." Avicenna retook this legend and linked it to that of the Aliph, an orb "the size of a speck, which contains the whole universe within." In modern times, Sir Richard Burton and von Slatin still register the mosque of Amr in northeastern Turkey. The idea of an all-seeing crystal has thus endured centuries and mutations to break into the present time in the form of ruins. But in Berkeley's words, "Ruins might have been always ruins; some human skeletons were never humans."

EXCERPT FROM V. LAURENTIS' *OF OUTER CIRCLES*. LUCERNE, 1679

& amongst those Devices employed by Sorcerers, Myrrors and Crystal Balls may be controlled by their Owners to watch over their Enemies; but some Artefacts have a Mind of their own. Crystals may be used to see through, whilst other Crystals are Eyes & they see by their Will. These Eyes do not spy solely on Men, but on Demons & Angels & Forbidden Things that Men are not allowed to see. & for this Reason the Book of Yaël warns, "Damnation to Him Who sees through an Eye, for the Eye sees within his Soul & weighs the Good and the Evil in it. & if It finds Evil in his Heart, Nightmares will haunt Him & the Knowledge of the Hidden World will creep upon his Soul like Spiders."

EXCERPT FROM F. RAYNAL'S *A TRAVELER'S JOURNALS*. LONDON, 1908

September 25th—Early in the morning, while Iskandar and his boy discussed the route, I sketched down the unnatural yellow sky over the Black Sea. They chose to lead us into the country along the border, which in this craggy region of knife-sharp mountains is but a line on the map freely trespassed by Turkish smugglers and Russophone Gypsies.

Just some yards inland, the path turned painfully steep, switching from shadowy valleys to magnificent vistas in a matter of minutes. From one of the latter we sighted another cave village across the Yavits River, and I insisted on exploring it. As soon as we took the long slope up, the dwellers swarmed out through the myriad holes in the rocky walls, like soldier termites running to defend their nest, and on our arrival the children took great pleasure in stroking our clothes and seemed immensely amused by my spectacles, while unveiled women offered us food and water. We could not but submit to their hospitality, so we stayed for lunch, which consisted of mashed legumes, cheese, bread, and tea. Gaumont offered the elders some Scotch, but they refused. They still observed some Islam traditions, and yet few of them spoke any Arabic.

The air was cooling when we waded across the river and returned to the main route through the Samzic chain. Gaumont sighted some distinct Byzantine ruins and we newly discussed the many affluent cultures that have shaped this country, from the Eastern Roman Empire, so unlike its Western counterpart, to the Persians, Turks, and Russians. A beautiful proof of this colorful substrata we found at the Azidz Pass: it was the Mosque of Amr, mentioned by Sir Alistair Boleskine in the last volume of his *Asian Travels*. The mosque (the noun is excessive) is but a sanctified peristyle square within the ruins of a greater Byzantine palace. The imam was delighted with our interest in the broken yet powerful architecture, and he led us downstairs into the foundations: the remains of an older site on top of which the palace was built. Gaumont was dumbfounded at the sight of those proto-Islamic arcs, clearly older than Muhammad and Jesus Christ.

Then the caretaker took my hand and guided me into the deeper end. I confess I felt uneasy wandering among those arcs and columns whose number one could estimate as infinite in the dark, blinded beyond the dwindling pool of light around the guide's torch. The cracked ceiling incessantly poured trickles of sand into the chamber, so that in the further end the floor was arisen and the capitals lowered to my reach, and the vaults were blackened by the seemingly frequent visits of torchbearers. The imam stopped by a pillar and instructed me to lean my hand on the capital. Despite being aware of a queer, vibrating sound in the dark, at the time I did not remember Sir Boleskine's mention of the unexplained prodigy I was about to witness: My hand touched nothing but ancient stone, and yet within that stone I felt what I can only describe as a frantic heartbeat. My guide referred to it as the Orb of Allah, and explained that it was kept inside the stone so that no man could see God through it. But once a year, at the sunrise of the shortest day, the Orb takes a minute's rest. Then a man can look inside and the Orb remembers twenty people of its choice, and these twenty will in time speak to Allah in heaven.

*

There were another two books that Caleb had produced, grossly over-estimating my command of Latin. I just skimmed through them and tossed them onto the pile.

"This is bullshit," I concluded.

"I know how it sounds."

"I'm not saying how it sounds; I'm saying what it is. It sounds worse."

"Do you believe in God?"

"No, Niamh does that. I'm the rational one."

"Do you believe in ghosts?"

I sighed, just to slow down the pace. "It is hard not to, in this house."

"Oh, so you saw it."

"Her," I corrected. "She's a girl."

He rose, in a resolute history-teacher fashion. The fireplace suited him. I was still on the sofa, Niamh's delicate head resting on my lap. My right hand played with her ear piercings.

He asked permission to smoke; on my granting it, he started to fill a pipe.

"That sphere," he began, pointing at the chair with my jacket and the darkly shining object beneath it, "came to Horace Wells in 1892."

"Did he pry it out of the pillar?"

"What? Oh, no, the one under the mosque is still there, as far as I know. There is more than one. The Suda says five; we have located three. This one he traded a revolver for from a fugitive in Bombay, where his father was stationed. He'd noticed the untouchable had carried it wrapped in a cloth and wore gloves; when Horace touched it with his bare fingers, he learned why. He spent the following year carrying it around India, until a savant back in Bombay told him what it was."

He lit his pipe. It stank in a very dignifying way.

"That is the Wells' version. As my own grandfather used to tell it, the fugitive told him about the Eye; then Wells wandered for a year searching for it, and on his return to Bombay he met the savant. In both versions this happened on December the twenty-first. That is when he saw the first Twenty."

"Twenty what?"

"Twenty people. Twenty visions. Twenty dreams, as you put it, that obsessed him forever. You can read his notes on them, if you wish; they're in the archive. The Wells have kept notes on every Twenty since 1892."

"What twenty?" I reversed. "What are you talking about?"

"The Eye's picks," he answered patiently, and pointed to the bibliography at my feet. "The Orb of Allah's memories while it takes its yearly minute's rest. During the year, the Eye shows nothing more than flashes and shadows. Touching it causes nothing but a violent jolt, and then that." (*Pointing at Niamh.*) "Through an insulator, one might perceive an entangled string of images and sounds and smells at unimaginable speed; then, seconds later, that happens too." (*He pointed at Niamh again.*) "But every year, at the dawn of the shortest day, the Eye stops its frenzied activity for a minute, and at this time, you can touch it. Then it chooses twenty events in the previous year; twenty milestones along the road—at least according to its enigmatic opinion—starring twenty people, anywhere in the world. A musician in Ibiza. A gun seller in Liberia. A bank robber in Mexico. A genocide victim in Rwanda. Most are remarkable, in a way. Many seem trivial enough. Some are delicious to the senses. Others are so atrocious, they overshadow the rest. The Eye seems to forget them all soon enough, back to its insect-speed watching. But the man who sees what the Twenty saw, feels what the Twenty felt, won't forget so easily."

"Wait, wait, wait, wait a minute," I cut in. "Are you . . . You're telling me that everything the ball shows actually happened?"

"Somewhere in the world, sometime in 1994."

"I saw . . . a person falling from, like, fifty thousand meters, plunge onto a tropical island, and stand up and walk, just like that. I saw a skeleton playing poker!"

Caleb just nodded and smoked, at peace.

"For centuries," he began, "sources on the Eye perplexedly described its visions as 'creatures' or 'monsters.' Of course, if the Eye chose an Eskimo, a Cherokee, or an Aborigine, to Muslim pilgrims in the temple of Amr it must have looked like footage from another world. Now the world is almost completely mapped—or so does the layman think. So for every Twenty, even within the realm of the remarkable, there are only three or four that strike us as alien."

"Mr. Ford," I insisted. "A. Skeleton. Playing. Poker."

"The best thing about the Eye is that it's not just an extraordinary thing. It's a window to extraordinary things."

I guess he expected my reason to simply collapse under the weight of the many arguments it would pull out against that.

"So that's it," I said. "A crystal ball shows it, so it must be true."

"It worked for your cousin," he retorted triumphantly. "Do you know why we're here? Because Horace Wells managed to locate a haunted house he saw in the Eye. The Ngara girl was number ten in 1896."

With that he sat down again, before adding, "Tens are all ghosts, by the way. That boy in Africa this year? The one who looks over his shoulder? That was a ghost he felt."

I said nothing. And he just rocked in his chair and smoked like a happy little hobbit.

"A remarkable deed, truth be told," he rambled now, in the way one would expect from a much older wise man. "Finding a ten. Elpenors are early quitters."

I didn't understand a word either.

"So it's true then," I said to steer the conversation back to minimum absurdity. "The Wells bought this house because it was haunted."

"Among other reasons. By 1900 Horace Wells knew he would devote his life to the Eye, to try to solve the mystery of the Twenty. He needed a quiet place, a stronghold to keep the Eye safe, and means to finance his research. So he moved to America, land of quick fortunes."

"And he chose the house with a ghost in it."

"Wouldn't you have done the same?"

"Yes," I replied swiftly.

"And why?" he inquired, his pipe accusing me like a state attorney.

"Because meeting the Ngara girl is the most interesting thing that's ever happened to me."

"Now you talk like a Wells," he said, lounging in his seat. "You understand why the Eye obsessed Horace, why it obsesses us. It is one of the few things in the world that trespasses the boundaries of our comprehension, that blatantly escapes mankind's consensus of what is real, of what is possible. Not an invisible puff of ectoplasm or a questionable abstract phenomenon: a real, palpable object that defies logic. It is an intruder from myths. A relic of the magical past that made its way to our time.

"Horace Wells had no challenges in life before. The son of a British officer, highly educated, distantly religious. His path was laid; his life was to be utterly mundane; he expected no surprises. And then India gave him one. A godly object. *The eye of a god,* some say—like that wouldn't make it a god in itself! It turned Wells' reality upside down. It gave him glimpses of extraordinary places, impossible people, transcendent things!"

"And he naturally longed for more than glimpses."

"Who wouldn't? The Eye does not just see—by the end of the year, it judges. For the first time, you hear an entity above man, a god, *speaking*. How can you ignore it? Anyone would do what old Wells did: spend his life trying to find those whom the Eye picked, to participate in their greatness, perhaps even to merit the Eye's attention. For the first time, somebody outside some old dubious sacred book is actually saying what is expected from man."

"Which is just as soon to solve Rubik's cubes or indulge in homosexual love as to rob, kill, or maim," I pointed out.

"The Eye knows no morality," he probably quoted. "It is unlike all religions. It is not a sacred object turned into a tool by priests who make up rules and ethics to keep the people on a leash. It is just the sacred object, period. It is a god . . . and we followers trying to figure out what it means."

We paused.

"The way you put it, it's beginning to sound less like a secret society and more like a cult."

"It might be," he admitted. "The Eye of Amr, the one described by Raynal, is in a temple. We have reason to believe that all the existing Eyes are related to that one; they were scattered at some moment in history. They must have been worshipped at some point. Today, they are little more than a legend, and not even a popular one. Some thousands in the world must have read about it, a few hundred have seen it . . . and as far as I know, only twenty people have been keeping track of its yearly verdicts for the last century."

"That's when Horace Wells founded the Society."

"Not *founded*, really. The Eye Society came up by itself. I think in the beginning Horace just wanted to share the revelation. The treasure was too big for one man. So every winter solstice there was somebody new attending the showdown—that is, the recall, the moment of the year when the Eye speaks. My grandfather was among the very first. Spears and Dagenais too; our families sailed together from England. But it wasn't a society at the time; the Eye was just the excuse for a Christmas gathering. Of course, they saw the magic convenience of expanding the group to twenty people. It was a good number: a *chosen* number. They reached it in 1908."

"And I guess at that moment it just seemed logical to distribute tasks: twenty visions for twenty members."

"Again, at the time, they probably didn't call them tasks. But yes, before 1910 the assignments had begun. Each member was given a vision to work with; their goal was to put it in context, find out where in the world, who in the world. Just as Horace Wells did in finding Axton House."

"Was there a prize?"

"No. I guess the prospect of meeting a chosen one, talking to him or her, was appealing enough. Not that he or she would have much to say; they are unaware of their cosmic relevance. Today, though, we've forgotten about meeting them; if you just have a name by the end of the year, it's a victory."

"Sounds like quite a challenge."

"And an addiction. It becomes a full-time activity. One can hardly cut down on it; besides, you'll dream with it anyway. As soon as he could, Wells quit his job in railway engineering, sold his stocks while they were high, which incidentally spared him the Depression, invested in land here, and became one of those jobless characters from Jane Austen's novels whose only work is writing letters. Other members did the same. That's why the Society was not founded; it happened. The Eye took over their lives, so why not at least formalize it? Some of them were British, after all."

"So the Society is just . . . an attempt to rationalize an obsession."

"And our obsession is to rationalize the Eye. In the Society we join forces to solve our common problem: What is this object, what is it telling us? The Society is like group therapy. We share our admiration and revulsion for the Eye. We play it down."

"Really?" I inserted. "Because from here it looks like with your codes and your secrecy you might be giving yourselves some importance."

"It is quite the contrary," he opposed docilely. "The secrecy is necessary, of course; an extraordinary object remains so only as long as it's not divulged. The rest is just us being melodramatic. Having fun in a British way, with social meetings and club rules. For the founders, it made the obsession easier to manage. They turned it into a game."

"A bourgeois pastime," I quoted.

"Certainly. Not everyone can afford a game consuming so much time. Or resources. Or health."

Niamh was stirring in her sleep, her head on my lap, my fingertips back on the fuzz behind her ears. Help lay by her side, his head down, eyes fixed on Niamh's face.

Caleb lit a new pipe. His tone had dropped an octave or so.

"You know how some young people seem aged or worn-out?" he asked bitterly. "I think it runs in our group."

It was funny that he mentioned it, for I had determined, at some not-that-interesting point of the explanations, that Caleb Ford looked like an old man of forty-two. He blamed the weariness. I'd say his clothes helped.

"Ironically, though," he went on, "the fatigue makes us all the more eager to return here every year—if not for the Eye, for the comfort of being among peers. Then, having caroused with old friends, repeated the old rites, released our worries, and dined copiously, consulting the Eye just seems the natural thing to do."

"Does it?" I was recalling the Prometheus letter. He said he was looking forward to seeing Ambrose again, but wasn't particularly keen about the reunion.

"The Eye only speaks for about a minute a year. Chances are too rare to forfeit. No one in my lifetime has declined an invitation to a meeting," he said with a smirk.

"Not verbally, at least," I slapped back, smirkless.

His eyes returned to *The Sacred Fount.* Mine to Niamh.

"What happens when someone deserts?" I asked, carefully picking the word.

"We have a list of runner-ups, so to speak: people whom members recommend, based on personal trust and availability. In Wells' case or mine, membership comes in families. But that is infrequent now. Most of us don't have families anymore. The game takes too much time."

This air of surrender dumped some extra years on him too. And the pipe, and the rocking chair.

"How do you allow it to?" I wondered.

"Oh, it is immensely gratifying when you win. Believe me. I just have the blues now because I recently learned that my best friend defenestrated himself. But to have a vision, to savor it, to dissect it, to extract a clue from it, to place it in space and time; then to travel to a country, a region, and finally to pinpoint the right person . . . it pays. To look at them and marvel at their uniqueness, which goes unnoticed by everyone around them, even themselves . . . It compensates for the nightmares, for everything. It's like a little victory over the Eye. It spotted someone in the world; it pointed me at a man in six billion." He in turn pointed at his briefcase. "And I found him. His name was Julien Mugiraneza."

"The torture victim," I said, on recalling the driver's license I had failed to identify. "He was a Tutsi. But you say he's dead now."

"Doesn't matter. I found a special person. I won."

"Just like . . . numbers 4, 7, and 15?"

"Yes. Four wins this year."

He fell silent then. After a while he added, wincing at the irony, "It would have been a good year after all."

"Have you ever found all twenty?"

"In our dreams," he said, chortling sadly. "Six is the standing record. And this is easier than ever now. They didn't have any crystal balls before."

"Oh," I said, spotting the start of a new subchapter. "So the others are just crystal balls."

"Sure, nothing mystic about those. They are man-made recording devices containing every year's showdown since 1973—something our fathers would have killed for. It all started when the Eye took Ambrose and Curtis to the Eastern bloc. Let me tell you, traveling there wasn't easy back then; you really needed a good reason. Anyway, in East Berlin they met a group of neuroscientists—"

"Dänemarr!"

"Very good," he acknowledged, positively impressed. "Dr. Dänemarr was searching for a medium to transmit electric signals that trigger specific ideas in the brain, sensations without stimuli, like what you see, hear, smell in dreams. Ambrose and Curtis listened to him and thought

272 | EDGAR CANTERO

that the Eye fit that description. Of course, secrecy forbade talking about it . . . But they reasoned it was in the Society's best interest to make an exception. They exchanged letters with Dänemarr, and referred him to some bibliography, like the one you just read. Dänemarr visited Ambrose in 'seventy-two; Ambrose visited him back in 'seventy-three and Dänemarr showed him a prototype. A crystal ball. With his resources he never got much further; he can't record but a minute's worth of oneiric activity, in a chaotic way at best. However, it happens to suit our needs like a charm. Perhaps because the Eye's electric signal is clearer than that of the human stream of thought, the visions are recorded to the smallest detail. So Ambrose exalted his work and offered to buy more crystal balls."

"So Ambrose sponsored Dänemarr's research."

"In a way, yes. His prototypes haven't evolved much, but they haven't gotten any worse either. They have been of invaluable help. Before 'seventy-three, we could only replay the visions in dreams, but dreams, as you'll know, favor only the most shocking visions in every Twenty."

"Too much of the pitchfork murderer and too little of the tomboy schoolgirl on the roof," I whispered darkly.

"We used to set clocks back then to wake us every sixty to ninety minutes, the usual time between REM phases, so as to retrieve the subtler episodes as we dreamed them. That's all we had: dreams and notes. The first minutes after the showdown were crucial. Have you ever read a crystal ball?"

It took me a while to understand that he meant just touching one. I remembered the one we first found in the secret room, how I neared a fingertip to it and the images jumped on me.

"That was a recording," he said, pointing at my thoughts. "Reading the Eye is more intense. Imagine pulling yourself out of that, grabbing paper and pen, and starting to take notes before it fades away. We still do that, but having a backup is a great comfort. Then we compare notes—if one doesn't obtain twenty, he must have blinked through one or had two muddled up. Then we discuss them while they are still fresh: Did anyone recognize a clear landmark, a language, or even a face? A public person seldom makes it onto the list; it happens with fifteens every now and then. And finally, once the Twenty are set, there's the draw."

"You draw the visions?"

"No, we draw lots. To assign the roles."

"Roles," I chorused. I was eager to get to that. "You mean the host, the secretary, and all that?"

"No, those are more like positions. I am the secretary, either for life or until I resign. Roles change every year."

"Leonidas, Hector, Archimedes, and such," I guessed again.

"Right. The role you land with decides which vision you work on: Leonidas takes the first, Hector takes the second, and so on. The names are a relatively modern invention. One of Ambrose's first, in fact—he was the one with the classical education."

"I know Ambrose was Leonidas; which one are you?"

"The twelfth. Phoenix," he replied, as if I were supposed to have inferred that. I guess I could have. Just two days ago I had given him up for dead in Africa. Now he was here in my music room, lighting his pipe again, which tended to go out during the longest monologues.

Later the true meaning struck me: Phoenix. *I'm in the dark for a million years hearing them giggling at my eyeball. Then I wake up and kill them.*

"Exactly," Caleb said. I wasn't aware of having thought that aloud. "Number twelves are consistently some of the worst. That's why we draw lots—nobody would ever choose to be the Phoenix. Although we all share and dream with all of the Twenty, it feels quite different to focus your efforts on the schoolgirl or the tortured man."

"Wait wait wait wait again," I begged, my mind pushing the fast-forward button through the escape from the torture chamber and the fuel tank–exploding scenes. "You mean, like . . . all number twelves are the same?"

"Pass me that book," Caleb said, with a sigh that seemed to indicate he was finally taking pity on my puzzlement. "The one with the metal straps."

It was one of the books in Latin I had pretended to read. I remembered having noticed it before in the library, on a shelf with other old, megalithic volumes. The leather binding was furnished with straps; the pages were worn thin as onionskin, and similarly colored. The type was small and thick, with hook-shaped lowercase *s*'s.

"The Wells were the ones to live with the Eye, so they studied it closely. Even before the Society had reached twenty members, Horace Wells had made out some patterns. Such as, 'The tenth vision is always someone who can't be seen': the Ngara girl in 1896. Number twelves are people on the verge of death who suddenly escape: the Tutsi, last year. Number thirteens are living people who can see ghosts.'"

"The couple in the poppy field," I said. "She was a ghost."

"You noticed. Eventually, Horace discovered the Eye's criteria."

He turned the book toward me now, open at a spread with print on the left page and an engraving on the right. The engraving showed a naked man holding a spear. The style reminded me of the pictures in the study upstairs.

"Each year's Twenty match the twenty signs of a millennia-old canon mentioned by Byzantine and Persian sources as a sort of zodiac, and possibly descended from Indian Brahmanism, where it represented the stages in the path of spiritual evolution. First, the Warrior."

I knock down the two policemen in under five seconds.

"The Watcher."

I pick up the grenade. The pin's off.

"The Sage."

I play the piano, one key at a time, and write ideograms.

"The Genius."

I stand at the altar between the liquid crowd and the UV lights.

"The Wizard."

I'm reading under the clopping kitchenware. The yuppie drops his chopsticks.

"The Nobleman."

The books falls out of my hand. A fountain sings outside the Moorish windows.

"The Mother."

Flies buzzing dumbly across the line between my shotgun and the countermen.

"The Twins."

Fling the stone through the teeth of the hideous man holding me.

"The Lover."

I smell her hair, the snow on my soles melting deep inside the bed.

"Soul."

The African boy peers over his shoulder, sees through me; his skin feels me.

"Bones."

The ocean expels me and my surfboard into a tempest of chrome clouds.

"The Phoenix."

I shoot at the fuel tank; the ball of fire roasts them alive.

"The Oracle."

The poppy flower disassembles at a kiss of her pellucid skin.

"The Fortune."

I lay a thirteen-letter Greek word across the Scrabble board.

"The King."

I shake his black hand; something explodes among the ramshackle rooftops.

"The Monster."

I fork him to the ground, see his organs collapse.

"The Wolf."

Pull the tubes; a Styx of blood trickles down my skin.

"The Crab."

I'm holding two fives. Poker face.

"The Juggernaut."

I crash-land on the tropical island. The cement cracks.

"And the God."

I solve the Rubik's cube. She smiles at me.

Caleb closed the book.

I felt an inexplicable joy.

"Any more questions?" he cued.

My mind was too crowded. I felt as if I were lucid-dreaming while being awake. I felt I was hallucinating. I felt I was too many.

I had to wait for them to fade away.

"Was the skeleton *Bones?*"

"No, Bones is number eleven; it was the surfer. The skeleton was the Crab. Don't ask why."

"Why?"

"Look, we only understand so much, okay? It's just a canon; the number and the general order fit, but some fits are obvious; some aren't. The King is always someone with power; Sages are scientists; Geniuses are artists. The Mother's a mother, seldom a father; the Twins are twins, sometimes just siblings. Souls are invisible. Wolves are often people just waking up. Crabs are . . . probably nonhuman. And Juggernauts and Gods . . . we never made any sense out of them, really."

Much to Help's delight, Niamh stretched her limbs like a tiny cute mountain and forced herself to wake up. She wrote on her notepad, her hand slanting as though the letters were falling asleep or tumbling like dominoes, *Did I miss much?*

I showed her the voice recorder. She nived.

Since she had been quiet enough for the last hours, I advised her to go to bed. On her exit, she wrote a farewell line for Caleb. He stood up and bowed.

"You are very kind, miss," he said. "I too am pleased to be back. Please go to bed; you will feel much better in a couple hours."

Help escorted her upstairs.

Caleb and I remained in the music room. Although our conversation had taken the best of the day, according to the grandfather clock, I felt far from satisfied. Caleb hadn't sat down again; he was standing by one of the French windows, watching it, but not through it.

He turned around and leaned his hand on a nearby chair. Not for support, more like comforting the chair itself.

"I should contact Curtis Knox immediately."

I realized then I've been retaining a message from Ambrose to Knox for weeks. I'll have to fix that soon. And come up with an explanation.

"Knox is convinced you're dead," I said in the meantime.

"I'll be bringing him news from the underworld then," he replied, his expression vicepresidentially empty. "A message from Ambrose. We have much to discuss."

"Really? What is to be discussed? Knox seemed determined to carry on. Do you think different?"

He turned to me. "Jesus, Ambrose is dead!"

The remark, albeit obvious, deserved a silence. I stayed on the sofa, unfazed.

"Please excuse me if I sound too bold," I began, "but this must have happened a few times before. How many suicides during your membership alone?"

He looked down shyly. "Two confirmed." Then, resolute: "But this is different. Ambrose wants us to stop."

"Yeah, like the others didn't care."

"Now you're being bold," he reprimanded me.

"Stay with me; I can be bolder. Ambrose didn't commit suicide. His letters say so. This was an accident. A recording sphere in the secret room rolled off a shelf and leaned on a gas pipe. Full spheres have some electric charge, about four to five volts; we measured it. The charge spread through the pipe to the bedroom above and onto the brass bed. The canopy acts like a sort of antenna, radiating on the sleeper. He wasn't dreaming like the rest of you: He was being subliminally fed the recordings over and over. He just thought his nightmares were getting more vivid this year, and felt the end coming because he was the age of his father when he took the leap, but it was overexposure that killed him."

Weak as it sounded for a consolation, that idea seemed to put down roots in Caleb's mind. He noticed too; he tried to rebel against it.

"Putting an end to the Society with his own life was not spur-of-the-moment. He planned it all his life. He chose bachelorhood. He chose childlessness. He meant to cut the line."

"That was his mind in February, when he wrote those letters," I fought back. "But he died in September. That's seven months to change his mind."

"How do you know he did?"

"What the hell am I doing here?!" I proclaimed. "If he wanted to cut the line, why did he come for me? Why would he suddenly start looking for a next of kin in another continent? Why would he hand me down everything, after having given you the keys? He wanted this. He wanted us to have this argument!"

With this I ended my exposition.

Caleb took a chair, this time to sit on it. I took his place by the window, and said nothing.

About two minutes later, I heard him fishing a paper from the mess of five-by-five grids and playing cards littering the table. He had retrieved the ledger page with the code names.

"This needs updating," he said, as he pulled a pen out of his waistcoat pocket.

I spied over his shoulder as he filled out some squares in his fin-de-siècle handwriting.

"Prometheus . . . I mean Silas Long sent a letter saying he gave up," I tipped him. "And also Tyche, Ken Matsuo. And a guy called Kingston; he sent a postcard this week."

"Kingston . . ." he reflected. "He was Coroebus, I think—he was after the surfer. Check."

"Also, some guy named Vasquez sent pictures of the redheaded twins. He found them in Ontario."

"Vasquez found his Twins? Good year indeed."

The document now looks like this:

1994 Quest Status Report—December

1	Leonidas		*Deceased*	
2	Hector		*On field*	
3	Archimedes			
4	Sophocles		*FOUND*	*Ibiza, Spain*
5	Zosimos		*On field*	
6	Socrates	*(Gone)*		
7	Cybele		*FOUND*	*Sonora, Mexico*
8	Dioskuri		*FOUND*	*Ontario, Canada*
9	Anchises			
10	Elpenor		*Quit*	
11	Coroebus		*Quit*	
12	Phoenix	*(Gone)*	*FOUND*	*Kamembe, Rwanda*

13	Amphiaraus		
14	Tyche	*Quit*	
15	Alexandros	*FOUND*	*Monrovia, Liberia*
16	Asterion	*On field*	
17	Chronos		
18	Prometheus	*(???)*	*Quit*
19	Heracles	*(Betty)*	*Quit*
20	Zeus		*Quit*

"'On field' means the researcher is traveling to the probable location," Caleb explained. "'Quit' means he has given up. You can always do that if you're completely lost or just exhausted. Many people just quit around this time of year. It's like taking a holiday. Busying yourself with other things is supposed to make nights easier."

"'Elpenors are early quitters,'" I quoted.

"That's Society jargon," he acknowledged. "The Soul is always a very brief vision—you can hardly scrape anything from it—so whoever lands with it ends up taking an early vacation. This year it was in West Africa, I think."

Shirtless man peers over his shoulder. He feels me.

"What does 'gone' mean?" I asked, tapping on the sixth line.

"That the subject is probably dead. Quite often, your final act is the one by which the Eye nominates you."

The book falls out of my hand. A fountain sings outside the Moorish window.

I pointed at the triple question mark on the Prometheus row. "Prometheus is number 18." *I'm holding two fives. Poker face.* "The skeleton, right?"

"Right. Hard to tell, isn't it?"

I had to smile at the tired resignation in his words.

"But . . . how do you accept that?"

"I have no reason not to. I just found a Phoenix. I entered the cottage and everything—what is left of it, at least. It was not a god's dream; it happened. The Eye sees everything happening on Earth. Actually, farther: An astronaut on the moon became the Nobleman in 1969; we never could tell whether it was Armstrong or Aldrin. We know who JFK's assassin was: the Eye made him King in 1963. There are secret streams of events you and I ignore running underground, a parallel history with its own battles and villains. And heroes: Recently, a kid prevented a terrorist bomb from going off in a crowded station in London; no one noticed; probably saved hundreds of lives: Watcher, 1991. So, the Eye says somewhere, right now, some people are playing poker with a skeleton. Yes, I accept that."

I looked back at the ledger page.

"'Betty'?" I pointed.

"Oh, yes, Betty. She's one of the Eye's favorites. Also one of the most traumatic almost every year. 'Heracles always quit,'" he epigrammed. "The Juggernaut's visions are too far-fetched to put in context. Especially Betty's. Her deeds, her life, her . . . universe is so otherworldly, you just don't know where to begin."

I plummet down to Earth. The highest altitude a pair of Puma training shoes ever reached. I crash-land on the rooftop.

"How can you be sure it's a woman? I can't picture her face."

"We have all seen her already. Besides, we know her shoes."

"How come I see that vision in the first person, and I do so when they pull my eyeball out, but then, in the Monster vision, I feel I am the victim, not the killer? And in the Twins, I can see both. It's like the camera changes."

"You must not think in television terms; it's . . . Well, it's not a camera. You can see everything, really; with practice, you assume some control to focus on the details you want. I think by default the brain just assumes the role it relates to. And most people witnessing a murder empathize with the victim, not the killer. We have seen Betty's face other years; I guess this year there were no witnesses of her action but herself."

"Why did you name her Betty?"

"The senior members say it's her name. As legend goes, one year, in a vision, somebody said, 'Betty,' and she turned. She is a peculiar case, though. Curtis, our historian, must have more accurate data, but I don't think we have seen more than two or three people who make it into the Twenty more than once in a lifetime. Whereas Betty . . . If I am not mistaken, she has been the Juggernaut sixty-six times since 1900."

"That makes her, like, a hundred years old," I objected.

He looked at me again, eyebrows arching naively.

"As I told you: realities you're totally unaware of."

The clock struck three. Caleb put down his pen and stood up.

"Whether we hold this year's meeting or not," he said, "Curtis Knox must be contacted immediately."

"By all means."

"And if we were to hold it, invitations ought to have been in the mail a week ago."

"You'd better get to work, then."

"And the exact time of the solstice must be found out to calculate the time of the showdown."

"Go ahead."

"And logistic preparations must be made."

"Niamh and I will take care of everything."

"And this doesn't mean the game is not over," he pointed out, inching a little closer. "Once they are all informed, the Society shall decide."

"If the game's over, I keep the Eye," I said. "No reason for you to have it."

He deliberated for 2.83 seconds.

"Deal."

And we shook hands.

BEDROOM SAT DEC-9-1995 23:59:00

NIAMH is sitting on the bed, all alone, her voice recorder playing on her lap, HELP curled up at her feet.

CALEB (REC):   And this doesn't mean the game is not over. Once they are all informed, the Society shall decide.

A. (REC):   If the game is over, I keep the Eye. No reason for you to have it.

[2.83 seconds blank.]

CALEB (REC):   Deal.

[Niamh victoriously pulls the whistle cord on an imaginary steam locomotive.]

PART III

ONE WEEK LATER

12/22/1995 14:02

A bald GIRL sits alone, facing the door. She wears a bulky anorak over an undershirt and heavy-duty boots. Her legs are naked. A vending-machine sandwich is neglected on the table before her.

> *[Door opens; enter Deputy TED Miller in uniform and Detective MORGAN Summers in plain clothes, reading from a report.]*

MORGAN:　　—roadblocks are on, but not nearly quick enough.

TED:　　Hey, we did what we could. The Ponopah sheriff was way out of his league. *[Leans on the table, back turned to the girl.]* Maybe we should give the troopers a chance; I don't feel like pulling out a statement from Miss Chemotherapy here.

MORGAN:　　Shut up.

TED:　　I'm serious. Did you know the house was rigged up with cameras? Well, she says she forgot to change the tape this morning.

MORGAN:　　There's no need to be rude.

TED:　　It's okay; she can't read me from there. She's deaf-dumb.

[The girl springs onto the chair and pitches the sandwich at Ted. Most of the bread bounces off, but lettuce and ham stick to the back of his head thanks to the adherent power of industrial mayo. He hardly flinches, his mistake sinking in as tomato sinks into his shirt.]

MORGAN:	*[Reading, quietly.]* Actually, she's just dumb—and I think they prefer the term "mute."
TED:	*[Sighs for patience.]* Yeah, well.
MORGAN:	Maybe I should take care of her.
TED:	Be my guest.

[Ted leaves the room, not even glancing back. Door closes behind him.]

[The girl sits down again. The detective takes a chair and relocates it to the suspect's left. He sits down, lays down the report and another pile of papers he was carrying.]

MORGAN:	Okay, Niyam … Is that how you pronounce it?
NIAMH:	*[Not looking, shakes her head, mouths something.]*
MORGAN:	Come again?
NIAMH:	*[Now looking up, mouths her name.]*
MORGAN:	"Niff." "Neeve!" I see. Okay. *[Reading the report.]* Well, Neve, I understand you waived your two phone calls … *[He mentally ascertains the absurdity of what he just said, then resumes:]* So, we're supposed to appoint a lawyer for you, but our juvenile was off today; he's on his way now. And we don't have a sign interpreter either, but … we really need a statement now.

[He waits for an answer. She just stares at the table.]

I have a daughter your age. *[Pause.]* She doesn't talk to me either.

[He leans back, then pushes the bulk he was carrying toward her—it turns out to be a whole pack of blank copy paper, which he tops with a pen.]

So, Neve, I think you have a considerable amount of prose to write. Do you think you could start ahead, and let your attorney check later?

NIAMH: *[She snorts: first sound she utters. Then signs assent and takes the pen.]*

MORGAN: Good. Thank you.

[She starts writing. At first, the detective seems to inspect her hand for a minute. Then he stands up, choosing to be useful.]

I'll get you another sandwich. And some pants.

[Morgan exits the room. She keeps writing.]

CALEB K. FORD,

Secretary of the Eye Society, acting in the Name of

AMBROSE G. WELLS, *Host*

requests your attendance to our Yearly Reunion & Recall,
which will take place at

12:44 A.M. on December 22nd 1995 (EST)

in Axton House, Point Bless, Virginia

You are invited to join us from 5 P.M. on the eve.

Please confirm.

Axton House
Axton Rd., 1.
Point Bless, VA 26929

753 965 4000
theeyesociety@lycos.com

VIDEO RECORDING

KITCHEN THU DEC-21-1995 17:00:00

The red-clothed counter is populated by a colorful banquet of garnished dishes like stars parading on a red carpet. A hefty cookbook is open between the casserole and the tuna-filled eggs. The oven is on. On the stove, pasta is boiling along with another two steaming pots. NIAMH is shaping meatballs. Her hair is completely buzz-cut, an ashen shade on her skull.

At her feet, tail wagging at more than ninety beats per minute, HELP waits for anything edible to fall on the floor.

> *[Niamh taunts him with a meatball, gives two short whistles. Help stands on his hind legs, yearning for the bite.]*

> *[DOORBELL.]*

> *[Help forgets about the appetizer, barking himself silly. Niamh tries to make him sit, to no effect.]*

A.'S DIARY

After Edward Cutler came an Asian man—Ken Matsuo. He is a second-generation member and the second-youngest at thirty-eight. He also looked the least Victorian so far. Whereas suits seem to pull Caleb and Cutler back in time, Matsuo's looked fashionable and slick, the kind that belongs in post-Oscar parties. I regretted having nothing better than jeans for the big evening.

"You're only the second to arrive; what's wrong with you?" Caleb greeted him while they hugged. Apparently, winners are usually the first to come in, eager to share their success.

"And you must be the new Mr. Wells," Matsuo said, bowing courteously before offering his hand. His smile reconciled a mournful reminder for the late host and an optimistic view on the new one. I liked him. "I had an easy and yet difficult task this year," he explained. "I was—"

"Tyche, I know. We got your fax. You chased the Greek Scrabble player. Not much to begin with."

"Even small countries look enormous when your only clue is a kitchen."

Cutler rejoined us and I guided them to the dining room. Niamh and I wanted to make sure that our preparations lived up to my predecessor's. They weren't disappointed. The table looked splendid with the low lights and the dusk behind the windows, and that peculiar blue glow behind the fourth window, which is blocked by the swimming pool.

"This is Help," I announced on the entry of the barking hurricane, inviting the guests to let him sniff their pants and get acquainted. "You must excuse him; he gets excited in the presence of other vertebrates. And this is my partner, Niamh Connell."

If they were baffled by her new hairstyle (or lack thereof), which she chose to adopt only yesterday, they hid it pretty well. Cutler was caught a little off guard, I think: He seemed to freeze for a second, a hand stretched out, staring at her as though he'd just seen the last thing he expected to meet here tonight. Which perhaps she was: a minor, a woman, and a cook, all in one person. But then, while shaking her hand, he was genuinely nice. He'd struck me as the kind of uptight gentleman who would frown disapprovingly at hippies in San Francisco (where he comes from), but he proved to be no challenge to Niamh's natural charm. He looked well over sixty, short but strong and good-humored. Most likely because he had won.

"Am I miscounting, or are there twenty-one seats?" noticed Matsuo.

"You're not miscounting," I answered. "This year we don't ditch the cook. She knows everything anyway."

Niamh skipped to a new page on her notepad:

Don't worry. I won't speak.

The doorbell rang again, and Help had a new seizure. Caleb went to open the door and ushered in Curtis Knox—a tense moment I was willing to avoid.

"Well, I think you two know each other already," Caleb said when we met in the foyer.

"Good evening," I said, shaking his hand. "Did you get that thing in the mail you were expecting?"

"I get lots of interesting things in the mail these days, yes," he acknowledged. "Thanks for asking."

Niamh greeted him too, then excused herself, gesturing that she had to put something in the oven, or give someone a ride in a rickshaw. Caleb asked Knox about Philip Beauregard, who still had not confirmed; it was Caleb's first concern at the moment.

"I'm afraid I don't have any news," Knox said. "I hadn't contacted anyone until two weeks ago; I had been waiting for a signal from Ambrose. And then, just as I reached out to Kingston, Stillwall, and Black to expose the problem, you returned."

"It has been a peculiar year," Caleb acknowledged. The euphemistic choice of the word didn't make up for his tone. "And yet a good one," he explained to us all. "Five founds this year."

There were approving *oh*s and nods from the others, except Knox, who spotted the perfect moment to bring forth the folder he was carrying.

"Six. Throw in a Nobleman too."

The ovation grew louder. We moved on to the music room, where Knox spread the contents of the folder over the piano. Among other things, there was a picture of a gravestone with a crescent moon, one of a Moorish house with arched windows, some Arabic newspapers, and a book.

"His name was Yusuf el-Tahtawi, a math teacher in Alexandria, Egypt. He died in his house at the age of sixty-nine upon reading the last verse in a compilation of poetry of Al-Andalus. His edition was different, but I think it's this one."

I couldn't make out a single character.

"Six!" exclaimed Matsuo. "We matched the standing record!"

"How rare is a Nobleman?" asked Cutler.

"I think Beauregard found one, like, ten years ago."

"How come you didn't report until now?" I asked Knox.

"Well, I knew Ambrose wasn't here, so why bother?"

"The finding is quite recent, then," put in Matsuo.

"Yes, I only was on field last month. I'd found his obituary on the Internet."

I excused myself while the others praised the new era of information.

I locked myself inside Ambrose's office, picked up the phone and Ambrose's red notebook, and dialed a number in Lawrenceville. I was hoping Knox had servants too.

"Hello?"

"Hello. Could I speak to Curtis, please?"

"I am sorry, Mr. Knox is away for a long weekend. Can I take a message?"

"Oh, I suppose he's still in Egypt."

"No, sir, he returned from Egypt two weeks ago. To whom do I have the pleasure of speaking, sir?"

"Oh, really? How long has he been away then?"

"Exactly a month, sir. From November the sixth to December the fifth."

"I see. Okay. Thank you. Please tell him I called."

"Sir, I didn't catch your—"

I hung up.

And probably swore in mumbles.

*

KITCHEN THU DEC-21-1995 17:43:28

NIAMH is stirring the contents of a pot on the stove.

> [A. wanders in, gazing at the food; he leans on the sink, pensive.
> She offers a spoonful of chowder to him.]

> [A ignores the invitation.]

A.: Be nice to Knox. He's not the bad guy.

NIAMH: *[Astonished; her nive has faded away. She shakes her head in disagreement.]*

A.: Knox went to Egypt the day after his first visit, November the sixth, and returned one month later. The break-in here was on November the seventh. He didn't do it.

NIAMH: *[Tosses the wooden spoon in the pot, goes for her notepad.]*

A.: I know, we said he could have hired someone, but no. Would you hire a housebreaker to steal something for you the same day you go on a trip? It's stupid. You'd wait until you come back; it's safer here, in our house, than in the hands of a rental burglar.

NIAMH: *[Frozen, hasn't had time to write a single line.]*

A.: We need another suspect. *[Beat.]* It's okay; they keep coming; we'll soon have a roomful of them.

NIAMH: *[Starts writing again, shows notepad.]*

*

—Maybe I'm overly suspicious, but Help going MAD.

—Yeah, I noticed. We should get him a room too. Put him away in the office, just in case one of them tries the safe again.

AUDIO RECORDING

[In the background: clink of glasses and silver and several conversations by the far end of the table.]

CUTLER: —nyway, but … I thought that it's the audience that makes it the best song in the world. The record is a different experience; it's evocative. But when I went to the club and saw her in person, and saw those people dancing to her beat, like …

well, it was ecstasy. Like a voodoo ritual. There I saw it. She's
a genius not because of the merit of her composition, but
because of the way she reaches into people's souls, into their
primitive core.

MATSUO: I am still coping with the idea of you visiting a club in Ibiza,
            Cutler.

A.:   Me too. If I get over that image, the Eye will hold no surprises
            for me.

[Plural chortle.]

KNOX: But Edward, you know the audience has nothing to do with it.
            Remember the Genius in New Zealand.

FORD: [Aside.] A few years ago the Genius was a teenager writing a
            poem in her diary; we never found it or her.

KNOX: She was alone in her room and probably no one has ever read
            that poem to this day. What made it the best work of art of
            that year? It can't be the public's reaction. It must be the
            poem itself. Its beauty, its technical perfection. Same goes for
            the deejay.

STILLWALL: [New voice: old male, Southern accent.] Oh, please. Are you seri-
            ously implying that an electronic beat with stolen notes from
            here and there can make a perfect musical composition?

MATSUO: What's wrong with that notion?

STILLWALL: What's wrong? Would you compare Mozart to a note borrower?

MATSUO: Yes! Please, times they are a-changing!

FORD: [Whisper.] Here we go.

MATSUO: Do you know what it takes to compose that? The only differ-
            ence is that a classical composer tells the orchestra what to
            do, whereas she has to use prerecorded instruments. They call
            their workplaces "labs"!

STILLWALL: Ken, Ken, please, you're thirty-eight. Stop playing the young
            rebel of the table.

MATSUO: And you're only sixty-nine; stop acting like you met Mozart!
            Let me tell you one thing about Mozart: He played to be
            listened to. If he were born today, he wouldn't be writing sym-
            phonies; he'd be on MTV. Music evolves!

STILLWALL: Oh, so now you have to be old to appreciate Mozart!

MATSUO: Well...yes!

[Hollering.]

FORD: Gents, gents, you're proving the basic axiom of music: Every
               generation believes that what their children listen to is
               garbage.

A.:   Well, my parents would be right; I do listen to Garbage. *[Mat-
               suo laughs, all alone.]* Sorry: next-generation joke.

MATSUO: You are the youngest at the table; what do you think?

A.:   Uh...well, I'm sure the Eye chose Mozart...sometime in six-
               teen whatever.

KNOX: I don't think so.

MATSUO: That would be too mainstream for the Eye.

KNOX: I bet it picked Salieri.

FORD: Please, I don't think you saw our host's point. The thing is that
               art evolves, and so does the Eye's taste. But that's what it is:
               taste. The fact that it likes a song doesn't mean we have to
               like it. The Eye is always looking into the present as it flows.
               So it is aware of the latest trends; hence it evolves like us.
               That doesn't make it objective truth. It's just some very well-
               informed opinion.

A.:   But you said the Eye was a godly object.

FORD: Well, gods can be wrong.

A.:   Oh. Really? Can your God be wrong, Niamh?

NIAMH: *[One knock on the table, close to the mike.]*

A.:   Okay. Didn't know that. Slow down; you're the cook; you're not
               supposed to enjoy yourself this much.

[Laughter.]

CUTLER: Everything is delicious.

MATSUO: I wager this is better than the noodles in Kuala Lumpur.

KNOX: I agree.

A.:   Noodles in Kuala Lumpur?

FORD: The Wizard this year? Cook in a stall in Kuala Lumpur?

MATSUO: The cook's reading a magazine while a customer is eating noodles at the counter and he drops his chopsticks in bliss after trying his meal.

A.: Oh, yeah. With, like, wooden spoons clopping above him.

MATSUO: That's the one.

A.: I hardly remember that one. It wasn't very remarkable.

MATSUO: Actually, Wizards are easy, right, Knox?

KNOX: It's the second-most-found after the King.

CUTLER: Sage, Genius, and Wizard, that's the lucky trio; they're always pleasant to work on.

FORD: The Wizard is almost always a cook, allegedly authoring the best meal in the world.

KNOX: And he's never British. *[Laughter.]*

FORD: *[Through a smile.]* The historian should know.

KNOX: Stats can't lie.

A.: How do you all know it was Kuala Lumpur?

MATSUO: You could see the Petronas in the background. Petronas Towers? With the bridge across? They were behind the customer on the right. Yeah, you had to look for them. It's okay; you'll get the hang of it.

VASQUEZ: *[Far from the mike, young baritone.]* As of tonight, Miss Connell will be the new Wizard!

CUTLER: Toast to that!

[Glasses jingling.]

A.: *[Whispering.]* Who is that again?

FORD: Who? Long hair? Vasquez; he found the Twins.

A.: Oh, yeah. That explains the mood.

MATSUO: *[Loud.]* Hey, Vasquez, you in for a dive in the pool after dinner?

A.: I'm sorry; we emptied it last week. The freeze could damage the structure.

MATSUO: Oh, pity!

VASQUEZ: *[Far.]* I would do it!

KINGSTON: *[Farther, dry, raspy voice.]* You'd freeze to death the second you touched the water.

VASQUEZ: On the contrary, the cold would preserve me long enough for the paramedics to perform CPR, like that Bones in 'ninety-two.

KINGSTON: Who said we'd call the paramedics?

[Laughter and clapping.]

A.: *[Whispering.]* That was ... Charlie?

FORD: Kingston. Coroebus. Sent you a postcard.

A.: Right.

CUTLER: *[Loud.]* Who gets the last stuffed egg?

FORD: Well, let's see; who spent eight months in Africa chasing a Phoenix? Oh, it was me. Thank you.

[Amused protests.]

MATSUO: Oh, come on!

CUTLER: He's going to brag like this all year.

KINGSTON: Let's appoint him Phoenix for life, since he's so good at it.

FORD: No, that's against the rules.

CUTLER: Or Asterion, let's see how you manage.

VASQUEZ: Hey, where is Philip, by the way? I can't believe he's missing this, of all people!

A.: *[Aside.]* Why is it against the rules?

FORD: You can't get the same role twice in a row.

KNOX: It would be unfair: some roles are consistently harder.

NIAMH: *[Warning whistle.]*

A.: What? Oh. Telephone. Excuse me.

[A chair screeches on the floorboards; steps run outside.]

*

I answered it in the office, just to check that Help was okay.

"Hello."

"Hello, I'd like to speak to Mr. Ambrose Wells, please?"

"Who is this?"

"Is this Ambrose Wells' house?"

I saw no reason not to come clean. "Ambrose Wells passed away last summer. This is his cousin."

He took an almost intolerable pause before continuing.

"Sir, this is Corporal Lowe, working with the sheriff of Pennaniket, Louisiana. Sir, do you . . . Are you acquainted with a Philip Beauregard?"

Swallow.

"Yes, he's a friend of my cousin's."

"I'm afraid I have some very bad news for you, sir. I am calling because the owner of the Dixie Motel here in Pennaniket found your number among the unclaimed luggage of a Philip Beauregard who went missing after checking in. We . . . we just found his body," he stuttered. "I am very sorry, sir."

"How did he die?"

"We found him outside town, in the woods—"

"*How* did he die?" I insisted.

"He was murdered, sir. He was in a common grave in an old farm. It is . . . hard to tell; we think he's been there for three months; but . . ."

"*How?*"

"He had a pitchfork driven through his chest."

And I fall. And my rib cage collapses in an explosion of blood.

Either I said, "God," or I gasped; I couldn't make it out myself. The corporal's voice quavered with fear or shame.

"Apparently, it's been going on for some years. Old Asa has been murdering hitchhikers and burying their bodies there. We're now contacting—"

"Is he dead?"

"What?"

"The murderer, did you kill him?"

"Yes," he answered. I pictured the man in uniform on the phone pulling a tear back into his eye, holding his head high. "He fired a shotgun at the arresting officers, so they shot back."

"Thank you," I whispered.

After a now intolerable pause, he replied, "You're welcome."

We hung up soon after that.

*

VASQUEZ: Hey, we could be before the first British Wizard!

NIAMH: *[Short, protesting double whistle.]*

MATSUO: She's not British, Vasquez; she's Irish!

CUTLER: *[Aside.]* Irish? Where from exactly?

[Footsteps approach the mike.]

A.:   Caleb. We need to talk.

A.'S DIARY

We decided to break it to the members after dinner.

Their faces were beyond description. The death of a friend is always a shock. But a nightmare come true—that's devastating.

No one said anything, beyond the early muttered swearing. Not even Caleb. He froze right after releasing the news.

About a minute later, Daniel Vasquez, the Puerto Rican, softly uttered the impertinent thought that had been hesitating at the tip of his tongue.

"We broke the record."

Other guests stared at him. He was a handsome man in his early forties, suave, with chin-length hair, and the only person in the room not wearing a tie, save myself.

"Philip found the Monster. That makes seven," he explained. "Did you get a name?"

"Yes. Old Asa," I said, and the multitude savored the name like a forbidden word.

"That's it. We broke the record."

"Who cares!" cried out Silas Long, aka Prometheus, the one who quit by letter in early November. He was a short man sitting on the other end of the table; he hadn't raised his voice until now. "God, Beauregard is dead, and all you can think of are stats?"

No one rebutted the accusation.

"This game is destroying us!"

"This was another accident," argued Knox.

"Oh, shut up!"

"No, I won't."

That took us by surprise. He showed remarkable authority without raising his voice. "Philip fell victim to a serial killer. An indiscriminate psycho. The game has nothing to do with it."

"He wouldn't have gone into the lion's den if the Eye hadn't showed it—if we hadn't told him to!"

Caleb intervened. "Silas, we're not responsible for this."

"Oh, yes, I know; it was luck. Any of us could have taken his place had we gotten the wrong ball a year ago." He scanned the room for reactions. People at his end of the table did not seem to disagree. I then noticed that most of the winners this year were sitting by my end. Vasquez was the only exception.

"So what, we keep drawing lots this year?" Long ranted. "See who gets to meet the next Monster?"

"Actually, we can't," said Eli Kingston, the one who sent the postcard from California. "There're nineteen of us."

Vasquez pointed at Niamh. "What about the cook?"

"A woman?" complained someone.

"It would be about time!" Vasquez insisted.

"Christ, listen to yourselves!" cried Long. "You're racing to your own death!"

At least two people agreed with him aloud. One of them was Jeff Stillwall, one of the oldest in the bunch. He came from Tennessee and had been Anchises this year—the one after the lesbian schoolgirl scurrying along the snowy roof. I remembered that because I had considered him lucky: That was a vision I wouldn't have minded focusing on.

"You can't see what the Eye is doing to you," Long resumed. "I too was blind, but now I see. I am not ready to continue this game for another year."

"We should vote," said Stillwall.

Caleb replied, "Why not let the host decide what to do?"

"Who made him the new host?"

"Certainly not you," I spat out.

No one said a word. Hey, if Knox can stun people into silence, so can I.

"Look, you can fight over rules and morality as long as you want. But in four hours the Eye is speaking again, and you can't prevent that. Now, as it will be my first showdown, I personally have decided not to miss it. Gentlemen, you are all free to do as you please. My hospitality does not bind you to any game, neither to one man's rules nor to democratic decisions. The vault opens at twelve thirty a.m. My house is your house."

With that I left, Niamh following.

*

—*You the alpha male!*

—Shuddup.

`KITCHEN THU DEC-21-1995 23:46:45`

A plethora of dirty dishes and leftovers fills every horizontal surface in the room.

Two Victorian gentlemen: CUTLER (sixties, stocky, balding), sitting on a stool, and VASQUEZ (early forties, long hair, Vandyke beard), standing across the counter. Vasquez is staring at something that just came out of Cutler's mouth. Possibly a word.

For a long time.

VASQUEZ: No way.
CUTLER: Way.

    [A second later, Vasquez chuckles, unbelieving.]

*

`SMOKING ROOM THU DEC-21-1995 23:47:05`

Three Victorian gentlemen playing pool: STILLWALL (oldest, white mutton-chops), REDBY (fat, bearded), KINGSTON (forties, Caesar haircut). A fourth (Silas LONG) sits with his right flank to the fireplace, a glass in his hand.

STILLWALL: At least I didn't do badly this year. *[Leans over for the shot, slowly; he's the oldest of the lot.]* I had mine located.

    [He shoots. One striped ball is pocketed.]

REDBY: It wasn't difficult. Probably Norway, or Finland.
STILLWALL: No. Arkhangelsk, Russia.

[He shoots again. No score.]

LONG: How did you find out?

STILLWALL: I spotted the building. Whose turn is it?

KINGSTON: Wait a minute. You had the building? The one with the tomboy capering along the roof?

STILLWALL: Yes. See, judging by the time the girls were put to bed, the sun, and the snow, I decided it had happened somewhere along the Arctic Circle. So I just ordered photo books on cities near the sixty-sixth parallel, hoping to recognize the skyline: Fairbanks, Reykjavík, Tromsø, Murmansk … It was Arkhangelsk. Saint Ursula, a boarding school for girls.

LONG: *[Very interested.]* And then what?

STILLWALL: Nothing. That's as close as I got.

KINGSTON: You had the name of the school, and you gave up?

STILLWALL: What did you want me to do?

KINGSTON: Man, you go to the school, check the class photographs, browse through student files, and you get their names!

STILLWALL: I can't just go to a boarding school in Russia and say, "Hello, tovarich, give me your files!" Let alone, "Oh, I hope it has pictures of the little girls!" And it was autumn! Do you want me to go to northern Russia in autumn for a damn picture?

REDBY: I would have tried.

LONG: Me too.

STILLWALL: Well, I'm sorry to disappoint you; I'm sixty-nine!

KINGSTON: God, and to think I was stuck with a surfer in the middle of the ocean and no point of reference whatsoever. I traveled for two months through the hot spots of Southern California, hoping to come across a face, while you had everything!

STILLWALL: God, two months on the coast of Southern California! My heart bleeds!

[Kingston stares at his sarcasm for a solitary second.]

[Then they all burst into laughter.]

LONG: *[Amused, exiting with an empty decanter.]* I'll go get more
               brandy.

✳

MUSIC ROOM THU DEC-21-1995 23:48:54

Caleb FORD, Curtis KNOX, Ken MATSUO, NIAMH, and A. sit at the corner table,
near the liquors. Other Victorian men gather in duos and trios at the far
end of the room. Scattered glasses and conversations all over the place.

A.:   The cops wanted to mail Beauregard's luggage. Doesn't he
               have any family?
FORD: *[To Knox.]* Didn't he have a sister in Boston?
KNOX: *[Exhales a drag from his Egyptian cigarette.]* I'm not sure they
               spoke to each other.
MATSUO: Wasn't he dating a psychiatrist in—
KNOX: They broke up. *[A second drag.]* Philip was a high roller.
A.:   *[After a brief pause to give somebody time to explain.]* Meaning?
KNOX: He lived for the game. No time for long-term relationships.
FORD: He was quite young, had money ... Traveled almost every
               year ... He's been in for ten years, and he won ... three times?
KNOX: And came really close twice. Playing this hard is incompatible
               with a family.

          [A third drag. The smoke drifts in baroque curls.]

A.:   Can't you share the burden?
KNOX: It's not just that. It's a stance. Long exposure to the Eye turns
               you into a cynic. Shows the best and the worst of mankind, but
               has a definite taste for the worst.
FORD: *[Beaten.]* Damn, Curtis, you'll make me pour myself another
               drink.
KNOX: *[Oblivious, to A.]* Did you know the Eye doesn't believe in
               marriage?

MATSUO: Oh, boy.

KNOX: Ever notice that the Twenty are actually twenty-one? Because the Twins are two. It is the only plural category. The Lover, however, is singular. The Eye focuses on one member of the couple. So the greatest lover is only one of the two. No matter how well he does, he'll never be fully requited.

[Caleb Ford raises up.]

FORD: Bourbon, anyone? *[Checks the ice bucket.]* We're out of ice.

[He starts for the door, but Niamh gestures him to stay and leaves for the kitchen.]

A.:   *[To Knox, after checking that Niamh is gone.]* Is the Lover more often a man or a woman?

MATSUO: I'd say it's quite balanced.

KNOX: I'd say the loved one is more often a woman.

A.:   That makes sense.

⋆

KITCHEN THU DEC-21-1995 23:51:02

CUTLER and VASQUEZ, in the same position we left them.

[Enter LONG, carrying an empty decanter.]

LONG: Gentlemen. *[Heads for the liquors.]*

VASQUEZ: Hey, Silas, you gotta listen to this.

LONG: *[Uninterested.]* I heard it already. It's crazy.

CUTLER: It's not! Just look at her face!

LONG: Edward, really, stop it. It's impossible.

VASQUEZ: I never saw her face.

CUTLER: Look, I've been playing this game for thirty-three years. I am well trained. I can focus. I saw her face then, and I saw it again today!

VASQUEZ: How can you be so sure? How long's it been, five years?

CUTLER: Four. I was Leonidas; I was after that black smiling hunter-gatherer girl in the desert, and right after that it was her!

LONG: Edward. Please listen to me. Do you know what the odds are of someone you've seen through the Eye just turning up by pure chance?

CUTLER: Well, I've seen quite a few already: twenty a year, for thirty-three years—

LONG: [Interrupting.] Twenty times thirty-three against SIX BILLION! It's impossible!

[Enter NIAMH. The conversation is interrupted. She smiles at the guests on her way to the fridge.]

VASQUEZ: Hello.

[The others just nod courteously; Cutler and Vasquez pick at the leftovers. Niamh gets a bag of ice from the freezer and exits with a new good-bye grin.]

[Once she's out, the conversation is resumed.]

VASQUEZ: Who was Hector that year?

CUTLER: Hyde just reminded me: It was Beauregard.

VASQUEZ: Damn.

CUTLER: [To Long.] Look, you don't believe it, let's check the Archives.

VASQUEZ: What for? The file will be incomplete: She was a quit.

CUTLER: There will be a recording.

[Long checks his watch. Then looks at Cutler.]

LONG: The Archives. Down in the vault.

[Cutler stays in affirmative silence. Long sighs, pours himself another brandy.]

*

MUSIC ROOM THU DEC-21-1995 23:52:33

FORD, KNOX, MATSUO, A., and NIAMH remain silent, drinks in their hands.

[A door opens off frame. Enter a new group of Victorian gentle-men. One of them carries a pool cue.]

HANDHELD CAMERA

Like amontillado seekers, the Victorian men flow along the flanks against the garden lights sifting through the basement windows, footsteps drumming on the concrete floor. The vanguard turns left around the wine racks, ranks closing in, clearing up again shortly after as they arrive at the shiny stainless-steel vault and form a semicircle around it by the aqueous green-blue light of the flooded end of the basement.

The camera tunnels through the crowd to reach the first row, right in front of the oblivious blond-mustachioed general standing ceremoniously by the steel door, watching the formation of gentlemen in suits, and the camera scans the men behind the general, zooming and panning through Stillwall's white muttonchops and Vasquez's corsairlike hair, and the slanted eyes of Matsuo, who smirks and winks at the camera before returning his attention to the general, who is just now receiving from A. the four-sided key.

And the key is placed and twisted in the cruciform lock, and the door coughs its hydraulic wheeze, and quickly the men on the right flank gather to pull it open, and the camera looks into the black depths of the vault as A. and the general step in and plunge into the blackness, and it hurries to follow them watching the Chucks jump over the step, and fades to black.

The light switch snaps. And the army, now parchment-colored in the medieval light of the spherical chamber, aligns again around the central stand topped by a blanket, which the general pulls to introduce the Eye to a public sigh of recognition, the crystal ball droning self-consciously, breathing imperceptibly, a mist of dark oceans and galaxies swirling across its surface. And over the Orb, Knox's blue eyes glare into the camera and he says,

"Welcome to the rest of your sleepless life."

*

Knox, as the historian, or perhaps unrelated to that role, was the one in charge of channeling the recall into a blank sphere, for which another supporting stand (another birdbath upside down, I'd say) had been pulled forward. In order to record, one needs to touch both spheres at the same time.

Caleb checked his watch and waved the others to gather. It's easy to get distracted in a room you step into only once a year; Cutler and Vasquez and some others were skimming through some unsorted files.

"Gentlemen," warned Ford, "the sun will rise in Amr at exactly . . ."

And suddenly something in the Eye faded out.

Do you know that feeling when a background noise you weren't aware of suddenly stops? This happened, but not only inside the vault. It was like a sound that had been going on for years, that I had listened to unconsciously all my life, was stolen from Earth.

"Quick, your hands."

The Eye is roughly the size of a volleyball, so twenty people cannot possibly place their hands on it at once; our fingertips would have to do (I guess they have, all these years). I shouldered my way in between Matsuo and somebody else; then Niamh squeezed in, after leaving the camera propped outside the circle, on a little desk used to revise the files. Her miniature hand hesitated in the vicinity of the sphere; her eyes queried me; I signed it was safe to touch now. The electric charge was minimal, the kind that gives metal the feel of velvet. It was awkward, but not unpleasant. Across from us, Knox, standing sideways, stretched his left arm backward to reach the blank sphere.

Caleb calls this minute "the recap phase." We spent most of it in silence.

I was about to bring up what Ambrose Wells wrote in his posthumous letter to Knox: "That some year, maybe not this one, hopefully not the next, but some year, it will be so dreadful, we will not last a single night."

"Fifty bucks says the Juggernaut's not Betty this year," said Vasquez.

"Deal," said three voices at once.

"Fifty the Mother's in Yugoslavia," said Kingston.

"Deal."

"Fifty the Nobleman's an American."

"Is that unlikely?" I whispered to Matsuo.

I never got the answer; the Eye spoke first.

*

—the jolt sweeps through their bodies, snapping their spines straight, shoving them apart while tying their hands together harder, and they twitch again in the first second, Niamh's legs almost failing, bald head pulled back, but her stretched arm stays anchored on the center of the circle with the others, eyes closed, and no one moves, or perhaps they do; maybe they're shaking slightly, trembling, but it might be that the camera has paused, and the halted head is reading the same frame in a loop, or maybe they don't, because you can see A. pulling his head farther back at some moment and separating his lips, and then there is almost a collective sigh, at which they all seem to realize at once that their lungs are still working, and some of them choose to take some oxygen in quickly, until a general gasp cuts their breath away, and A.'s arm is now clearly shaking between his frozen torso and the middle of the circle, whence a new gasp is generated. And then a jerk of pain. And a snort. And a jerk. And a sudden multivoiced cry. And then nothing. And then—

*

The current spit us back to crash against the walls.

Everyone rubbed their faces, folding. I understood what the buckets were there for.

"Caleb, you liar!" I cried. "You said it would only last a minute!"

"It did," said Matsuo, checking his watch. "Actually, less: about fifty-five seconds."

"It seems longer because your brain is being fed more stimuli per second than it gets from the senses," Knox lectured.

Niamh's hands grabbed her bald head like spiders climbing a rock.

Luckily no one felt an urge to use the buckets. People cleared their throats, wiped their sweat, welcomed air into their bodies again.

"That was Betty, wasn't it?" polled Vasquez, fingers raking his hair.

"Yes."

"I feared so." And he pulled out his wallet.

VIDEO RECORDING

BEDROOM FRI DEC-22-1995 02:55:36

A. writing in bed.

[Enter NIAMH, closes door behind her.]

A.: Did you change the tapes?

[She nods. He continues to write. Niamh sits on her side, takes her shoes off, her skirt, her leggings, her sweater, her shirt. She finally sits on the bed, staying in her undershirt, smiling to herself, looking particularly zingy and not in need of rest.]

[A. notices.]

Are you not taking notes?
NIAMH: *[Shrugs indifferently, then points at his notes.]*
A.: *[Understanding.]* Yeah, you have mine already. You should go to college someday; you truly have the spirit. Was there anything you recognized?
NIAMH: *[She shrugs again, shakes her head.]*
A.: Yeah. It was a long shot.

[He continues to write. Niamh looks straight at the camera with a mischievous snigger.]

[She then snatches his pen and, reaching across the bed, she turns his side lamp off.]

[A. massages the bridge of his nose, tired, while Niamh gets in the bed. They pull up the sheets; then his eyes meet hers.]

[Quoting.] "Welcome to the rest of our sleepless life."

[Niamh remains quiet for a moment. A lively nive begins to blossom.]

No.

[She pops out of the bed to pull the bolt across the door. Turns around, a definite smile now on her mouth.]

Niamh, we talked about this. No.

[She switches off her lamp. DARKNESS.]

[A sudden whine from the bedsprings. An agitation of blankets.]

Niamh, NO! *[Softer, remembering the guests.]* Niamh, I'm telling Aunt Liza.

[The clothes slowly settle.]

[…]

Okay, I'm not telling her this.

BEDROOM FRI DEC-22-1995 06:24:28

The camera must still sit on the dresser, now half-tumbled off a book or some low support, for the image is tilted a few degrees to the right, and all blue. Morning twilight hardly brims in through the tight shutters, somewhat dispelling the darkness around some of the canopy and the mattress.

[A body twitches, the shock wave shaking the bed to its foundations.]

[Heavy sniveling.]

A.:   What time is it?

[A digital watch screen glowworms in the dark.]

[Sheets stirring; a switch is snapped on.]

[Again.]

[Again again again again.]

        Try your lamp.

[A single, equally unproductive snap.]

[A.'s blue silhouette gets up, opens the window, then pushes the shutters open. The bedroom is now completely charted in ashen chalk: canopy, sheets asprawl, two useless bedside lamps, everything save some deep shadow regions in the corners, together with A.'s complete profile near the window and the bald-headed girl sitting up on the bed.]

NIAMH: *[Suddenly alert.]* Shh!

[Index finger raised like a dog's ears.]

A.: I didn't hear anything. *[Suddenly he looks straight into the camera, points at it.]* How come that thing's working?

NIAMH: *[Retrieves her notepad from the bedside table, writes, shows.]*

A.: *[After reading.]* We have an emergency outlet? Cool.

[He rubs his face, but stops midaction.]

[Looking around.] I did hear that.

[He and Niamh exchange looks.]

[Niamh sprightly scuttles off the foot of the bed and toward the dresser, in panties and a loose tank top. In no more than one and a half maneuvers, she slips into one of A.'s shirts, turns on her voice recorder and fits it into the breast pocket, grabs the handheld video camera.]

Don't forget your proton pack.

[She laughs a blank, widemouthed laugh, jumps into some shoes, and capers for the door; tries to open it, remembers to draw the bolt back, tries again, and exits.]

HANDHELD CAMERA

Dark.

Night-vision mode toggled on. Video is enhanced to a green rendering of a corridor, darkness pushed back to the attic stairs, beyond the door to the study, on which A. is now knocking. He waits for an answer, shivering lightly, wearing nothing but a shirt and jeans. He calls in a low voice,
  "Caleb?"
and leans his head closer to the door, eyes checking the camera, naked floorboards groaning under his bare feet, and then he says,
  "He's still out of it. Better check the circuit breaker,"
as he passes the camera, which turns a hundred and eighty degrees and glides to the other end of the corridor into the vast stair hall sunken in the heure bleue *pouring through majestic windows,*
  "and you should let Help out before he pees on Ambrose's chair."
and the marble floor makes a squelchy sound under A.'s feet, but when he reaches the wooden stairs the steps creak gently, and so they do under the Chucks as well, descending into a complete darkness that the night vision has to fight off. And when it does, A. is revealed unexpectedly close, hands on the walls, right-hand fingers finally finding a corner and guiding the body down the final steps to the second floor landing. And the landing has no windows, but the library doors are open, and so are the ones at the far end, and the shutters along the gallery are all open, so that the image enhancement is weakened again and the green dye is dispelled, natural colors trying their best to glow in the dull light of early winter morning, the camera encouraging them, hovering into the library away from the squelchy steps, zooming in on the closer shelves, on the leather spines of books, but the letters on them look all astigmatic and disordered like letters do in dreams, so she pans away to let the books sleep. And she returns to the darker landing and looks both ways, first toward the faint light in the smoking room, then to the black doorway into the south-wing corridor where the luckiest guests sleep, and after that it resumes its way to the stairs. And then, after a regular footfall, it stops.
  And remains stopped.
  And she breathes.

Then the camera moves on, perhaps slower, into the dark stairway, but the night vision takes longer than usual to set, and the darkness resists and whispers eerie thoughts into the microphone, and the breathing on this side is slow paced, humanlike, but deeper, emptier, like gentle waves washing onto a beach of very fine sand. And finally the image enhancement switches on, exposing the open hand on the wall, a loose-fitting sleeve perching off the arm; then the camera descends to the platform between both floors and gazes over the hall, which is too dark for colors at this time, and too solemn anyway most of the day, and the camera, devoid of night vision once again, is unable to decipher the high ceiling, and it desists altogether as it reaches the ground floor.

"Hey Niamh!"

says a voice in the distance.

"Something happened to the kitchen cam."

Now the camera must lean close to the wall to reveal the closed door under the stairs, camouflaged with the paneling, but on even closer examination, on squeezing the most lumen out of any wandering photon in this corner of the house, it turns out that maybe the door's ajar half an inch, and at a half-hearted push of the hand it opens with a moan of very ancient wood, and some sifted twilight pours out. And on the carpeted floor rises a short series of steps, but the Chucks hesitate to tread on them, and the breathing billows.

A very small window at the top of the steps illuminates this hallway of the servants' quarters, and when the camera turns left into a tributary corridor, the night vision again takes a while to come back; only after a few more sea-wave breaths the sensor awakes, but the encompassing shadows are hardly pushed back more than three or four yards, enough to reveal the first two doors left and right. And the camera inches forward, and so the darkness recedes. But if the camera withdraws, as much the darkness reconquers.

And the Chucks have noticed this, and walk now very slowly, fearing to step outside of the tenuous pool of light in the center of the frame, and they make no sound at all on the carpet, although the sea-wave breathing is now slightly louder, if not faster, as though it took more effort to keep it on a leash. And long before reaching the door on the right, the hand stretches forward and knocks gently and waits for an answer, not for too long, before knocking again now with all four knuckles. And impatiently the fist unfurls and the resulting hand grabs the handle, perhaps hoping for a bolt to stop her, but there isn't—breathe—there is only dark and some slits of filtered light behind curtains—blue curtains, after the light-enhancement mode goes to sleep again for altogether insufficient reasons. And the camera stares into the dark, crying for light, but there is none, and only through will the camera makes out the shapes of men sleeping on the twin beds.

And then the light comes back, a whole lampful of it, shining yellow and unnatural in the blue twilight, artificially rendering the whole room of the servants' quarters, the blood-splashed beds, the nonbreathing men sleeping with their eyes open staring at the camera.

And the waves break the pattern to pieces. They accelerate, they curl backward, they collapse into one another, and the camera turns around, jumps out into the corridor, waves surrendering to panic, hand pushing a new door open, the slam sounding like the first real sound in decades, and then the room light is switched on, and Vasquez's body is sprawled on the carpet, a dead hand reaching for the door, facedown, drowned in his blood, and the breathing is at its loudest, maddest, desperately trying to inhale enough air to finally throw out a wild, thunderous WHISTLE that saturates the microphone and bursts through the walls, and the camera runs out into the corridor again, feet drumming on the carpet, WHISTLE, longer, and then possibly out into the hallway, down the steps, just bouncing off the walls and the carpet and the ceiling, not knowing where it is, and WHISTLE, and A.'s voice far away, and then the landing, and the mercenary in a balaclava and a GUNSHOT.

And the camera drops to the floor.

A.:   Niamh! NIAMH!!!

HANK: STOP! Hold it right there!

A.:   Niamh! Niamh, you okay?! *[Rustling of clothes against the mike; voice very close.]* Niamh. You all right!

HANK: Come here—

A.:   *[Wrestling.]* What the fuck—

HANK: Shut up!

DONNA: *[Background.]* Eighteen! Got eighteen!

HANK: There! On your knees there!

A.:   Who are you?!

HANK: Got the other two right here!

A.:   Who are—

HANK: Oh, sorry, wanna see my face? No problem now.

[A second's worth of silence.]

A.:   Wait … Scar … The snowplow guy?!

DONNA: *[Closer now.]* All clear! *[Gun cocking.]* Was that you whistling? You're supposed to be mute!

A.:   What the—What are you doing here?

KRAUS: *[Farther, floorboards protesting, heavy footwear approaching.]* Don't worry, kid.

[Now closer: a lighter. Burned paper. A puff.]

           Most of them died in their sleep. A luxury you can't afford.

A.:   Wh—

           Wha—

           [Gulps.]

           Why?

KRAUS: Why, why …

DONNA: It's nothing personal, honey. We just do the job for a reasonable fee.

[Door opens somewhere in the distance. Another gun's hammer cocking, much closer: this time sounds like a revolver.]

KLAUS:	Silencer off. I think I want to hear this one.
GLEW:	Hold it.

[Pause. So that everyone can check who just spoke there.]

A.:	YOU!
GLEW:	As expected, you fucked up. You got the wrong sphere.
KRAUS:	Hank?
HANK:	It was in the vault, exactly where he said it'd be. There's a whole collection.
GLEW:	I don't care where it was; this is not what I'm looking for. The one I want is slightly bigger and it's supposed to hum.
A.:	Glew!
KRAUS:	Okay, try the safe again. Last door on the left.
HANK:	Fuckin' blow that bitch away. *[Jackboots stomping away.]*
A.:	GLEW! Look at me!

[A gap of wordlessness.]

GLEW:	Oh, shut up. Someone dies, and a brat in Europe wins the jackpot? It was a matter of time before the tables turned.
A.:	*[Angry.]* Why? Just tell me why?!
GLEW:	*[Impatiently smooth.]* Please don't be pathetic. Let's just say that some people are ready to pay unimaginable sums for what they believe to be evidence that God exists. And here I am apprised that an idle millionaire who just kicked the bucket held one such object. I looked everywhere for it. But I failed. Even Kraus here couldn't find it after what he called a ninja break-in.
KRAUS:	It was a ninja break-in. Whistle bitch here has Daredevil hearing.
DONNA:	Didn't hear eighteen muffled shots, though.
GLEW:	Yeah, well. I hear the first sleep after is pretty deep.

A.:   *[Appalled.]* But...ALL OF THEM?

GLEW: Yes, you see, we had to wait until the one day in the year when the treasure comes out of the chest, even though the house would be—

A.:   Who told you about this? Knox?

GLEW: No names. Anyway...

A.:   Then who? Nobody outside the Society knew anything, and nobody has parted the Society to this day.

GLEW: God, you just can't shut up, can you? I'm in the middle of my villain speech and you—

A.:   Dänemarr?!

[Standstill.]

[Then, very far, very loud:]

HANK: Fuck!

[In the distance: a body slamming down, vicious snarling, cries of pain.]

GLEW: What the hell is that?!

HANK: *[Far away.]* Ah! God! My face! AAAAH!

[Snarling approaches at great speed, pawed feet galloping on the floorboards.]

[GUNSHOT.]

NIAMH: *[Untranscribable.]*

A.:   NO, HELP! FUCK!

DONNA: *[Bursts out laughing.]*

KRAUS: Man, did you hear that?!

GLEW: Jesus Christ, look at this! I have dog brains splattered all over my pants!

A.:   *[Sobbing.]* Oh, God!

KRAUS: Was that you? Is that really your voice? That squeak? *[Chuckling.]* Did you hear it? Do it again! Come on! Is that really what you sound like? God, you're disgusting!

A.: SHUT UP, YOU HEINOUS CUNT!!!

[GUNSHOT.]

[A. yells out a gurgling burst of pain. Continues shouting throughout the next lines.]

GLEW: *[Calm.]* Is this really necessary? I shouldn't really be here, let alone see this.

KRAUS: Did you see that? She didn't utter a sound. She squeaked for the dog, but didn't even moan when I blasted your knee off. How does that feel?

[A blood-splattered, tearful pause.]

Hey. I said, how does that feel?

A.: *[Panting, softer than his own breath.]*

KRAUS: What? Sorry, I can't hear you.

A.: *[He just pants, words trying to swim out of a pool of saliva. Seconds later, like floating debris from a sunken ship, consonants begin to emerge in a somber line.]* ... beg for your life.

KRAUS: Sorry, what was that?

A.: *[He swallows.]*
   [Now the words are gurgled out again, louder.] You'll die begging for mercy, you parent-abused wreck.

KRAUS: Okay, I've had enough of you. *[Revolver cocking.]*

GLEW: Wait!

[...] [Wait.]

We don't have the Eye yet.

KRAUS: *[Bored.]* It's in the safe.

DONNA: *[Far.]* It's not in the safe!

KRAUS: Oh, give me a break.

DONNA: *[Closer.]* Hank doesn't look very well either.

KRAUS: Oh, he'll have a new scar to boast about.

DONNA: Yeah, well, he'll need a new nose and upper lip too.

GLEW: *["Hello?"]* Gentlemen?

KRAUS: Yeah, sorry. You. Stop crying. Where's the ball?

A.:   *[Snorts.]*

KRAUS: Where's the ball or I blow her head off.

A.:   Bedroom. *[Swallows.]* In the chest.

DONNA: Must be the locked door upstairs.

KRAUS: Okay, raise up; you're gonna show me.

A.:   *[Shouts in agony.]*

DONNA: He can't climb upstairs; he has no knee.

KRAUS: *[The voice of resignation.]* God, one of these days…

[Brainstorming.]

Okay. You, Squeaky, come with me. Show Uncle Kraus your room.

A.:   Don't fucking touch her!

DONNA: Man, come on.

KRAUS: *[Easy.]* What? We're gonna get the client's stuff. He can't come upstairs, but she has nice working legs.

DONNA: Yeah, but … I mean, c'mon. She's like … fourteen.

KRAUS: So what? I'm just going upstairs. Besides, she's more like … fifteen. Can you squeak your age, sweetie? Anyway, I mean, fourteen, fifteen, she already bleeds.

GLEW: Great, very glamorous. No wonder you were the cheapest on the list.

KRAUS: You're coming too; see the dragon balls for yourself.

DONNA: Man, we really should drive the fuck out.

KRAUS: It's okay; we'll be out in a minute. Take Hank to the van; we'll be right there. Come on.

A.:   If you so much as touch her—

[WHACK!]

KRAUS: SHUT UP!

GLEW: Just—hold yourself, until I've got the ball!

KRAUS: Okay, okay! Donna, put him in the basement. He can't climb
         stairs, but he can roll down some. I'll deal with him when the
         client's satisfied.

A.:   You fuck—

DONNA: Up!

A.:   [Shouts through gritted teeth.]

*

—*coming nearer, and then the female, even closer:* "Yes, please, tell me if
I'm too rough," *and footfalls approach the blank wall where the wooden
paneling is interrupted by the slit of the door, which now is pulled open,* "Aw,
God!" *and unfocused and somebody grabs the camera* "Up, I said!" *and
paws the microphone and STOP.*

VIDEO RECORDING

BEDROOM FRI DEC-22-1995 06:45:13

The lamp on Niamh's side of the bed is on.

On the right half of the picture, GLEW holds a sports bag. KRAUS—big man
dressed in military surplus—holds a revolver in one hand, NIAMH in the
other.

The latter glares at the lawyer as only lawyers can be glared at.

The chest is open.

   [Glew, using a scarf as an insulator, reaches into the sports bag.]

GLEW: This is it.

[He zips it closed.]

KRAUS: Good. Go now; I'll catch up with you.

[Glew stops halfway to the door. He looks questioningly at the mercenary. His hand on Niamh's shoulder is twice as big as her hairless head.]

GLEW: Are you serious?

KRAUS: *[Easy.]* Yeah, go with Donna and Hank. I'll take care of these and take one of the cars outside. See you at the meeting point.

[Glew waits for a dismissive laugh.]

            Would you rather see me execute them now?

[But no. He's serious.]

GLEW: Jesus Christ.

[Exit.]

*

Paws on the microphone and smudgy shadows, the lens waking and sobering up, finally making out his contused face, a large bruise summoning on his left cheekbone, sharper now, open pores shiny with smeared blood, then zooming out a little and booming up, revealing his right wrist handcuffed up high to the steel shelves in the basement, his chest heaving with panic.

    Eyes look into the camera, one of them still red.
    "Niamh."

Tongue swipes the bottom lip for blood. Outside, water drops click the seconds away.

"If you get to see this,"

A pattern of blue-green undulations reflects on his skin.

". . . the following will have been worth it."

The camera is shelved away, now spying him from his right side. A pipe overhead drips water seconds on him. He'll have to stand up to reach it, but keeps tilting to his left as he tries. He pants.

"Come on,"

he whispers, not for the camera anymore, and he tries to crawl up the wall, with his back to it, from sitting to standing position, without standing, because the knee that has just come into frame is torn apart, and he winces when his weight falls on it, so he must take a leap of faith and grab the pipe and hang from it, let his body loose, which is little relief, until the pipe finally snaps with a sound of coughing metal and he falls back and water pours over his head, and he immediately shouts, and restrains a second shout, because the water is cold as December outside, and his panting increases in volume and speed, for he needs some strength to reach to his left and drag over a box that was lying there all the time, body tilting for it, both arms stretched out, left hand pining for the damn thing, lips summoning it, already changing to purple-blue. But finally the fingers touch it, pull it, manage to tip the box over, and then run for the top edge again and tip it once more, make it roll over until he can finally draw it next to him, and then open it and extract something from it—a smaller box. And he stabs the sealing tape with his fingernails in a frenzy before the cold eventually congeals his blood and the adrenaline stops rushing, and his fingers pluck through the cardboard, and he tears the box open; he thrashes the box. And inside, he finds a third box.

*

BEDROOM FRI DEC-22-1995 06:48:43

KRAUS stands by the window, glancing outside, listening for car engines. Golden Gate–size tendons anchor his neck to his shoulders.

NIAMH stands, head held high, back turned three-quarters, naked legs under a loose shirt. Ninety pounds, being generous.

[Kraus looks down to her.]

[He holsters his revolver, making sure Niamh gets the point. He takes his beret off.]

KRAUS: Okay, here's the deal.
NIAMH: [She won't blink.]
KRAUS: Do that sound again. The squeaking thing. And I'll spare him.

[Niamh darts for the door; the soldier blocks her in under a second, both falling to the floor; the camera trembles.]

*

And a crystal ball rolls out of the torn box, and he grabs it, but his fingers whip back at the zap from the crystal ball soaked in ice water, its surface the color of a large emerald, charged like a cattle prod, he just realized, and he has to pant three times to realize that he shouldn't care, and grab it again, shout in consonants, command his fingers to stick to it, his hand to raise it, lift it in the air, strike it on the floor crying, "BREAK"—optic nerve snapping—and then lift it again—a spit dropping toward the planet—"BREAK"—pitchfork driven through the rib cage—lift it—the highest altitude a pair of Puma shoes ever reached—"BREAK"—the hotel explodes—lift it—free-falling at flesh-tearing speed—"BREAK"—two policemen down—lift it—a tropical island and seagulls watching—and "BREAK!"—watching Betty kaboom-land on the roof!
    The ball's smashed to pieces.

And as he grips a shard of emerald glass, amid the lingering visions in his eyes he finally sees it—through a seagull's eyes.

And the epiphany catches up.

"Oh, fuck me."

And a late, sick smile lights up his face.

"FOUND."

—and the woman in lingerie smiles.

*

BEDROOM FRI DEC-22-1995 06:49:17

> *[KRAUS and NIAMH struggling on the floor, her back against the wall, bile oozing through her gritted teeth.]*

KRAUS: What, you angry? You think you scare someone with that bald head?! You think you look tough?!

> *[Niamh manages to set her hand free, throws a slash at his face.]*

>   Gaaah!

*

And with the victory smile still on his lips, he wields a shard of glass and stabs his handcuffed wrist with it, once, twice, thrice, laughing like a maniac, until blood spurts out of the sliced vein, and the frenzy still lasts enough for him to grab the shard between his teeth and tear open his free arm, the first squirt of blood splashing on the lens, all this in hardly ten seconds before the adrenaline flows out of the body, and he's left sitting in a corner of a basement, handcuffed to the shelves, burning-cold water pouring onto his head, soaked shirt squirted with blood stuck to his chest, blue skin showing through, blood flow slowing down, organs shutting down, lungs and vocal cords now running on pure inertia through a mindless, exhausted mantra: "Come on. Come on. Come on."

∗

BEDROOM FRI DEC-22-1995 06:50:03

> *[KRAUS has his back turned to the camera now; NIAMH is cornered against the foot of the bed. She has lost her shirt. But not her defiance.]*

KRAUS: Last chance. Do the sound.
NIAMH:

> *[He stands up, breathing hard.]*

KRAUS: Okay. I'll squeeze it out of you.

> *[He grabs her and slams her down on the mattress.]*

∗

The wavy reflections appear more excited as the pool on the floor grows, and water keeps chugalugging onto his head, now turned away from the camera, fallen.

Blood has long stopped flowing out of his handcuffed arm.

Lights flicker.

The head moves. The fluorescent tubes now drone louder, glow brighter, light shining on the blood streams on his skin. He opens his eyes to an expected view. A nive on his purple lips.

The first time they articulate the words, no sound comes out. He notices that. Then he tries harder.

"Help her."

Water keeps pouring out, like a chirping fountain outside a Moorish window.

"Don't just stand watching. You can do something. Please."
The light is brighter now; the waving wall is electric blue.
"You've done this before. Go."
The lips keep quivering between sentences.
"Go. I beg you. Go."
The head can no longer hold its own weight.
The lips mutter, "Go," one last time.
And he sinks a little deeper into the blue-green pool.

✳

BEDROOM FRI DEC-22-1995 06:50:32

Mattress screaming; NIAMH squirms under KRAUS' weight, her fists pounding his back.

The bedside lamp flickers.

KRAUS: *[Muffled.]* Stay put, you fuck—

> *[The bedside lamp lights up, a hairstring of sound just this side of the audible spectrum growing suddenly so loud that it deafens the camera. Kraus looks up, immediately driving a hand to his eyes.]*

> What—

> *[The light pulsates, as if trying even harder, before Kraus stomps in that direction and slaps the whole appliance off the table; the bulb explodes.]*

> *[The lamp on the other side (which was off) is now coming to life.]*

> What the fuck.

[And so is the ceiling light, first blinking itself awake, then growing brighter, screaming on the verge of ultrasound—]

Who is this?!

[—white sheets welding into whitened walls, spreading to the whole room ablaze, inflamed, nuked out, supernovaing, and in the blaze of released energy devouring the bodies you can guess the adumbrated skeletons of the three people in the room: Niamh rolling off and under the bed, the mercenary peeking over his arm at the third one, a residual shadow staining the left side of the picture.]

Stay there!

[A bulb explodes.]

[The mercenary draws his weapon: SHOT in the general direction of the camera; dresser mirror shatters to pieces; he steps back: SHOT at the left side of the tape, SHOT, SHOT, light spreading and engulfing him, sound rising, tape burning.]

[CRASH.]

*

The water has stopped. Cyan waves dance gently across his skin. His hair is soaked. His arms are tracked by streams of blood.

His eyes are closed.

*

BEDROOM FRI DEC-22-1995 06:51:10

The ceiling lamp lies dead on the floor, a glistening pool of glass spikes and metal. Sparks pour out of the wires above. KRAUS is still holding onto the canopy, where he climbed to pull the lamp down. He stays perched there like a large ape, a useless revolver in his free hand.

He stares at nothing in the general environs of the camera. His eyes are red.

KRAUS: What the fuck.

> [NIAMH rolls out from under the bed; she grips the broken, power-belching bedside lamp.]

> [Kraus realizes, pulls the trigger: CLICK.]

> [She cattleprods the bed: ZAP.]

> [Kraus is thrown off the bed and through the window. CRASH.]

> [Smoke rises from the point where his hand clutched the canopy as a thud comes from the garden.]

> [Niamh runs out of the room.]

> [She reappears, picks up the revolver, exits.]

*

The sound of her footsteps precedes her by a good ten seconds before she comes into frame in a sprint, Chucks splashing in the pool, and her bald head's cool enough for her to check for his vitals before anything else. But he's stopped moving, and *he's sunk deeper into the freezing pool, whole body hanging from his hand-cuffed, slashed wrist, which makes a very unsuitable position for CPR, so she has to pop off frame, yank something out of the shelves, return with an ax, try to strike at the cuffs, stop, aim first, then strike, let his hand drop, and now she starts massaging his heart, while he's almost completely under-*  *water, cold enough so that his vital organs might have been preserved and there might be a chance; she pounds on his chest with all her weight—one, two, three, four, five, six, seven, eight, nine, ten—then puts her lips on his purple lips and forces air into his lungs, and once again, one, two, three, four, five, six, please, eight, live, ten, try his mouth again, force air into his lungs, push it, restart the heart, one, two, please, four, useless, six, please, eight, live, ten, make him breathe wake up massage his heart look around is that a broken crystal ball are those dreams and nightmares on the floor*

It looked bad.

Of course, the swimming pool was supposed to prevent a fatality in the eventuality of somebody leaping out of the third-floor window. But the pool was required to be full of water in order to fulfill that function. And in liquid state, preferably. That morning it contained about five inches of melted snow from the previous day, which had frozen again during the night into a diamond-hard layer of compressed ice. Kraus broke both his legs against it. Very badly. You could see the splintered bone piercing through the thighs. Even he didn't dare to look.

Of course, the view was hopeless anywhere he looked—trapped in the bottom of an empty blue container, six feet, three inches deep, both legs broken, crawling on ice. He'd lost his revolver. There were auxiliary steps on the shallow end of the pool, but whether he'd be able to climb them using only his hands was yet to be ascertained. His left hand, incidentally, was burned in a very peculiar way; you've never seen anything like it. The flesh on his palm was roasted, more like microwaved. On the back, black spider veins poked through. It smelled like chicken. And he didn't feel it. So he'd have to climb on one hand. And if he made it out of the pool, he'd still have to crawl around the house and slither into a car before anyone arrived.

He had hoped that at least the cold would somehow relieve the pain. It didn't. He was crying. His good hand was scraping the ice when Niamh hung the ladder and climbed inside. That seemed an eternity later, despite the evidence of the parallel tracks of blood from his legs showing that he had crawled about two feet.

She jumped in, landing soundly on her Chucks, walked two steps, checked his belt for a fresh cylinder of ammo, and loaded the revolver.

What with the excruciating agony and all, Kraus missed the irony.

"Please."

The violent recoil made her lose the gun. Kraus' brains were splattered over the ice.

SECURITY VIDEOTAPE: POINT BLESS POLICE STATION

07:59 AM

[A minor disturbance in the street causes Officer LINNEY to look up from the counter for a second. A passerby outside judged it worth stopping by the window, her sight line pointing at the black Audi that just flitted past from Market Street and must have parked near Musgrove, but Linney does not grant it that much attention and soon returns to his paperwork. A new form is loaded into the typewriter and he starts typing.

The door slams open: A head-shaved KID in an anorak comes to the middle of the room, and there she stops, undecided between Linney on the counter and Corporal JACKSON's desk, and the impetus that carried her in is wasted. Linney and Jackson and the passerby outside the window stare at her. She's wearing nothing but panties and an undershirt under the anorak. And those are splashed with blood.

Right before Linney and Jackson awake and run to help, she collapses onto her knees, face contorted in a blazing scream—but there's no audio to the recording.]

12/22/1995 20:14

Dixie cups and candy wrappers have gathered around NIAMH's end of the table while she stays, arms folded, waiting for Detective MORGAN Summers (standing, propped on the table) to finish reading her statement. A whole school of cigarettes has washed up in the ashtray too.

> *[Morgan puts out the last cigarette (not in the ashtray: on the table, three inches away, but he doesn't notice) as he modestly hurries through the final lines.]*

> *[Unmoved, he glances at the thickness of the statement and unloads it on the table.]*

> *[Only then does he look at his witness.]*

MORGAN: Not bad. I liked the character development.

> *[Enter Deputy TED Miller with papers in his hand, to prove he has something to say.]*

TED: I just talked to the sheriff of Franklin, North Carolina. They got a Hank S. Blagowitz, aka Scar Bee. Apparently his mates dumped him at a hospital, where he was arrested. *[To Niamh.]* Your dog bit his nose off. That'll make a nice scar story.

MORGAN: *[Skimming through the papers Ted brought.]* As long as he omits that the dog was a collie.

TED: There's another thing. Last night's videotapes of the house show two men, one woman in balaclavas crossing through the kitchen at twelve forty-four a.m.; then one shoots at the camera. CSIs think they hid in the coal room during the night.

NIAMH: *[Snaps a finger for attention, then draws a letter P in the air.]*

MORGAN: What?

NIAMH: *[Encore.]*

MORGAN: P-what? Oh, pee. Sorry. *[To the door.]* Anderson? Would you please accompany the witness to the ladies' room?

[A FEMALE AGENT has appeared at the door; Niamh leaves with her.]

[Morgan hands the statement to the corporal, but he's pushed back by the hefty volume.]

TED: So, is she clean?

MORGAN: *[Sighs.]* Well, she's good. They killed everyone save her because she providentially locked the door to her room, and she shot one of them.

TED: *[Shrugs.]* Okay. Case is clear, right?

MORGAN: Perhaps.

TED: *[Less reflective.]* We got footage of Kraus' people breaking in.

MORGAN: Circumstantial.

TED: We got Hank's weapon. That will account for at least half of the bodies.

MORGAN: Yes, and her prints on a revolver will account for at least another one.

TED: In self-defense.

MORGAN: Point-blank to the head.

TED: On her property.

MORGAN: Actually, she pushed him out of the window, then went down-stairs and shot him.

TED: *[Not seeing the point.]* So what? Come on, "disabled underage white girl shoots an ex-con merc and sex offender"? The jury will build her a shrine!

MORGAN: *[Scoffs.]* Yeah, wait, it gets better: The thing is, she'll never step into a courtroom. She's a minor with Irish citizenship.

TED: So what? She's a U.S. resident.

MORGAN: No, she's not.

TED: *[Perplexed.]* She has a green card!

MORGAN: *[Smirks.]* No, she doesn't. He did. She accompanied him with a tourist visa, expiring in January.

TED: Then her guardian is responsible.

MORGAN: You're gonna love this. *[Checks another paper.]* Father's dead, mother's unfit, so the custody falls to an aunt Liza, who is already pulling strings to bring her back at once. And when her juvenile attorney heard that, he phoned the embassy so hard he almost sprained his dialing finger.

TED: Hey, hey, hey, hold your horses. If she can't make a phone call, how does the auntie in Ireland know about all this?

MORGAN: *[Proudly adding the cherry on top.]* She *e-mailed* her before going to the cops.

[Silent ovation.]

TED: *[Folding arms.]* Wow. She *is* good.

[Still standing, he leans on the table, mimicking the detective.]

Okay, so what have we got?

MORGAN: Oh, plenty of things. Lots of unanswered questions, for a start. Like who would hire mercenaries to steal some jewels, or how can a ninety-pound girl fling Hulk Hogan out of the window. Plus a noseless suspect, a dead criminal wanted in six states, one fugitive, a missing lawyer, seventeen people in the morgue, two in surgery, and lots of paperwork.

[Ted lights himself a cigarette, offers one to Morgan.]

TED: Will the ones in surgery make it?

[A drag.]

MORGAN: God willing.

Christmas passed by, and then the snow washed away and so did the dismal clouds, and there followed a few days of that unearthly blue air of winter, too pure to breathe. And the woods looked still shrouded in stone, but high above, on top of their stretched limbs, their fingertips dreamed already with spring and longed to swing in the sunshine.

Some yards short of the woods, far enough to look monumental, two twigs made a cross in the front yard. Niamh had dug the grave herself, by the marble plaque on the ground that marked the solstice when the shadow of the weathercock fell on it. She had wrapped Help's remains in his own blanket and left them in a shadowy corner in the snow, waiting for the funeral. The bulk looked so small, laid in the bottom of that hole. A hero had died. A pet was being buried.

She shoveled the earth on him before the prayers; even shrouded, he wasn't a bearable sight. Then she dedicated him some words. They must be still pinned to the cross, if it stands, on a page from her notepad.

HELP
Guardian's Guardian

She stood there not crying for a long while, until the sun had fallen behind the house, and the brightness of the sky had faded away, and a red-and-violet ribbon of dusk tapered in the west like the music of a rock concert far away.

Then I called her in and told her to pack.

MUSIC ROOM DEC-31-1995 17:12:51

Dusk.

A pile of bags and suitcases lurk among the shadows in the foreground. The only lit lamp is the one on the piano meant to light up the score. Now it beams on A. sitting on the stool, reading from a folder.

> *[Enter NIAMH, holding something behind her back—the camera sees it; A. doesn't.]*

A.:   Hey.

> *[He closes the folder, turns to her, strokes his left leg. It's bandaged around the knee, twice as thick as the right one.]*

> *[Their eyes stay locked for a while.]*

You know, all this time I was wondering why you were supposed to protect me. I just got it.

> *[He opens the folder again, spreads a few photographs and typewritten pages over the piano lid.]*

The funny thing is, Caleb mentioned the case. "A kid prevented a terrorist bomb from going off in a crowded station in London." It must have been his subconscious, because he never got any farther. But then, while I was in the hospital, I remembered how Edward Cutler looked at you when you two first met. Of course, it was so many hairdos and a puberty ago, but one out of twenty was bound to recognize you. It was Cutler who did. I recalled him and Vasquez and someone else browsing through the file cabinets in the vault right before the showdown. I've just been there. I think this is the one they were looking for.

[Niamh is going through the photographs, mildly interested. A. reads from the file.]

Blah, blah, blah, "The kid dumps the suitcase inside the pool and disappears into the crowd ... No one notices." "Watcher, 1991." "Quest assigned to Philip Beauregard, quit."

[His free hand points at the photographs. He wears another bandage around his wrist.]

He found the place: King's Cross Station, London. He even identified the terrorist: Dan O'Bailey, a rogue IRA, trying to buy an extension for the Troubles. But they never identified you. *[After a pause.]* You're a Watcher. Did you even know this?

NIAMH: *[Shakes her head, indifferent.]*
A.:   But Aunt Liza knew.
NIAMH: *[Shrugs: "I guess."]*
A.:   *[Noticing the object she's concealing.]* What are you carrying?

[Niamh produces a small present box, fitting in her porcelain palm.]

[A. stays put, not trying to take it.]

[Cool.] Wow. What's the occasion?

[Her fingers tap the piano keys: "Jin-gle bells / Jin-gle bells / Jin-gle all the way ..."]

Oh. You're right; we missed it.

[She keeps playing with a single finger: "Oh, what fun . . ." But then the notes become the opening of the "Bridal Chorus" from Wagner's Lohengrin: "Treulich geführt / ziehet dahin" . . .]

[Astounded.] What?!

[Niamh stops playing, kneels down, her hand still offering the bowed box, exultant smile shining in the twilight.]

[A. stares down at her, wordless.]

	Niamh. You're kidding, right?
NIAMH:	[She holds his amazed stare.]
A.:	No, you can't be serious. Are you?
NIAMH:	[She shakes the box in her hand: "Come on, open it."]

[A few seconds fly by.]

A.:	Niamh, there are primitive civilizations in the Horn of Africa who know this is wrong.
NIAMH:	[Stands up, shakes the box in his face: "Open it, you twat!"]
A.:	Okay, okay. [He takes the present, unties the box, opens the ring case . . .]

[. . . Then there's a dramatic pause . . .]

[. . . Then he scoffs.]

A.:	God.

[He picks up the hexahedral object filling the small hexahedral box; then he twists one of the pieces, and he twists it back, and for a while he just gazes at the little Rubik's cube between his fingers. And then at Niamh.]

Thanks a lot.

[She opens her arms. They hug.]

[Very tight.]

   [Muffled by her anorak.] Thank you, Niamh. Love you so much.

[Night's fallen.]

Locals blame ghosts for Point Bless massacre

By Alison Cullen

Clayboro.— The horror-struck community of Point Bless, which awoke to the news of the multiple homicide in nearby Axton House on the 21st, seems to be dredging up old legends and ghost tales as a means to cope with the tragedy.

"There's something crooked about that house," says Sam Mitchel, 51, a hardware store owner who claims to have visited the crime scene only some weeks ago. "You could smell the evil."

The secluded mansion that recently achieved fame as the scene of the Point Bless Massacre used to belong to a family of slave traders whose abusive ways were known across Ponopah County. Since the turn of the century, the mansion has been the home of a long line of secretive scholars versed in "dark matters." Mitchel described the present dwellers as equally "non-talkative" and having "a gloomy air about them."

According to Sheriff Joel M. Harris, "neighbors have often reported nocturnal noises and lights" in the house, which is said to be haunted by the vengeful spirit of a child slave, the "Angola Girl."

Meanwhile, State Police pay little attention to "folklore," in the words of Dep. Ted Miller from the Emporia station. Investigation continues on the events of the 21st, where 18 died, including one of the suspects. The only person under arrest is negotiating to avoid the death penalty in exchange for assistance in the hunt of a third suspect.

However, Pointblessants refuse to attribute the unexpected tragedy to common criminals, blaming instead spiritual forces. "It's wrong to mess with certain powers," says Monique Brodie, 62, a local farmer who also linked the victims with Freemasonry.

EPILOGUE

"Ken Matsuo lived," I began, my hands surrounding at long last a cup of non-American coffee. "He's still in the hospital, but doing well. The third intruder, the woman, is missing. Glew left the country the same day."

Niamh sat by the window, having white chocolate. She seemed focused, less juvenile in spirit, but as eager for adventure as she did back in the beginning.

"Anyway, we have reason to believe that Glew was only in for the money, acting as a director in the field. The real mastermind is someone else. Probably Isaak Dänemarr. That was the guy who came up with the dream recorders. The Society had pointed him to the legend of the Eye, from which he took some inspiration, but I guess in the end he grew tired of replicas and became obsessed with the original. He must have deduced that Wells and his friends had one, or perhaps Ambrose himself showed it to him."

Niamh slapped a word on her notepad for my eyes only: *Money!*

"Yeah, true. The only thing that doesn't fit with this theory is that a scientist from the former Eastern bloc doesn't strike me as able to produce the big sums of money that Glew mentioned. So maybe he's just a pawn too and there's a sponsor behind him. Anyway, Glew surely cut expenses by hiring low-life thugs like those."

Aunt Liza's eyes checked the crutch propped on my chair.

"I'm so sorry you two had to go through all this."

"It's okay. The truth is the Society would have met again for the showdown anyway, and Glew would have sent the killers in, whether we were there or not. That couldn't be foreseen."

"There was the bed, though. That was dangerous."

"I had Niamh to protect me."

"I could do something about your knee, you know."

"I'm sure you can." I chuckled. "But no, thank you. I'll handle it. I have a year of rehab ahead. But hey, my therapist is remarkably hot." I flinched at my good leg being kicked. "And by remarkably hot I mean seven on a scale from one to Niamh."

Liza laughed. Her skin was perfect, both now at her apparent thirty years old as at any age she wanted to look; she was gorgeous, out of the Niamh scale. Perennially beautiful like something carved at the prow of a galleon.

"You did great," she said. "Both of you."

"We lost the Eye," I regretted.

"That was never the point. We never wanted the Eye. We knew nothing about Eyes or crystal balls in the beginning."

"But you knew it was a crystal ball feeding me the dreams through the brass canopy."

"I figured that much after checking the bibliography on conductive telepathy. Unlike you, I do read German. But I didn't even know that the crystal balls or the Eyes existed. All I knew was that someone, or something, or somethings, were spying. And one was spying from Axton House. You two found out what it was. I'm glad I trusted you. You were the right choice."

"Yeah, well, I only recently caught up with you on your choices. It took me a while to figure out why Niamh was the one doing the protection."

"She was the only Watcher I knew," said Liza.

"Okay. That explains why her. But why me?"

"She chose you."

She and Niamh shared a significant nive.

I turned to Niamh. "Well, thank you then. It's been . . . illuminating."

Outside, the world of truly old streets, bicycle bells, and buildings without fire escapes ran gray and unaware of our presence. It felt cozy to watch.

"What I'm most sorry about," I said, "is that we never apologized to Knox. We suspected him all the time because he suspected us. Meanwhile, we never noticed Glew because he never suspected our cover. No one did, really. Strückner mentioned that Ambrose had been contacted by someone around May regarding his relatives in Europe; he said they'd met in Clayboro, but his discretion prevented him from inquiring any further. At times, I think . . . it's like even Ambrose believed I was his second cousin twice removed."

"I am sure he wouldn't have minded," said Liza. "When I confronted Ambrose in May, he was convinced he was about to die and nothing could be done to prevent it. It could, as you two proved later, but at the time he was resigned to following his father's path. He would die another victim of their game, and his friends would mourn him for a day and continue to play, ignoring his last wishes. That's why he agreed to this deal: I watch over the Society, or have someone do it for me, and in exchange I learn everything: who is watching me, how, and why."

"Pity we failed at the watching-over-them part," I said bitterly. "Still, it was such a big deal he offered you. I bet he was crazy about having found you."

"Actually, he hadn't. He'd been poking around, and I found him. But yes, he seemed pleased to meet me." Liza smiled away in modesty. "After all, he'd seen so much of me already. He'd seen me at my best."

"I know," I said, in awe of her many unknown facets. "Sixty-six times since 1900. By the way, you made the Juggernaut again this year. Congratulations, Betty."

"Thank you," said Aunt Liza, playing with a ringlet of dark brown hair. "I work hard for it."

Edgar Cantero is a writer and cartoonist from Barcelona working in Catalan, Spanish, and English. He was born in 1981.